NO MAN'S LAND

Sally Malcolm

Copyright © 2024 by Sally Malcolm

All rights reserved.

No portion of this book may be reproduced in any form without written permission from the publisher or author, except as permitted by U.S. copyright law.

Acknowledgement

This book started life in 2016, during a fun weekend spent with my writing partner, Laura Harper.

Ostensibly working on a different book, we found ourselves spinning up ideas for a series of contemporary stories about an ancient society dedicated to the control of paranormal Britain. A society as old as the Norman conquest, informed by a shadowy twin of the Domesday Book – a thousand-year-old inventory of all the supernatural creatures on our islands.

Our premise was that all the stories would feature genuine folklore. That's an idea I've stuck to in this book, weaving together old London legends with the new myths that exploded into life during the collective trauma of the First World War.

Alas, Domesday has yet to come into being. But No Man's Land is set in that world, and I'm grateful to Laura for allowing me to play with our joint creation.

Chapter One

Flanders, September 1917

The first time Josef Shepel met the man who would change his life, it was among the dead at a forward dressing station in the Ypres Salient.

He'd been working all night, rattling along the rutted road with the ambulance headlights dark. And nothing to guide him but the poor sod slogging along ahead of them holding a white handkerchief behind his back. Must have done half a dozen trips already and there were still nearly twenty stretcher cases awaiting evacuation to the clearing station.

Josef squinted at the brightening horizon as he climbed out of the ambulance and stretched his aching back. After a long night, the pre-dawn grey was welcome even if it did open up the threat of German guns. To his left rose the dark shape of the bombed-out farmhouse the Royal Army Medical Corps had co-opted, its windows and doors long ago blasted away and its walls pockmarked by shrapnel. Ahead, the skeletal remains of barns and woodland emerged from the night, stark silhouettes against a paling sky.

With a shiver, Josef reached for his cigarettes.

Corporal Johnston was barking at the SBs, getting the worst of the casualties loaded into their van. It would take twenty minutes, probably, so Josef slid around the side of the farmhouse in search of five minutes' solitude. Leaning back against the wall, he closed his eyes and took a long drag on his gasper, releasing a weary smoky breath. This was his fifth—no, sixth—night without sleep, driving the ambulance back and forth from the clearing station to the dressing station. And there hadn't even been a big push, just the usual grinding attrition of the salient.

A sudden flash of brilliance startled his eyes open. On the horizon, a sliver of clear sky had allowed a spear of sunlight to pierce the crouching clouds, lighting their bellies in russet and scarlet. Like fire, or blood. Beneath them stretched the scarred, alien landscape of the battlefield, distant but visible beyond the ruins of the farm buildings and a forest of limbless trees.

And at Josef's feet lay the dead.

He hadn't noticed in the dark. Hidden from the road, behind the farmhouse, was the dying ground. Men brought back from the lines who hadn't survived the journey, or hopeless cases passed over by doctors stretched beyond their limit trying to save those who stood a fighting chance. There were, perhaps, thirty men on the ground before him, covered in blankets or just their coats.

God but it was a pitiful sight.

Taking the cigarette from his lips, Josef felt a surge of sorrow, swiftly followed by fury for these sons and fathers and brothers and lovers left here like meat to rot. Oh yes, fury was so much more useful than helpless aching compassion. Heedless of the risk, Josef reached for the camera he kept hidden in his breast pocket. Sliding it out of its case, he flicked open the catch, relishing the smooth release of the lens on its struts. In this bright dawn sunlight, he could take his shot. Crouching, he adjusted the aperture and shutter speed, then lifted the camera to frame the photograph. He centred it on the deathly face of a young man with closed eyes and slack bloodless lips, his gored arm thrown across his chest. Behind him, the bodies stretched out in ramshackle ranks, but they'd blur in the photograph to draw the eye to the image in the foreground. Holding steady, Josef pressed the shutter release and listened to its satisfying click and whir. He just hoped nobody else heard the telltale sound. Glancing over his shoulder, he quickly lifted the flap to scratch the date onto the autograph film and expose it to the light. But, damn it, that had been the eighth and final exposure. Luckily, Josef always carried a spare film in his pocket.

Tucking his smoke into the corner of his mouth, he quickly wound the film on and opened the back of the camera. It took a moment to retrieve the spool from inside the film and the new film from his pocket. He'd done this a hundred times or more, and the fiddly job didn't take more than a minute. Once the camera was closed again, he wound the film on until the first exposure was ready. Checking he was still alone, Josef moved closer to the bodies and tried for a different angle. This time, the silvery sunlight limned the pale faces of the dead, rendering them ghostly. If the photograph captured that, it would be spectacular.

He was just slipping the camera back into its case when he heard a hoarse whisper.

"Water."

His head shot up, and he met the gaze of the very man he'd photographed. His eyes were a strange, glassy blue.

"For God's sake, water..."

Josef's heart wrenched. Shoving his camera back into his pocket, he swung his canteen around from over his shoulder as he stepped over another man's body to reach the poor bastard still living. Kneeling, Josef unstopped his bottle and lifted the man's head. "Easy, there," he murmured as the man cried out in pain, setting the bottle to his dry lips and watching as he drank greedily.

God, but he looked young. Younger than Josef's twenty-six years, certainly, his waxy skin clear and boyish beneath its pallor. His uniform was dark with blood over his abdomen, and there was a nasty wound on his left forearm where the sleeve had been torn away. Already blackened and putrefying, it stank like the devil.

It was a miracle, or perhaps a tragedy, that the lad was still alive.

When the water started to trickle, undrunk, from the boy's lips, Josef lowered his head back down. His mouth moved, then, as if he were speaking. Josef leaned closer, trying to hear, almost gagging on the stench from the wound. He thought the boy might have a last message for his mother; they often did.

"Don't," he whispered, "leave me..."

Josef's throat thickened. "All right," he said and reached down to press his palm to the young man's cheek. "I won't."

"They come—" Fingers scrabbled weakly for Josef's wrist. "—for the dead. Don't let..." He gasped with pain, then moaned low in his throat and sank back.

"Hush now." Josef stroked a hand over the young man's forehead, brushing his mousy hair away from his face. "I'll stay with you. I promise."

The boy didn't respond, although his face was still scrunched in pain, drifting in and out of consciousness.

"I say," called a crisp voice from behind him. "Is that chap alive?"

Startled, Josef twisted around. A figure stood on the far side of the bodies, silhouetted against the dawn. Josef raised a hand to shade his eyes and recognised the shape of an officer's uniform and cap—as if the cut-glass accent hadn't already given it away. "Yes, sir," he said.

He expected to be ordered back to work and braced himself to refuse until the boy was past caring, but to his surprise the officer started to pick his way through the dead men towards him. Josef rose to meet him. He was a tall, well-made man with refined, aristocratic features and the arrogant bearing to match—yet the effect was softened by a troubled expression as he looked down at the suffering man. "Ah, poor boy," he said after a moment's pause, and bent to examine him.

Josef noticed he wore an armband of the RAMC and captain's stars on his shoulder. "Are you a doctor, sir?" he said, crouching too. He didn't hold out much hope for the wounded soldier, not after lying here all night, but if this man was a doctor...

The captain didn't answer, seemingly absorbed in examining the wound on the man's arm. He reached out a gloved hand to lift the arm, making a face at the stench but, nonetheless, studying it closely.

Josef averted his gaze. He'd become hardened to horrific injuries, but whether it was the stink or the black putrefaction, something about that wound made him shy away. Instead, he studied the captain. Beneath his forage cap, Josef saw a glint of dark hair in the sunlight, his square jaw and straight nose rather perfectly drawn, and strong thighs stretching his trousers tight where he crouched. Not that Josef had time for men of the captain's sort—no more than they'd have time for a socialist troublemaker like himself—but he couldn't help noticing. Even when his mind should be on other things.

Guiltily, he turned his attention back to the wounded man. Poor sod appeared insentient now, but nonetheless, Josef brushed his fingers over the boy's forehead again and into his hair, the way his mum had done when he was a lad and sick in bed. Josef wanted him to know he wasn't alone. "He asked me not to leave him," he explained to the captain. "I'd rather stay until...Well."

"He spoke to you?"

Surprised by the sharp tone of query in the captain's voice, Josef looked up. "He did, yes, sir."

"What did he say?"

"Umm...nothing much." Disturbed by the intensity of the captain's gaze, he looked back at the boy's face. He had become very still now, but his chest still rose and fell with a tenacious hold on life. One thing he'd learned here was that men clung on until the last knockings. You wouldn't credit how long a man could keep breathing with his guts spilling out.

The boy moaned, and Josef bit his lip against another twist of pity. God, but this was unbearable. Usually, he poured his feelings through the lens of his camera, letting his photographs capture the pain so he didn't have to feel it, but this boy's chill skin was under his fingers, and there was no ignoring that.

"Tell me," the captain pressed. "Tell me everything he said."

The note of command in that cool aristocratic accent felt like the touch of a hot iron to a raw nerve. "Why?" Josef snapped. "What does it matter to you?"

Silence.

When Josef glanced up, he found the captain regarding him with a single, cocked eyebrow. Clearly, he wasn't used to having his orders challenged. But Josef wasn't a soldier, and he wasn't particularly fond of following orders.

"I should like to know," the captain said after a moment. He set the man's wounded arm down over his chest. "But if you have some reason for keeping it secret, then I shan't pry. You and he were...friends?"

There was a slight emphasis on 'friends' that put Josef on guard. "No," he said quickly. "I never saw him before today. Don't even know his name."

"No?" The captain looked doubtful. "Then you're always so tender with your patients?"

Josef looked down at his hand, still stroking the lad's hair. "Who'd do less? He's just a boy." The captain didn't reply, and after a moment, Josef said, "He was rambling. Delirious, I suppose. He asked me not to leave him and said…it was something like 'they come for the dead'. He was afraid, I think, of being taken away prematurely as…as a…"

As a corpse. Poor bastard.

When he glanced at the captain, to see if he'd understood, the man's mouth was pressed into a tight line. The sun had disappeared behind the bank of steely cloud, and the cold light turned the captain's colour to ash. "Hellfire," he spat with vehemence. "Hellfire and bloody damnation."

Josef was astonished by the outburst, but before he could respond, the boy gave a thin, pitiable cry, convulsed badly, and fell still, blood erupting from between his lips. His strange blue eyes were half open but unseeing, and Josef stopped the movement of his hand, letting it rest on the boy's fine hair.

The captain felt for a pulse and let out a breath. "He's gone," he said softly, and swept a hand over the boy's eyes, closing them. "That's a mercy, at least."

"Ha!" Angry tears pricked Josef's eyes and thickened his throat. "A mercy, you call it?"

"I do, yes." The captain rose fluidly to his feet, and Josef looked up at him, squinting against the cloudy sky. "There are worse things than death."

Josef pushed himself to his feet and found himself not quite eye to eye with the captain, who was rather tall. "Like what? Dishonour? Cowardice?"

He was sick of hearing that bullshit from people who should know better.

"I meant suffering, of course." A pause. "Your kindness to him was a mercy, too."

Josef glared, then looked away, scratching a hand through his tangled curls. Stupid, to take out his fury on this man; he didn't even know him. His anger drained away in a rush, leaving only the hollow exhaustion that lay beneath. "I wish..." He sighed and shook his head, unable to find the right words. He wished what? That this bloody war would end? God, he wished it had never started, but what use were wishes? If he wanted things to change, he'd better go out and change them.

"I wish too," the captain said, surprising him again. "But here we are."

Josef turned back around, and the captain smiled tightly. "Winchester," he said and offered his hand to shake. "RAMC."

Surprised, it took Josef a moment before he took the captain's proffered hand. "Shepel. Red Cross."

"Well." Winchester held Josef's eye. "Take some advice, Shepel, and stick with your pals when you're out after dark. Can't be too careful."

"Careful of what? It's a bloody war."

Winchester smiled. "Just stay out of the shadows."

Strange advice and Josef didn't know what to make of it, but he didn't have time to ask because at that moment Corporal Johnston poked his beaky nose around the corner of the farmhouse. "Shepel! Move your bloody arse. We're heading back."

Josef cast a final look at the boy at his feet, resting in peace now, he supposed. Or as close to it as possible in this hellish place. He regretted not being able to photograph him again, to record his passing, but with Winchester standing right there, it was impossible. Instead, he gave the captain a nod of farewell and headed back toward the ambulance. There were still a dozen stretcher cases waiting outside the dressing station, and he knew he'd be back again before he saw breakfast or a place to lay his head.

He glanced once over his shoulder as he turned the corner, to see Captain Winchester bending over the dead man. As Josef watched, the captain pulled something small from his pocket—a coin?—and touched it to the man's mouth. Then he straightened, gazing down for a moment before tugging the blanket up from the boy's legs to cover his body and face. For some reason, that simple gesture touched Josef. He wished he'd thought to do it himself.

It was several days before Josef saw Captain Winchester again.

He was in the resuscitation tent when it happened, bringing a casualty in straight from the ambulance for an emergency transfusion. Pale as a ghost he was, as Josef helped transfer him from the stretcher to the cot, and the doctor began the business with needles, tubes, and a bottle of blood. They were the stuff of miracles, transfusions. Although Josef didn't much fancy the idea of another man's blood running through his veins—seemed unnatural—there was no arguing with the results. He'd seen it bring men back from the dead.

He was moving aside, giving the doc space to work, and rolling his aching shoulders—you wouldn't credit the dead weight of a man in a wet and sodden uniform—when he heard Winchester's voice. "Over here," he said. "Look."

Josef glanced up and saw Winchester bending over a bed on the far side of the tent, examining a man who lay motionless. Unlike some of the other tents, filled with the moans and groans of the wounded, the resus tent was silent as the grave, and Josef could easily hear Winchester's words even though he was speaking quietly. But the man he was talking to made Josef look twice: a tall, rangy Indian sepoy with a fine moustache and a deep frown beneath his turban as he looked where Winchester pointed. He gestured to the patient and said something in a language Josef didn't understand. To his surprise, Winchester nodded and replied in kind. They carried out a hushed conversation for a few minutes, none of which Josef could understand but which was clearly heated. When Winchester finally straightened up, he said, "Nevertheless, I believe we have to take action."

"That," his friend replied, in an accent no less plummy than Winchester's, "is what you always say."

Winchester grunted, turning toward the door to the tent. In doing so, he caught Josef's eye. Bugger. It was too late to pretend he hadn't been watching, so Josef brazened out the uncomfortable moment by lifting a hand in a wave. "Morning, Captain."

"Shepel." One corner of his mouth lifted, and Josef felt a flush of pleasure at being remembered. Which was galling; he made it a point of principle to care nothing for the good opinion of brass hats like Captain Winchester. "Staying out of the shadows, I hope?"

"Not so much," he said, bending to retrieve his stretcher from the floor. "I find I prefer them to the enemy guns when I'm out and about at night."

Winchester looked him over with aristocratic assurance and turned to murmur something to his companion. Josef instantly found himself subject to the other man's scrutiny, which was scalpel-like in its precision and sharpness. He made a comment to Winchester, eyebrows lifting, and Winchester shrugged. "Why not? Life's short," he said and touched his cap to Josef in a rather un-soldierly manner, and the pair of them strolled out of the tent.

Josef watched the flap settle back into place, then carefully set the stretcher back down next to his patient, who was already starting to lose the grey cast to his skin. With a glance at the doctor, still busy with the transfusion, Josef made his way through the rows of beds to the man Winchester had been examining.

He lay on a heated pallet, his face sickly and body lifeless. One arm and both legs were covered with loose dressings, none of which did anything to mask the stench rising from the wounds. Josef glanced about, saw that the doctor was still busy with the transfusion, and gingerly lifted one corner of the dressing on the man's thigh. He reared back, dropping it almost instantly. What the devil? The same black putrefaction that he'd seen at the dressing station crept along the man's leg.

He retreated a step, revolted. More than revolted, disturbed.

He'd seen mustard gas wounds. That stuff could burn away half a man's face, but this was something different. He'd never seen anything like this rancid rot until the other night. Was it a sickness—or some terrible new weapon?

Either way, you could bet the brass hats would keep it hidden from the fighting men. Truth was bad for morale, you see. And God knew nobody at home would read about it over their morning tea because the censors had seen to that at the start of the war. The only newspapermen at the front these days were a handful of government propagandists.

At least, the only official ones.

Josef put his hand to the breast pocket of his jacket, settling his fingers reassuringly over the little VPK camera hidden there. He wished he could take a photograph of the man's wounds, but it was too dangerous in such a public place. Two years ago, he'd heard about a respected journalist, working for a national newspaper, being threatened with the firing squad before being shipped home from France. Josef doubted the army would be as lenient with him—a socialist from Spitalfields—and didn't fancy putting it to the test.

No, a photograph here was out of the question. But that didn't mean he would let it drop.

Heading back to collect his stretcher, he lingered for a moment until he could see the doctor was finished administering the transfusion. Reaching down for his stretcher, Josef said, "He's looking better."

"Aye," the man said, with a soft Scots lilt. "He'll do."

Josef smiled. "That's good news." He nodded, casual as you like, toward the man Winchester had been examining. "How about him? Doesn't look so good."

"Bearman? No." The doctor rubbed a hand over his weary face. "He came in last night, raving. Poor lad spent eighteen hours in no man's land before his company could retrieve him. We'll do what we can."

Eighteen hours in no man's land. Poor bastard. "What causes that, then?" Josef said. "That kind of infection?"

The doctor gave him an old-fashioned look. "What do you think? You wouldn't keep swine in the conditions these boys endure. They're infected the moment they're wounded."

Not like that, Josef wanted to say. That wound was different, sinister in a way he couldn't explain. And as the salient's only independent reporter, Josef felt a duty to investigate.

Had he known then where his investigations would lead, he might have made a different decision. As it was, Josef made a point of keeping his eye out for Captain Winchester, and when he saw him next, in the bar at Toc H, he saw his chance to dig deeper. Saw it and took it.

Chapter Two

Toc H—soldier parlance for Talbot House—was one of those rare establishments where officers and enlisted men mixed freely. It had been running for a year or so in the nearby village of Poperinge, a transfer station for thousands of soldiers, and was part bar and part place of reflection and rest.

Josef was most interested in the bar.

But a trip to Pops also allowed him to visit the elderly Belgian gentleman who developed his films. He was keen to see how the photograph of the dying young man came out. If it was as good as he hoped, it would be a powerful image.

M. Verbeke's pharmacy was on a picturesque little street only five minutes from Toc H, which had so far escaped any of the shell damage inflicted on other parts of the village. Josef doffed his cap as a couple of black-clad elderly women left, each of whom paused to give him a level and uninterpretable gaze. The people of Pops were used to the heavy British presence, but Josef saw no reason they would enjoy it. He slipped inside once they were gone, pleased to find the shop empty.

Mdm. Verbeke stood at the counter, but when she recognised Josef, she called over her shoulder in Flemish for her husband. Josef had the impression that Mdm. Verbeke didn't approve of her husband assisting him with his illicit photographs. Or perhaps she found the subject matter distasteful. And it was—the whole damned war was distasteful.

"Hallo, Josef," M. Verbeke said, appearing from the back room. "Hoe gaat het met jou?"

He was a small, stooped man with a round bald head, ruddy cheeks, and sparkling eyes. Almost the opposite in every way to his tall, stern wife who, with a curt nod for Josef, disappeared into the back.

"Zo en zo," Josef replied, as he always did. So-so was the best he could manage these days. It was also the limit of his Flemish. "I have another film for you, M. Verbeke. Are you able to develop it?" He reached into his pocket and handed it over.

"Joat," he nodded. "Next week, I will have it for you." He turned the film over in his hand, studying it. "So many photographs of dead men, Josef. What will you do with them all?"

"Publish them, of course. Back in London."

M. Verbeke looked surprised. "They will let you?"

"No." He smiled. "But...the newspaper I work for doesn't much care for the propaganda laws. And I say the people have a right to know the truth."

After eight months with the Red Cross, Josef had a stack of shocking images. And when he returned with them to London, he had every intention of shouting the truth from the rooftops. If that meant he went to gaol, then so be it. He couldn't think of a worthier cause.

M. Verbeke nodded along, but said, "You would leave us to the mercy of the Germans, then?"

Ah. Well. Sometimes, Josef forgot that not everyone shared his pacifist perspective. He said, "I hope, monsieur, that there's a man like me behind the German lines, too. Showing the truth to the German people. Then, perhaps, we can have peace."

M. Verbeke looked doubtful. "I hope you are right," he said, just as the door behind Josef opened with a soft tinkle of bells. Mr Verbeke slipped Josef's film beneath the counter, and Josef heard English voices before he turned around to see a couple of Tommies lurking in the doorway. Given the entertainment most men sought in Pops, it would have been clear what the young men were after even if their furious blushes hadn't made it obvious. But if either of them knew what to do with a real live woman, Josef would be surprised. Neither of them looked more than seventeen.

He left them to their stumbling requests. "Saluu, M. Verbeke," he said, before slipping out of the shop.

Dusk was falling by the time he reached the market square and from there headed over to Toc H. Its white frontage and long, narrow window shutters looked a little grimy, but the sound of laughter spilled out along with yellow electric light, and Josef's spirits lifted. There were few comforts in the salient, but everyone found solace at Toc H.

Despite the distant rumble of the guns, inside he was met by calm: a fug of tobacco smoke and unwashed men, the air thick with laughter, and someone on the piano bashing out an old Vesta Tilley number.

Josef headed directly for the bar. He wasn't a soldier, and Toc H wasn't strictly his turf, but he'd never had trouble being served here. Soldiers on the line knew the value of the Red Cross. It was back home where his status as a conchie caused problems. Not that he cared. What did a couple of rough shoves on the Underground matter, or a coward's white feather thrust at him by a group of angry-eyed women? He'd watched his fellow socialists go to gaol for their beliefs, and he would have joined them had May not suggested signing up with the Red Cross so he could take his VPK to the front and photograph the truth.

Soon, he'd be home again—only six more weeks—and then they'd start printing.

He ordered a beer, which wasn't real English beer but a light Belgian lager, and found a table to himself in the corner. Fishing out a cigarette, he amused himself by flipping through an old copy of the Wiper's Times—he'd written a few sardonic pieces for it himself, earlier in the year—and studying the occupants of the room. It was the variety of people he enjoyed most about Toc H, and although the officers and enlisted men tended to keep to themselves, there was more mixing here than anywhere else—except in the line, or among the dead.

And as far as Josef was concerned, the more the classes mixed, the better. Harder to persuade a man that you were his superior by birth when he'd seen you drooling into your whiskey. Or pissing yourself with fear.

Josef liked to think of his interest in other people as a journalist's eye. May said he was just a nosy bastard. Either way, Josef enjoyed watching people, which was why he noticed immediately when Captain Winchester and his Indian companion stepped into the room.

They went straight to the bar, talking only to each other. Not even a friendly wave for their fellow officers. Winchester was a little taller than Josef, which was to say neither tall nor short but somewhere unremarkably between the two. But his companion was tall. The effect was exaggerated by his turban and the fact that Winchester had removed his cap, exposing glossy dark hair swept back from his forehead. He leaned one arm on the bar, casting a bored eye over the room as he talked to his friend. Josef looked down at his newspaper to avoid making eye contact, turning the page without reading a word. After a moment or two, he glanced back over. Winchester was holding a glass of something amber, his companion sipped a mug of tea, and they were deep in discussion. Arguing, he would have said, except that Winchester's face was alight with humour. His friend's was not.

They were a curious pair.

As he watched, the Indian officer set his mug on the bar, leaned forward to murmur in Winchester's ear, and took his leave. Winchester only smiled to himself—then, without warning, looked directly at Josef and lifted his glass in salute.

Ridiculously, Josef flushed. With a curt nod, he turned away, picked up his beer, and took a long draft to douse his embarrassment at being caught blatantly staring. So much for his journalistic talents.

"Mind if I join you?"

Surprised for the second time, Josef set down his glass and looked up. Winchester was already pulling out the chair opposite, setting his drink and hat on the table between them.

"Doesn't look like I have much choice."

The captain smiled as he sat down. It was rather a dazzling smile, wide and engaging. Josef wished he hadn't noticed. "You're not waiting for anyone, I hope?"

He could have said yes—he dearly wanted to puncture the man's self-assurance—but he also wanted to investigate the mysterious and horrifying wounds he'd recently seen, and since Winchester appeared to know something about that, Josef simply said, "Not tonight."

"Good." The captain smiled again and lounged back in his seat. Beneath the table, their knees touched, and Winchester caught his eye, holding it rather longer than necessary. He said, "I'd hate to be in the way."

Well, well. Pulse spiking distractingly, Josef couldn't keep from smiling himself as he said, "Not at all. I'm glad you're here, in fact. I wanted to talk to you."

"Did you? How fortunate; I wanted to talk to you too."

Not about this, I'll warrant.

Josef folded his hands on the table before him but didn't move his knee, growing warm now against Winchester's. "In the resus tent the other day, I saw you looking at that man's wounds—Bearman. They were the same as the boy we watched click it at the dressing station."

Winchester's smile faltered, jarring like a truck bouncing over a rut. "I see a lot of wounded men," he said, but Josef could see his discomfort and jumped on it.

"Me too, but I've not seen anything like that before. What causes it?"

After a pause, the captain said, "I've twenty-four hours' leave. I'd rather not spend it talking about the damned war."

"Is it a new weapon? It doesn't look like mustard gas, but—"

Abruptly, Winchester sat forward, placing his hand over Josef's wrist, and looking directly into his eyes. "I saw straight away that you were a clever and curious man, so I shan't trifle with your intelligence and pretend I don't know what you're talking about. In return, you must believe me when I say that I cannot tell you anything about it. And, furthermore, that you can't try to find out."

"Or what? I'm no soldier, Captain Winchester. You can't give me orders."

"Which is a shame." His lips ticked up at one corner, rueful and wry. "I'd rather like to try."

Josef held his gaze, very aware of the weight of the man's hand on his wrist. "I'll bet you would."

Winchester gave a little huff of laughter, letting go. "Either way, it's in your interest to have nothing to do with this matter. But you can trust that those who need to know do know."

"I don't have a lot of faith in 'those who need to know'." Josef gestured around them. "They brought us all here, after all."

"This is different."

"Is it? How?"

He made an exasperated sound. "Just be grateful you can leave this mess to others."

"I'm not a very grateful man. And I happen to believe that hiding messes makes them worse."

Winchester barked a laugh, raking one hand through his glossy hair. "Dutta said you looked like trouble."

"Dutta was right."

"He usually is." Winchester's smile faded. "But sometimes secrets are best kept secret. As I think you well know."

And now they were talking about something else.

Winchester's knowing look set Josef fizzing; the excitement of being seen for who he was never failed to light a fire. His heart began to race. "Perhaps I do."

Beneath the table, Winchester rubbed his knee more surely against Josef's. Eyes sparkling, he said, "So...?"

Josef reached for his beer, swallowed the last mouthful, and set it back down on the table. Naturally, he knew Winchester was distracting him, but what did that matter? It was all a bloody game, and they could both be dead tomorrow.

Slowly, deliberately, he lifted his eyes to Winchester's—they were dark blue, like the night sky an hour after sunset. Attractive. He was an altogether attractive man, and it had been a long time since any man had crossed Josef's path with such eager intent. Only a fool would look such a gift horse in the mouth. Offering him a bedroom look, Josef said, "Oh, definitely so."

"Well then." Winchester picked up his cap, toying with the brim. "Perhaps you'd care to take a walk, Mr Shepel?"

"What did you have in mind, Captain Winchester?" What Josef did not have in mind was a rough fondle in some back alleyway, looking over his shoulder the whole time. He had more respect for himself than that, and if Winchester thought otherwise, he could shove it.

But the captain held his gaze again and said, "Perhaps, on this matter, you could bring yourself to trust me?"

"That'll depend on whether you deserve it."

Winchester considered for a long moment before he said, "Number eighteen, Priesterstraat. Give my name at the door and they'll let you in. I'll meet you there in fifteen minutes." With that he rose, nodded, and sauntered out of the bar.

Leaving the ball firmly in Josef's court and with plenty of time to reconsider. He appreciated that.

But he didn't reconsider. He wasn't the sort of man who second-guessed himself. Besides, his blood was up, and the thought of returning alone to the field hospital and his narrow cot was unappealing. And while Winchester might congratulate himself on distracting Josef from questions about the new weapon—which was Josef's current best explanation—two could play at that game.

Plenty of secrets, among other things, had been spilled in bed.

Chapter Three

Ten minutes later, Josef found himself walking along Priesterstraat—an unlit, narrow lane leading toward Poperinge's medieval church. Heavy cloud hid the stars and moon, breeding deeper shadows in the alley. Most houses were locked up for the night, their windows dark, Pop's weary inhabitants hiding from both the German guns and the British soldiers. Josef didn't usually mind; he wasn't afraid of the dark. As he'd told Winchester the first time they met, he preferred the shadows when he was out and about at night.

But tonight, something felt different. He felt uneasy, as if he were being watched.

Was it possible that someone at Toc H had noticed his conversation with Winchester? Unusual in itself for an officer and a man like himself to socialise, but had they signalled their intentions too clearly?

He glanced over his shoulder but saw nobody there, just the square of light at the other end of the street. Quickening his pace, he hurried on, squinting through the dark at the numbers on the building.

A sudden stench stopped him in his tracks, drifting on the air for a moment and then gone. But unmistakable. It was the stench of the black putrefaction he'd seen on those poor dying men. He sniffed the air again, but all he could smell now was the damp and the chill of the night. Wet stone, clean mud. He shook himself; he must have imagined it, thinking too much about Winchester's secrets.

Ahead, the lane opened out onto a wider street, but just before that, Josef found number eighteen. It turned out to be a very discreet guesthouse with only a small brass plaque on the door displaying its name as Jägers.

The door was locked so he rapped lightly, and it was answered immediately by a neat, grey-haired Belgian woman. Josef gave Winchester's name, no questions were asked, and he was admitted. Inside, he found a cosy parlour to his left with a crackling fire, shelves crammed with books, and several easy chairs. A small reception desk sat in the equally small foyer, and a dark dining room stood to the right. Ahead rose a narrow flight of stairs. The place was elegant, seeming untouched by the war, and certainly the nicest place Josef had visited in Belgium.

Well, truth be told, it was the nicest place he'd visited anywhere.

If this was how the officer class lived, it was no surprise they wanted to keep it for themselves. Not that he could see any officers around, the only other guest being a rather pale older gentleman reading in the parlour.

"Captain Winchester is expecting you, Monsieur Shepel," the housekeeper said. "Room eight, two floors up."

He thanked her and took the stairs two at a time. When he reached the right floor, he saw a short hallway either side of the stairs leading to two rooms each. Winchester's was on the left, at the front of the house.

Light bled from beneath the door, and Josef found himself hesitating, heart thumping in anticipation. This wasn't the first time he'd taken pleasure with a stranger, but it was the first time he'd risked such a thing with a man of Winchester's class—a man who'd hold all the cards should things turn sour.

The question was, could he trust him?

And the answer, which surprised him given his general antipathy towards officers, was yes. For some reason, he trusted the man.

He hoped he didn't live to regret it.

Lifting his hand, he knocked softly on the door, and a moment later, Winchester opened it. "You came," he said, smiling. "I wasn't certain you would."

"Neither was I." It wasn't exactly the truth, but Winchester didn't need to know that. "But here I am."

"Here you are." Winchester took a step back, inviting him in with a sweep of one arm.

The room was as fine as the rest of the house. Not enormous, but clean and richly decorated with a thick carpet and expensive-looking furniture. A small vase of fresh flowers sat on the armoire, and heavy velvet curtains covered the window. A fire burned in the small fireplace, and two comfortable chairs were set around it. But Josef's eyes were caught by the sizeable bed behind them, and his racing pulse shifted up a gear.

"Let's have a drink," Winchester said, taking Josef's hat and coat and hanging them on the back of the door. He himself was only in shirtsleeves, sleeves rolled up to reveal forearms dusted with dark hair. His collar was unbuttoned too, and he padded over to the mantelpiece in his socked feet.

Josef bent to untie his heavy boots, enjoying the feel of the luscious carpet beneath his toes. "This is fancy," he said as he stood up. "All the officers stay in places this nice, do they?"

"No, this is a private arrangement." Winchester had his back to him, pouring a drink into two short glasses. "Do you like brandy? I hope so because it's all I have."

"Brandy's fine," Josef said, taking the glass as Winchester turned to hand it to him. The room was gently lit by two gas lamps, and the soft light gave Winchester's skin an appealing golden glow. He was altogether very appealing—for a toff. Josef lifted his glass. "What shall we drink to, Captain?"

Winchester smiled and touched his glass to Josef's. "To secrets worth keeping," he said.

They both drank, the brandy a warm sensation in Josef's chest and belly. "Do you live here?" he said, taking one of the chairs by the fire. "Or just entertain?"

Winchester took the other, rolling his glass between his hands. "Neither. I'm...passing through."

"Ah." He tried not to let the flare of disappointment show. Even if Winchester had been stationed here, it was unlikely this would be repeated; they both understood this was a one-night affair. "Where to next, then?"

"London, for a while. Probably. Then...wherever I'm needed."

"For your work with the Intelligence Corps?" Josef asked innocently.

"My work...?" Winchester chuckled. "Well, if I did work for the Intelligence Corps, I would hardly tell you."

Josef mimicked making a note. "Captain Winchester neither confirmed nor denied the rumour..."

"Captain Winchester has something more interesting in mind." He set aside his glass and leaned forward in his chair, laying a hand on Josef's thigh. "What do you say?"

The sudden heaviness between his legs was answer enough, but he said, "Tell me your name, first. I won't fuck 'Captain Winchester.'"

A considering silence, then, "It's Alex."

"Alex." He liked the shape of it on his tongue, soft and easy. "I'm Josef. Some people call me Joe."

"Josef." Winchester lifted a hand and touched his jaw, running fingertips over his skin. "You're very beautiful, Josef Shepel. My God, but your lips are lush. And those eyes. I've never seen eyes so dark. Soft and dark, like a doe."

"Then you should visit Spitalfields more often," he said, alarmed by how breathless he sounded. "You'll find loads of eyes like mine around there."

Winchester—Alex—smiled, threading his fingers into Josef's curls, cradling the back of his head. "I've wanted to kiss you since the moment we met."

"Really? We met among the dead."

"Do you ever shut up?"

"No, I—"

Alex kissed him, gentle but unyielding, fingers tugging at his hair with tingling pleasure. And Josef kissed him back, rising to the challenge as he always did. God, but Alex tasted tantalizing—tobacco and brandy, a hint of menthol toothpaste. And he kissed well, with vigour and intent. Josef enjoyed a man who knew what he wanted. A strong arm slipped around Josef's waist and pulled him close, hard against Alex's firm body. For a moment, Josef feared for the safety of his camera, crushed as it was between their chests, and he pulled back a little.

"All right?" Alex asked, so close now that Josef could see flecks of green and grey amid the dark blue of his eyes.

"It's getting a little...restricting in the uniform."

Alex's lips twitched. "It is, rather, isn't it?" Then his expression grew darker, more intent, and he leaned in to nuzzle Josef's neck above the collar of his tunic. "Christ, I want to bloody ravish you."

Josef laughed—and then gasped as Alex's lips and tongue did something extraordinary to his ear. "Christ! Be my guest."

"I shall, but first..." Alex let go, sitting back on his heels, breathing quickly. "Get into bed."

"Is that an order, Captain?"

"I wouldn't bloody dare."

"In that case..." Josef rose and began to unbutton his tunic, slipping it off and taking a moment to drape it over the back of the chair to keep the camera safe.

When he turned back around, Alex was standing up and captured his face with both hands, bringing their lips together again. This time, the kiss was accompanied by a frenzy of unbuckling and unbuttoning as they half staggered, laughing towards the bed. Finally, Josef kicked off his trousers and socks and Alex swept off the covers, revealing white sheets and plump pillows.

Alex was glorious naked. Dark hair dusted his chest and limbs, his body virile with the muscular strength of an active man. His prick was full, hard, and ruddy.

Josef felt wiry by comparison, though he could hold his own in a fight—and frequently did. But Alex seemed to like what he saw, running his hands over Josef's chest to his shoulders, then down his arms and back to his waist. "Beautiful," he murmured, pulling him in. "And this?" His fingers closed around Josef's prick, thumb running over the head. "My mouth's watering."

Josef returned the favour, sliding his hand around Alex's prick, relishing the silken strength and the way Alex's eyes half closed, heavy-lidded with desire. "Get on the bed," Josef said. "On your back."

Alex complied, lying spread-eagled and unashamed amid the pillows, one hand lazily stroking himself. "Come on then," he said. "I'm waiting."

"I'm watching," Josef countered, giving his own prick a little attention, enjoying the way Alex's eyes darkened further. Oh yes, Alex liked what he saw. Good. So did Josef. He wished he could snap a picture, capture those debauched aristocratic features in the warm gaslight, the play of shadows over his fine arms and shoulders. Impossible, of course, but tempting.

He gave his prick a slow tug. Tempting too, to draw this out, to make Alex wait a little longer, but the truth was that Josef didn't know how long he'd last. It had been an age since he'd had this much fun. He moved closer, crawling onto the bed between Alex's spread legs, smoothing his hands along his muscular thighs. He liked how it made Alex quiver, little shocks that rippled across his belly and made his prick twitch. Perhaps it had been a long time for him too.

Alex was uncircumcised, and Josef enjoyed watching the head of his prick peek out from beneath his foreskin. It would be sensitive, he knew. Very sensitive. Leaning down, he flicked his tongue over that exposed flesh, and Alex sucked in a sharp breath and clasped the base of his stand.

"Jesus, the sight of you," he said harshly. "Do you have any idea what you look like, with that hair and those eyes? And that bloody sinful mouth."

Josef smiled, kept his eyes on Alex, and bent to suck him. Because, yes, he knew exactly what he looked like. He was no fool.

"Jesus, fuck, and all the saints," Alex whispered, quivering with the effort of not moving. "I'm afraid this might not last long at all."

"I know the feeling," Josef said, his own prick painfully hard and his climax already beating its wings in his ears. "Let's try this." He moved, turning himself around and straddling Alex's body.

"God, yes," Alex growled, seizing Josef's hips in both hands.

Josef leaned down, this time taking the head of Alex's cock into his mouth and groaning as he felt hot lips close over his own prick. And fuck, but Alex had a clever mouth and a bloody genius tongue. Not to mention those fingers, caressing his balls. It was increasingly difficult to concentrate on his own end of the business, opening his throat and swallowing Alex down.

They carried on like that for a few misty minutes until Josef felt his climax begin to boil, and Alex's cries got louder as he thrust helplessly into Josef's mouth. By unspoken consent, Josef pulled up and off, rolling over to lie panting on the bed next to Alex.

Too soon, it was too soon to end it.

After a few moments, Alex sat up. His lips were pink and glistening, his hair wild—as if he'd been clutching it—and his eyes were dark as midnight. Bloody gorgeous.

"You're a fucking angel," Alex growled. "Better than an angel."

Josef laughed. "Is that a god?"

With a grin, Alex pounced, their mouths crushing together in a kiss that tasted of musk and sex. Legs and bodies tangled and tussled, wrestling for dominance and release. Josef flipped him at the last moment, sliding his slighter frame over Alex's broader body and then sat up, straddling his hips. "I want to watch you," he said, his voice like gravel, like someone other than himself.

Alex nodded, lustful as Josef took both their pricks in one hand, slick and hot, and began to work them together. After a moment, Alex joined in, threading their fingers, controlling the pace. It was a beautiful agony to be held on the cusp—almost, almost, almost there. Josef could feel his release building, coiling in his thighs and belly as he watched Alex tense, back bowing, mouth falling open as their hands kept working. And then Alex cried out, loud enough to wake the whole bloody house, and a stream of white erupted over their joined hands, his face flushing in a wild rictus of ecstasy.

God, it was perfect.

As Alex's boneless hand dropped away, Josef was free to hit his own pace, and a moment later, his climax detonated. He unloaded with the force of a fucking howitzer, striping Alex's chest. And then the world went blank, and he barely managed to slide sideways, fighting for control of his wobbly limbs before he collapsed in spent relief onto the bed.

Next to him, Alex started chuckling, his hand landing heavily on Josef's hip. "Bloody hell, that was marvellous."

"I hope your landlady's deaf," Josef said, laughing too. "You were making a right bloody racket."

"No need to worry about that." After a while, he sat up, examined his belly, and made a face. "Excuse me."

Josef watched, too languid to contemplate moving, as Alex strolled naked across the room and disappeared through a door Josef hadn't even noticed. A private bathroom? The sound of running water confirmed it, and a few moments later, Alex returned wearing a silk dressing gown. Well, of course he bloody well did. "Stay," Alex said, sitting on the edge of the bed. "Take supper with me."

"Supper?" Josef levered himself up on one elbow. "That's not very discreet."

Alex waved that away with one hand. "Nobody will care, I promise." He leaned across the bed and pressed his lips to Josef's bare shoulder, kissing it lightly. "We'll recover our strength and then..." His dark eyebrows twitched. "Round two?"

"Well," Josef sank back into the pillows, luxuriating in the feel of feathers and clean linen, "when you put it like that, how can I say no?"

They ate a delicious supper of beef stew and frites in the chairs by the fire, washed down with Belgian beer, and then rolled back into bed together. This time, they brought each other off at a slower but no less satisfying pace, and, afterward,

Josef let himself sink into a heavy sleep with the warm weight of Alex's hand on his back.

When he woke, much later, the room was pitch black. Next to him, he could hear Alex's steady breathing, and for a while Josef lay there, listening to the sound. He hadn't had the luxury of sleeping alone since he left England, but sharing a bed tonight felt almost as indulgent as solitude.

Outside, it was quiet. Even the guns were silent. But something drew him out of bed, an uneasy restlessness born, perhaps, of working night after night. His natural sleep pattern had been wrecked months ago. Alex didn't seem to have any trouble sleeping, though, and Josef didn't want to disturb him, so he slipped from under the covers and groped his way to the window to see whether he could calculate the time.

The room was chilly, the fire burned low, but Josef didn't steal the blanket from the bed and couldn't find his abandoned clothes in the dark. He didn't mind a little cold, though. Without tripping over anything, he reached the velvet curtains and lifted a corner enough to look out. Nobody would be able to see him, but he could watch the street below. From his vantage point he could see the corner of the lane and the wider street beyond, and, to the right, the dark shape of the church. The sky was still night-dark, no hint of dawn on the horizon, and the streets were mostly empty.

A few lights burned here and there, other restless souls like himself still awake, and he spotted a couple of figures walking together further up the road. Soldiers, almost certainly. On leave, perhaps, and looking for company—of the paid or unpaid variety. Much like Josef himself, he supposed. Only his night with Alex hadn't felt transactional; it had felt mutual. Friendly, even. And, in the quiet of the night, he could admit to himself a certain amount of regret that it wouldn't be repeated.

Still, you took what you could get and made the best of it. That was true in life, and doubly true in war.

The two soldiers disappeared, into a brothel maybe. Or down an alley to find pleasure together. Or perhaps for some entirely innocent purpose Josef's gutter of a mind couldn't imagine. But as he watched, he realised another man stood on the street outside. He looked somewhat the worse for drink, leaning heavily against the building on the corner opposite. But then he turned toward Josef, his eyes catching the light strangely, and for a moment Josef thought he recognised him. His heart skipped, an odd chill rippling over his skin and stirring the hair at the back of his neck. Impossibly, the figure looked like the boy who'd clicked it at the dressing station—same boyish features, same fine hair. Same strange pale eyes.

Josef peered closer, blinking through the dark.

And a hand touched his shoulder.

"Shit!" He jumped, dropping the curtain as he spun around.

Alex stood behind him, hands up in surrender, watching him in amusement. "What are you doing? It's the middle of the night."

"What are you doing? You frightened the bloody life out of me." Irritated, his heart still skipping about, Josef turned back to the window. But outside, the street was empty.

Alex crowded in behind him, his body deliciously warm against Josef's back as one arm snaked around his waist. With his free hand, Alex pushed the curtain back further. "Did you see something?"

"Nah, just a soldier. I thought—" He dropped the curtain and turned around, enjoying the sensation of Alex's arm sliding around his waist as he moved. "Doesn't matter. He's gone now."

Alex's gaze went to the window and back to Josef's face. "Good," he said, pulling Josef hard against his chest, arms tight and hands roving up and down Josef's back. "Come back to bed. It's cold."

Josef canted his hips forward, rubbing their soft pricks together. "What do you think, Captain? Shall we try for round three?"

He felt Alex's growl of approval chest to chest, and in the warm pressure of his lips against his shoulder as Alex sucked a bruise into his skin. "I think we should certainly make the attempt."

When he woke the next time, Josef was alone, and the curtains had been cracked to allow the morning light into the room. He sat up, disorientated and a little disappointed to find Alex gone. On the mantelpiece, the clock told him it was almost seven o'clock. Time enough to catch the train back to the hospital before he had to report for duty.

Sitting up in bed, he looked around for any signs of Alex, but there were none. His clothes were gone; the bathroom was silent and empty. Their plates and beer glasses from the night before sat where they'd left them, on the hearth by the now-cold fire, and the room held a depressing aura of abandonment.

"What did you expect?" he asked himself aloud. "Roses?"

Throwing back the sheets, Josef got out of bed—made good use of the bathroom and its supply of hot running water—and dressed quickly. But when he slipped on his uniform tunic, his heart stopped.

His camera was gone.

Panicked, he put a hand to his breast pocket, but it only slapped against his chest. Where the hell was it? Had it fallen out? He looked around frantically, but there was no sign of it. He checked all his other pockets, flung the sheets and covers off the bed, lay on the floor to look underneath the furniture, but there was no sign of it.

On weak legs, he sank down onto the edge of the bed, reeling. He'd lost his camera, his most precious possession in the world—financially and spiritually.

But no, he hadn't lost it.

That thieving bastard, Winchester, had stolen it. There was no other explanation.

With a furious cry, Alex kicked out at the nearest chair and sent it crashing over. He'd been a bloody idiot, trusting him. What had he been thinking? Well, he hadn't been thinking, had he? He'd let his prick do the bloody thinking.

"Fucking hell." He dropped his head into his hands, scrunching his fingers into his hair. No camera meant no more photographs, no way to capture this insanity but in his own poor memory, with his own poor words. He felt blinded, muzzled by its loss. Stupidly, his eyes began to burn, his throat growing thick. Had someone lopped off his right arm it would have been less painful. And the fact that Alex had done it, that Alex had tricked and made a fool of him, made it so much worse.

He'd liked Alex, and he'd thought Alex liked him. But all along... What? He'd been plotting to steal his camera? Why, for the love of God?

Out of nervous habit his hand went to his breast pocket, checking for the camera that was gone, and this time he felt a crinkle of paper beneath his fingers. Reaching inside, he found a note. It was a single piece of paper, folded. On it, in the elegant hand of an educated man, were written two lines.

Take nothing home but yourself; souvenirs are dangerous. And stay out of the shadows. A.

That was it; that was all. But it was enough.

"Bloody hell," Josef said, staring at the note. "He was bloody Intelligence Corps."

Who else would issue such a threat? If so, it meant Alex could have dropped Josef into some very hot water. He hadn't. He could also have turned a blind eye to the camera, considering that they'd spent the night fucking, and he hadn't done that either.

For a long time, Josef perched on the edge of the bed in that empty room and stared at the note. Then he got up, tucked it into his pocket, donned his coat and hat and left, closing the door quietly behind him.

Threats be damned. If Captain Winchester—or any other sodding arse in the Intelligence Corps—thought Josef could be intimidated out of publishing his photographs, then they'd better think again. Because in six weeks he'd be back in London, and then the world would know the truth.

Chapter Four

London, November 1917

"The thing is," said May Capper, "the world doesn't want to know the truth."

Josef had been home from the front for two weeks and sat now in the cramped offices of the Daily Clarion with a selection of his photographs spread out on the desk before him. He pushed one towards her. "You can't mean that you won't publish any of these."

May sat back with a sigh. She was a young woman, older than him but not yet thirty, and spoke with a strong Manchester accent. Her lips pursed as she quoted the Defence of the Realm Act to him. "No person shall by word of mouth or in writing spread reports likely to cause disaffection or alarm among any of His Majesty's forces or among the civilian population."

"Since when do you give two hoots for DORA?"

May had no qualms about breaking the law; she'd been imprisoned several times for disorderly conduct and assaulting the police during Suffragette protests. She'd even been on hunger strike.

"It's not that I'm afraid to publish them, Joe." With one hand she indicated the photographs, some of his most urgent and harrowing work. "My God, they're desperately important. But if we publish any of these, the police will be round here before you can say Jack Robinson. The government are just looking for an excuse to shut us down. And what good will that do?"

"At least people will have seen the truth. That was the point, wasn't it? That's why I spent ten bloody months in that...that nightmare." His gaze roved over the images he'd captured, shying away from the memories they invoked—still too real, too visceral to bear unless through the filter of his camera lens. "What the hell was it all for if we don't publish? I might as well have gone to prison with the others."

"We have to walk a line, Joe. Say enough to inform people, but not so much that we give the censors reason to prosecute." She met his gaze across the table, her own softening. "But it's not just that." With her fingertips she moved the pictures around on the desk, examining each in turn. One, the boy lying among the dead at the dressing station, she drew closer, examining the lad's deathly face and the eerie gleam in his eyes. "This is some mother's son, Joe. Do we have the right to use his image to shock? I'm not sure."

"We do if it shakes people up enough to end the slaughter. We'd be saving countless other sons." He pulled the picture back towards himself. An error in developing the photograph had left a slight double shadow over the boy's face, as if his ghost already watched from behind those startlingly open eyes. Behind him, the dead blurred, indistinct mounds in the early dawn light. And suddenly, Josef could taste the cigarette he'd been smoking that morning, feel the clammy air on his skin, smell the stench of the putrid wound on the boy's arm. His stomach roiled, and he looked away, back to May's face. "If we hide the truth, then we're complicit."

"The countess wouldn't thank us for getting shut down."

The countess. Muriel Sackville, fervent campaigner for women's suffrage and the Labour Party, was the money behind the Clarion. Without her largesse it would have folded at the start of the war, when the public appetite switched from the Clarion's traditional socialist campaigning to the richer, more jingoistic diet provided by the Daily Mail, and other such rags. Although Josef didn't much like the idea of an aristocratic patroness, the countess's money kept him in work, and he wasn't the sort to look a gift horse in the mouth. Not even a posh one. He supposed toffs could develop a social conscience as well as anyone else.

Even if most of them turned out to be secretive, sneaky bastards.

Not that he was thinking about any particular toff, you understand.

"What you've seen and suffered won't be for nothing," May said. "One day, your pictures will be a vital record. People will know the bloody truth of this imperialist war. But for now... Do you have any images that are less shocking?"

Josef folded his arms over his chest. "Like what? Good old British Tommies playing footie behind the lines? No, I don't. I left that crap to the 'accredited reporters' and the propaganda machine." Angry, he pushed himself to his feet and paced to the other end of the office. "I thought we wanted the truth, May."

Through the grimy window, he looked down into the street, damp and foggy this November morning. The poor sods would be freezing their asses off at the front, and he was meant to be helping them, exposing the truth to the complacent world back home so that the people would rise up and demand an end to the slaughter. That had been the deal, the bargain he'd struck with himself when he'd taken non-combat work instead of going to gaol as a proud conscientious objector. But now... A knot tightened in his throat, a ball of guilt and horror and sudden hopelessness. God, but this war would go on forever, grinding up men into mince while everyone at home got blind drunk on patriotic zeal.

How could he stand it? How could he bear to do nothing when he knew what was happening over the channel? When he had the evidence but couldn't—?

"Joe." May's hand landed on his shoulder, but he didn't turn around because he could feel his churning anger and didn't want to lash out. She squeezed. "All right, listen. What about a pamphlet? We print it anonymously, distribute it by hand. Leave copies on the tube, hand it out in the street..."

He turned cautiously. "A pamphlet?"

"Choose, say, six of your most hard-hitting photographs and we'll put it together." She framed the headline with her hands, as if seeing it written in the air. "War: The Hidden Horror. We'll keep it between us. Six photographs and some words to go with them."

"It should be the front page of the Clarion, May."

"I know, but it can't be. Ending the war isn't the only thing we're fighting for, Joe. And we can't impale ourselves on that one issue."

He rubbed his hands through his hair, still bitterly disappointed. But he trusted May, he liked May, and deep down he knew she was right. After everything he'd witnessed at the front, ending the war overshadowed all other issues in his mind. But for May, for the countess, and for many others who worked for the Daily Clarion, the struggle was wider: universal suffrage and education, workers' rights, the advance of international socialism. They were fighting for a future where men and women everywhere lived with dignity and respect, and ending this imperialist war was only part of their fight. "A pamphlet is better than nothing," he conceded, and softened his ungrateful response with a smile. "But I want to write it too."

"Joe..."

He held up a hand to stop her. "I know I don't write as well as you, but it has to be my words. It has to be someone who was there."

Her lips pursed, but after a moment, she said, "All right. But the editor gets the last word, and no arguing."

"I wouldn't dare."

"Good. Now off with you. I've work to do. As do you, by the way. I need a picture of this evening's menu at the Ritz for a piece we're running about food shortages. Think you can manage it?"

"I dare say I can charm my way into the kitchens." He smiled, but it felt wan as he gathered his photographs from the table and slipped them back inside their envelope. "I'll bring a print over tomorrow."

May stopped him before he left, grasping his arm. "Bring one of your less-shocking pictures with you, too. We'll run a piece about conditions at the front."

"And the casualty figures. They're lying about that, May. And they're lying about the new weapons, too. The gas and... I don't even know what. Something worse, maybe." Something that left hideous, rotting wounds that he could have photographed further if Winchester hadn't pinched his bloody camera. Which, he suspected, had been the point of the theft. Too bad for the captain that Josef had already dropped off his film with M. Verbeke, because the picture of that boy had been every bit as powerful as he'd hoped.

He thought about it as he stepped out into the foggy evening. Truth be told, he thought about it a lot. For all the death he'd witnessed, that nameless boy's suffering had been the most intimate. And the most shocking.

Winchester's involvement only made it worse.

Perhaps that was why, as he turned up his collar and headed down Carmelite Street towards the Embankment, he thought he caught the scent of decay in the air. Not for the first time, either, since his return to London. Not ordinary decay, you understand, but the specific putrid rot of those vile wounds he'd seen in Flanders. Today, the stench seemed to linger in the fog. He rubbed his nose with the back of his hand as he walked along the narrow pavement, dodging around people as they loomed out of the murk.

The fog was even thicker down by the river, the mournful hoots of invisible ships only adding to the strange sense of dislocation. When Josef was a boy, his father had told him the tale of a docker who'd disappeared one foggy night down at the Port of London. Nobody knew what became of him until, when the fog cleared, the desperate scratches of his fingernails had been found on the side of the dock where he'd struggled to climb out of the icy river before he drowned. Apocryphal or not, the story had terrified Josef. He'd hated the fog ever since.

It was almost six o'clock by the time he reached the Ritz, its golden light beaming into the night as if wealth and privilege could beat back the dark. Maybe it could; it seemed like money could perform miracles. Why else would those who had it fight so hard to keep it all for themselves? Through the windows of the Ritz, Josef glimpsed the men and women within as if visiting an exhibit: The British Upper Class at Play. Colourful, exotic creatures in their tank, separated by glass from the cold, dank London streets. Separated by an even greater chasm from the struggles and fears of people like himself. And from the men dying at their behest in the salient.

Absently, he rubbed his nose. Was he imagining that bloody stink? Maybe it was the river. Eager to be out of the weather, he headed for the staff entrance at the back of the hotel and wheedled his way into the kitchens. He and the maître d', Floréal Bisset, were old friends. And by friends he meant 'friends'.

"Josef," Floréal gushed, kissing him on both cheeks in the continental fashion. "What a pleasure. I did not know you were back from the front." Floréal had a thick French accent which Josef was sure he actively preserved; he'd worked in England for at least thirty years, after all, but still sounded like he'd just stepped off the boat. "How are you?" Hands resting on Josef's shoulders, Floréal studied him, and Josef felt warmed by the genuine concern in his friend's face. A little more lined than before, a little more strained. But so were they all; it had been a hard few years. "You look thin," Floréal said. Then he smiled, his eyes crinkling. "Mais toujours aussi beau."

Josef squeezed his arm. "It's good see you too, Florrie. I'm afraid I'm here to beg a favour."

"Ah." Floréal's enthusiasm dimmed. "Go on."

Josef explained what May wanted, pulling his camera—his new camera, thank you very much Captain bloody Winchester—from his satchel. "It won't take a moment, and obviously, your name won't be mentioned in the piece."

Floréal rolled his eyes. "I see you're still fighting the 'imperialist elite'."

"I see you're still serving them."

Floréal's shrug was very French. "But every day I dine like a king, and you are very thin, so... Mince, Josef! Come on, I will fetch your menu. And something to eat, too. Put some meat back on your bones, mon poulet."

And so Josef not only got his photograph of the extravagant and frankly excessive menu, but he got to sample a dish of sole and lobster drowned in a creamy white wine sauce. A substantial meal on its own, and undoubtedly the best one he'd eaten since his supper with Winchester, but just one course for those who dined at the Ritz. His hackles rose at the sight of all the cream sloshing about the kitchen when food shortages meant that ordinary men and women struggled to buy a pint of milk.

That was the point of the article May was writing, but when he thought of the tins of Maconochie stew being cracked open at the front by soldiers fighting and dying in a war propagated and prolonged by the men who feasted here... Well, his blood boiled.

Which was when Floréal booted him out to cool down.

"Come back later, eh?" His gaze lingered in that specific, knowing way. "It's been too long, my friend."

"It has," Josef said, reaching into his coat pocket for his fags. Truth was, he'd not been much in the mood for that kind of thing since he got back. Too much else on his mind, he supposed. He lit up and offered Floréal an apologetic smile. "Thanks for dinner."

"De rien. And stay out of trouble, eh?"

Josef smiled and sketched a short bow as he began to walk away. "I'll do my best."

Unfortunately, his best lasted only a few minutes.

With the fog still thick, it was slow going along Piccadilly as he headed for the tube—sod walking home in this muck. He'd just reached the station when he heard a commotion up ahead. Nothing unusual about that in London, especially in the fog, so he paid no attention at first as he stopped outside the entrance to Dover Street and ferreted in his pocket for change.

The sudden shrill blast of a police whistle made him jump. And piqued his curiosity. He hesitated, eyeing the warmth and light of the Underground on one side and the foggy darkness on the other. As usual, his curiosity won the argument. Taking a bracing drag on his gasper, he went to investigate. As he walked toward the sounds of alarm, he couldn't see much except that someone was waving a light about—a hand torch, by the look of the steady electric beam. The police whistle blew again from up ahead, followed by the pounding of running feet as an officer sped past him.

Josef quickened his pace until the lumpy shapes in the fog resolved themselves into a small crowd of people, their low murmurs of consternation muted by the dank air. One of them—the police officer, probably—wielded the electric torch. Josef could see its beam flashing through the fog. He hurried forward but stumbled to a halt when his nose filled with that dreadfully familiar stench of rot.

This time he knew he hadn't imagined it because he could see two ladies holding their handkerchiefs over their noses and mouths. Josef's heart kicked with a sudden sense of dread. "Excuse me," he said, shouldering his way through the small crowd. They let him pass, eager to draw back.

And he understood why when he saw the dead man sprawled on the pavement.

A tramp, by the looks of his ragged clothing. Josef had seen more dead men than he could count, so it wasn't the old man's deathly stillness that troubled him, or his rictus of horror, peg-toothed gums bared. He'd seen far worse. No, what had Josef recoiling in shock was the putrid black wound on the man's arm and shoulder. He reached immediately for his camera and crouched down, then cursed the lack of light. Impossible to photograph anything in these conditions.

"Stay back, sir." The policeman stood on the other side of the body, keeping his distance like the rest of the crowd. "We're fetching an ambulance."

"Bit late for that," Josef muttered. More loudly, he said, "What happened?"

From behind him, a woman said, "Looks like something took a bite out of him."

"Maybe there's an animal on the loose?" said another. "A wolf or something, escaped from the zoo."

"There are no wolves loose in London, madam," said the unimaginative constable.

But wolves or not, the woman was right. The flesh did look as if it had been eaten away. Torn out. Which was unlikely, of course, but Josef's eyes saw what they saw. And God almighty, the stink! He tucked his mouth and nose into the crook of his elbow. "I've seen this before."

"Now, now," the policeman protested. "There's nothing to say this is anything like the other one."

Josef's head jerked up. "What other one?"

After a pause, the constable said, "Move back from the body, sir."

"Are you saying you've seen a wound like this before? In London—?"

"Excuse me, officer," interrupted a cultured voice. "Is there some kind of trouble?"

At which point Josef's thoughts scattered entirely because, to his complete astonishment, he recognised that voice. And sure enough, Captain Winchester appeared out of the mist behind the constable, flanked by two other men who, like him, were dressed in impeccable evening wear. One of them was the tall, Indian officer who'd been with Winchester in Flanders. The other Josef didn't recognise.

Still crouching by the body, Josef absolutely stared. No chance this was a coincidence. Not a single one.

"Nothing to trouble yourself with, sir." The policeman touched the brim of his helmet with the instinctive deference Josef loathed. "The ambulance is on the way." As if to prove him correct, the ding-ding-ding of the bell crept along the street behind them. "Poor wretch succumbed to the cold most likely."

The cold my arse, Josef thought. Did the cold chew a rotting hole in his arm?

Winchester's gaze was fixed on the body, so intent that he didn't appear to have noticed Josef. All to the good. "Very sad," Winchester said coolly, but he was looking at the wounds—bites?—on the body's arm with avid interest.

Now was not the time for Josef to speak to Winchester, not in front of all these people. Besides, dressed up to the nines as he was, the captain was clearly more of a toff than Josef had realised back in Poperinge. Any kind of familiarity between them would raise questions difficult to answer and potentially dangerous to them both; it wasn't the done thing among men of their sort to subject a lover to the risk of exposure. Even when said lover was a lying thief.

And so, Josef kept his head down, hiding his face beneath the peak of his cap.

"Seen your fill, you ghoul?" said one of Winchester's friends, a shorter slight chap with a top hat so tall it looked like he was overcompensating. "Come on. If we don't leave now, they'll give away our table."

"Mind your backs!" called a woman's voice, accompanied by the chug of a motor. The LCC ambulance had arrived, the driver leaning out of the window as she parked at the side of the street. The policeman began to move the small crowd aside, and Josef used the general shuffling around to hide himself as he stood up and mingled with the watchers. He kept his eye on Winchester, though. Well, he was hard to miss in his glistening topper and long, elegant overcoat.

Dashing, Josef's mind supplied unhelpfully.

The ambulance women took charge immediately, bustling about, assessing the casualty. Well, corpse. Josef found himself watching them with professional interest and admiration. The entire London ambulance service was staffed by women these days, much to May's delight, and from what he could see, they knew their stuff.

"Poor old boy," one of the women said, crouching next to the man's feet. She was a full-figured woman with a crown of red hair peeking out from beneath her hat. "Alright, Lottie. On three, now." She took the man's feet, her colleague took his shoulders, and together they hefted the corpse onto the stretcher. Then she fetched a blanket to cover his body and face.

The war dead were accorded much less dignity, Josef reflected. Except that Winchester had covered the face of the dead boy; it had been the first thing Josef had liked about the man.

"Give us a little space to work, please, sir." The ambulance woman was talking to Winchester, hustling him back a step or two as she lifted the stretcher.

"I say," said the man in the tall top hat. "Hardly appropriate work for ladies."

"Oh, don't be so Victorian, Percy," Winchester replied, his gaze still fixed on the blanket-covered body.

"All right then, that's your lot, ladies and gents," said the policeman once the women had loaded the body into the back of their ambulance.

The crowd began to disperse, but Josef hung back, glad now for the fog, and watched as Winchester and his friends set off along Piccadilly towards the Ritz. Odd that Winchester just happened to be passing when this body had been found.

Odd to the point of incredulity.

Before the mist swallowed them whole, Josef set off after them. He kept his distance, lurking as far as the concealing fog would allow. But when they'd left the policeman and the rest of the onlookers behind, he risked calling out, "Captain Winchester."

Winchester's steps faltered, but he didn't stop. Neither did either of his friends.

"Winchester!" Josef called, louder this time. Too loud not to be heard, but still Winchester didn't react. "Hey, I'm talking to you, mister!"

After a few more steps, Winchester slowed, paused, and then turned around. He regarded Josef with such blank incomprehension that for a moment Josef wondered whether he'd somehow been mistaken. "Are you addressing me, sir?"

A man could injure himself on the sharp edges of that cut-glass accent.

"You know I am. That body—"

"I say." The short man—Percy?—stepped forward like an aggressive little spaniel. "Who the devil are you?"

Josef spared him a disparaging glance. "My name's Shepel. Captain Winchester and I—" he glanced at Alex, "—served together. In Flanders."

Percy gave a haughty look down the length of his narrow nose. "I don't know who the devil you think you're talking to, man, but there's nobody here of that name. You have the honour of addressing Lord Rafe Beaumont." When Josef didn't react, he added, "Brother of the Duke of Chester."

Well, well. Josef met Winchester's gaze. "Funny. You look the very spit of the captain."

Winchester's expression remained entirely expressionless, save for a slight tightening around his eyes. Perhaps he feared Josef was about to expose the sordid truth of their liaison. "An honest mistake, I'm sure," he said, and touched the brim of his top hat.

"Good evening, my lord."

Winchester didn't answer, giving only the scantest nod acceptable.

Percy turned and began to walk away, the Indian gentleman taking a longer look at Josef before following. Winchester brought up the rear, swinging his cane with an angry swish. Josef watched the fog swallow each one in turn, chilled by more than the dank night.

Stupidly, he felt disappointed.

If he'd imagined meeting Winchester again in London—and, alright, perhaps he had imagined it once or twice—their meeting had involved considerably more warmth and fewer clothes than this chilly encounter. Certainly not a cold dismissal. Or the discovery that the man went by more than one name. But Josef supposed that was no surprise if, as he already suspected, Winchester worked for the Intelligence Corps.

He was mulling over that, and what it might mean that Winchester had shown up at the scene of tonight's discovery, when the man himself returned. Half lost in the fog, he was little more than a dark shape in the shifting shadows as he said, "It's a wretched night to be out, Mr Shepel. If I were you, I'd stay safely by the fire. The forecast is shocking."

With that strange meteorological advice delivered, Winchester turned and disappeared into the night, leaving Josef alone on the street. Alone but fired up, every journalistic instinct alight, as though he'd plugged himself into an electrical socket.

Something fishy was going on. Winchester—or 'Lord Beaumont'—was in it up to his nutmegs. And Josef was going to find out what the hell 'it' was.

It never occurred to him that he might come to wish he didn't know.

Chapter Five

Contrary to Captain Winchester's advice, Josef did not go home and sit by the fire. Instead, he hopped on the tube to Westminster, then pegged it over to St Thomas's Hospital.

He didn't beat the ambulance, but it was still there when he arrived, idling outside the hospital. An ambulance train must have just arrived at Waterloo Station because a fleet of Red Cross vehicles were pulling up at the hospital—St Thomas's having hundreds of beds set aside for the wounded—and while the critical patients were being admitted, nobody had time for an old dead vagrant. So the ambulance was waiting.

Which was lucky for Josef.

The crew were talking together, the driver's door open and the two women leaning against the side of their van while they watched the parade of injured soldiers being stretchered into the hospital. Josef watched too, an anxious churning in the pit of his belly that he couldn't fully explain. Maybe it was because he could have accompanied some of those very men on the first leg of their journey, carried them back from the dressing station to the field hospital. And now here he was in London, watching them finally make it home. Poor sods. And these were the lucky ones.

"Sobering, ain't it?" he said, addressing his comment to the red-haired woman he'd noticed earlier that night. He liked her round, open face.

"At least they're home." She took a drag on the end of a cigarette, dropping the stub on the ground. "Two of my brothers are at the front."

Josef said, "So was I, two weeks ago."

Her eyes flicked to him, and he saw her intelligence immediately. "Yeah? Which regiment?"

Bracing himself, he said, "The Red Cross."

"You don't look like a doctor."

"Ambulance driver."

"Ah." Her expression shifted, cooling noticeably. "You're a conchie, then, are you?"

His hackles rose, and despite all his antiwar principles, he felt a flush of unwarranted shame. "I've played my part," he said, and could have said a great deal more about the futility of this imperialist war. But arguing wouldn't help his current cause. Besides, if she had two brothers at the front, she wouldn't want to hear his arguments. "I was just thinking that I probably carried some of these boys to safety. I was working with a CCS in Lijssenthoek."

"And you was up at Dover Street half an hour ago, an' all."

He didn't try to deny it; she'd obviously recognised him. "Where I was admiring your professionalism, ladies."

"No need to sound so surprised." This came from the driver, her accent closer to Winchester's than Josef's, chiming like a silver bell. Her eyes were just as bright. "I think you'll find there are plenty of jobs we 'ladies' are more than capable of performing."

He tipped his hat to her. "I've no doubt of that, miss. My boss is a woman, in fact. At the Daily Clarion."

"You're a journalist?"

"I am. Josef Shepel, at your service."

The women exchanged a glance. Then the red-haired one said, "I'm Violet. Vi, for short. And that's Lady Charlotte."

"Lottie," the other woman corrected with a roll of her eyes.

"It's a pleasure to meet you both." Josef dug out his fags and offered them around. Vi took one; Lottie didn't.

"My old man reads the Clarion," Vi said, letting Josef light her cigarette. "He's a union man. But don't tell me you're writing about wounded soldiers coming back from the war. That's hardly news."

"I'm more interested in the poor blighter in the back of your ambulance, as it happens."

Again, the women exchanged a look. Neither said anything.

"What do you make of it?" Josef prompted. "That wound on his shoulder, I mean."

"It's stinking out the van," Vi said. "Why do you think we're standing out here in the freezing cold?"

"Before you got there tonight, the police constable said he'd seen something like it before. I was wondering whether you had, too."

"Well..." Lottie was watching Vi carefully.

"Happens we have," Vi confirmed. "Couple of days ago. A Gotha bomb fell over on Old Castle Street back in July and damaged the sewers. They're doing works there now to mend it."

"I know," Josef said, surprised. "I live around the corner."

"Well, the men turned up Tuesday morning for work—I think it was Tuesday."

"It was," Lottie confirmed. "Definitely."

"Well then, they turned up Tuesday morning and found..." Vi dragged deeply on her fag, spinning out the tale. "They found a body in the sewer. Like him, it was, all rotted and... chewed-up looking."

"In the sewer?" Josef rummaged in his satchel for his notebook and pencil. "And was the dead man old, like this? A vagrant?"

Vi shook her head, and Lottie said, "He was a soldier, in uniform. Private Andrew Sykes according to his tags. Police think he was probably blotto when he fell into the sewer—the fencing around the hole had been knocked over, and it would have been dark."

"That don't explain how his arm got chewed, does it?"

Lottie gave her a quelling look. "Rats, so the police say."

"And whoever heard of rats eating people?"

Josef had. Rats ate the dead at the front, gnawed at the unreachable bodies decomposing in no man's land. In Flanders, the rats grew fat. He supposed the same could have happened here, if some poor sod had blundered, drunk, into the sewer. And perhaps to the old vagrant, too, who'd succumbed to the cold and provided a feast for a fat English rat.

Talking of English rats, none of that explained the extreme coincidence of Winchester showing up both times Josef stumbled across a man with this strange, rotting wound.

No, there was more to this than vermin, unless the Intelligence Corps had taken to breeding killer rats. Frankly, he wouldn't put anything past this government; if they could unleash deadly gas and let it creep across the battlefield to murder men while they slept, why not killer rats? Still, it stretched his weary credulity.

"You mind if I take a closer look?" he asked, nodding to the back of the ambulance.

Vi and Charlotte shared another look. Then Vi shrugged and said, "No skin off my nose, but you might want to cover yours. It bloody reeks in there."

She wasn't wrong. The enclosed space intensified the stomach-turning stench, making it almost impossible to breathe. And even with his army-issue hand torch, it was too dark to see much when he peeled back the blanket, but enough to confirm that the flesh had been eaten away by something.

Unlike Josef, Vi and Lottie hadn't seen a man's body ruined by mustard gas. He knew there were more things than God's creatures that could consume a man's flesh. Gangrene and trench foot did it, too. But this...?

He fished out his camera and did his best to take a photograph, shining the torch with one hand. God knew whether it would come out, but at least he'd tried.

By this point, his eyes were watering with the stench, and he was forced to scramble out of the van and suck in great lungfuls of air to keep himself from throwing up his expensive Ritz supper.

Vi smirked as she strolled over, dropping the stub of her cigarette on the pavement. "Need a stronger stomach than that in this job, Mr Shepel." She closed the ambulance doors. "We've to drive around to the other entrance. Take him in that way, straight to the mortuary."

"Listen, if you see anyone else with the same wounds, will you let me know?" Josef pulled out a business card for the Clarion. "You can send a note or telephone that number and leave a message."

The ambulance's engine coughed into life, belching fumes. Vi waved a hand in front of her face, clearing the air. "Why are you so interested? What is it you think's happening?"

"I'm just curious." He attempted a disarming smile. "It's my job to be curious."

"Then you should be careful, too." She took his card and smiled. "You know what they say—curiosity killed the cat."

From the front of the ambulance, Lottie leaned out of the window. "Vi, come on!" she called. "They're signalling for us to drive round."

Doffing his cap with a flourish, he watched the ambulance pull away. And be immediately replaced by a drab Red Cross vehicle, unloading wounded fresh from Flanders. Josef made himself scarce, surprised by how his heart galloped at the sight of the still bodies on stretchers. Too familiar by half and pressing painfully on a wound he hadn't realised was open.

Walking back to Westminster tube station, he filled his head with the current problem instead of unpleasant memories. Vi and Lottie had been more helpful than he could have hoped, but it was obvious they knew no more about what was happening than he did.

Which meant Josef had no choice but to track down the one man who clearly did know something. Whether Winchester—or 'Lord Alexander Beaumont'—would want to explain it to him was another matter entirely.

But sod what the man wanted. Josef wasn't in the mood to take no for an answer.

Chapter Six

"Look him up in Who's Who," May suggested when Josef popped into the Clarion the next morning with his print of the Ritz menu. "If his title's real, he'll be in there."

"The title might be real but that doesn't mean he's not a phony," Josef pointed out, but it was a good suggestion. Who's Who was at least a place to start.

May looked up from studying the photograph. "This is excellent, Joe. We'll run it in the Saturday edition. Leslie's eating there tonight, so he'll write up something excoriating." She shook her head over the menu. "There are women struggling to buy milk for their children, and these men feast like kings."

He'd developed the picture last night in his room at the Cohens'. It was cheaper, and safer, to develop his own photographs, and he'd been happy with the way this one had come out. Happier still that his shot of the dead man's wound had been clear enough to see details, even if it was slightly marred by the same double exposure that afflicted the picture of the dying boy in Flanders. He intended to compare them later, although at the distance he'd taken that shot, the wound was difficult to make out. There might be something in it, however. Some connection.

Something he could use to challenge Winchester.

If he ever found the lying sod.

"I'm heading over to the library," he decided, standing. "They keep a copy of Who's Who."

He'd often wondered about that. How many people needed to reference Who's Who on such a regular basis it was worth keeping a copy in the public library? But perhaps there were plenty of aristocrats running about under assumed names, stealing other people's personal possessions. He wouldn't put it past them; historically speaking, theft had always been the favoured pastime of the ruling class.

Overnight, the fog had thickened into a viscous smog, and Josef was coughing by the time he reached the library on Charles Street. He'd promised Mr C that he'd help in the shop that afternoon, so he didn't have long for his research. Luckily, it didn't take long to find the Duke of Chester's brother: Lord Ralph (although Percy had pronounced it 'Rafe') Alexander Twisleton Beaumont. Twisleton! The entry told him that the family's principal residence was Beaumont House in Cheshire, that his lordship had been educated at Harrow and then Cambridge, that he worked as a private secretary in the War Office, and that he was a member of all sorts of toffee-nosed clubs with stupid names like the Savage Club and the Winconian Society.

There was no mention of his military service as a captain in the RAMC, nor any suggestion that he was a trained medical doctor.

Frankly, Josef doubted the man he knew as Captain Winchester was the same man as the chinless aristocrat described in Who's Who. Winchester had seemed too... human. Nevertheless, Josef wrote down the names and addresses of the various clubs as a place to start looking. If nothing else, he'd be able to confirm that the man posing as Beaumont was a fake.

Turning up his coat collar against the cold, he plunged back into the fog and headed home. Well, not home home, which was the two overcrowded rooms on Goulston Street he'd shared with his parents and six siblings, but to a small and gloriously private room above Cohen's Ironmonger on Leyden Street. Mr and Mrs Cohen had taken him in six years ago, after the general strike in the Port of London. Josef, a union official, had lost his position as a warehouseman when the strike collapsed, and his father had thrown him out; he'd refused to harbour a 'radical' under his roof. So, in exchange for room and board, he'd helped the Cohens in their shop, spending his evenings writing furious pieces for any of the union or syndicalist newspapers who'd let him, before finding paid work at the Clarion. These days, he still helped in the shop when he could, even though he paid the Cohens a decent rent. They were getting older now and found the heavy work of lugging around pots and pans, coal scuttles, and tin baths difficult. But he suspected the real reason they kept him on was because having a younger man in the shop made them feel safer.

Especially after the war had started.

Normally, Josef would have saved himself tuppence and walked home but given the fog he forked out for the tube instead. Blackfriars Station was quiet in the middle of the day, with scarcely anyone on the platform as he waited for the train. The cold made his nose run, and when he blew it, his handkerchief came away sooty. Bloody smog. He scrubbed at his nose with his coat sleeve and suddenly caught that dreadful stink in the air again. Dropping his arm, he wondered whether it had somehow clung to his coat but, no, he could still smell it. And for reasons he couldn't explain, the hair rose on the back of his neck. Moving closer to the edge of the platform, he peered down onto the track. Movement caught his eye, over to the right toward the tunnel entrance, and he recoiled at the sight of a huge brown rat scurrying beneath the elevated rails.

He watched it snuffling around as the air began to stir with the oncoming rush of a train. It came rattling through the tunnel towards him, pushing the air ahead of it—warm air from the deep tunnels. Thick with the same stench. Gagging, Josef put his hand to his mouth. And froze.

Something watched him from the dark of the tunnel, a gleam of eerie blue eyes.

Josef jolted in horror, oppressed by a sudden, paralysing dread. Then, suddenly, there was nothing but the yellow glare of the train's lantern as it burst out of the tunnel, brakes hissing and squealing as it slowed and stopped at the station.

Heart pounding, Josef made his way to the third-class carriage and sank shakily onto an empty seat. A young woman dozed at the far end of the compartment, her head on the window and hat askew, and two men in uniform stood at the other end of the carriage in deep conversation. One of them glanced at him, clearly taking in the sight of a young man of fighting age not in uniform, and ostentatiously turned his back. He heard "yellow belly" thrown out, intentionally loud.

"Conchie coward," agreed the other soldier.

Josef bristled, face heating, but he didn't respond; he was too shaken for a scrap. Besides, what did he care what they thought of him? Once your own father had disowned you, spitting insults into your face in front of your neighbours—'You fucking coward! You're a bloody disgrace to your family!'—the words of strangers lost their power.

Well, mostly.

As the train moved out, the stench dispersed, and Josef's horror subsided. He told himself he'd been imagining things because he could not have seen eyes in the tunnel. That was impossible. If he had, whoever they'd belonged to would have been pulverised by the train. But the devil of it was that he'd seen that eerie blue flash of eyes before—the night he'd spent in Poperinge with Winchester. He'd seen them in the dark street outside the hotel, and they'd been watching him then, too.

His throat contracted, and he coughed because it was too dry to swallow.

Stupid. He was letting his imagination run away with him, that was all. As a rationalist and an atheist, Josef didn't believe in anything that couldn't be explained by cold, hard reason. But maybe his nerves had been damaged worse than he'd realised by ten months wading through the bloody carnage of war? He wouldn't be the first man to start seeing things; that was for sure. Plenty of poor sods had their minds more injured than their bodies at the front, and he knew damn well those men weren't malingerers or cowards. No, the horror of it could damage a man's mind. He'd seen it happen.

The idea that it had happened to him, that his mind was playing tricks on him, was ... genuinely frightening.

But was his nose playing tricks, too? Because that stink had been real enough.

He curled his fingers around the edge of his seat, focussing on the roughness of the rattan beneath his palms, and told himself to think straight. Whatever was going on here had a rational explanation, and the only hair-raising thing about it would turn out to be that the government had invented yet another appalling method of mass slaughter.

Still, he couldn't shake a deep sense of unease that clung on until he'd left the Underground and emerged into the biting chill of the foggy afternoon. It was a five-minute walk from Aldgate East to Leyden Street, and Josef did it in three—despite the weather. He just wanted to get away from the tube and out of the dank day.

Working his way through the crowded market at Petticoat Lane calmed him down, though; the cheerful press of strangers and the familiar noise and bustle of the market were comforting. And by the time he saw the window of Cohen's Ironmongers glowing with yellow electric light, he'd calmed down enough to smile as he opened the side door of the shop. "I'm back!" he called, shucking his coat and hanging it on the coat hook. The shop was warm, the air thick with the acrid scent of iron polish, and the kettle whistling for the Cohens' afternoon cuppa. Josef relaxed, taking a deep breath as he unwound his scarf and hung it over the hook with his coat and cap. A cup of strong tea was what he needed, and for that he'd come to the right place.

Mr Cohen, smart in his immaculate overalls, bustled about the shop ensuring that everything was 'just so'. The shop was his pride and joy, and a cleaner, tidier, more correct place of business you'd struggle to find. Had they been blessed with a son, this would have been his legacy, but there were no Cohen children—no son had marched off to war; no daughter waited at home for her brother or husband to return. Josef often wondered whether the Cohens, in suffering one grief, had been spared another, deeper pain. Either way, they were alone, and Josef had become the beneficiary of all their parental affection.

"Joe!" Mr Cohen smiled broadly as Josef ducked in from the back of the shop. "There you are."

Since he'd been back from the front, they greeted him like this every day—as if still surprised he'd returned in one piece. He knew they'd missed him, even though he'd written as often as possible and sent them money for the rent to ensure that his room was still his when he returned. At least, that's what he'd told them. Truth was, he knew they relied on his three shillings a week, and he didn't want them having to find someone else to take the room. Who knew what kind of chancer they might take in?

"Just in time for tea," Mr Cohen said. "And you look like you need it, Joe. The fog's like soup out there today."

"More like pease pudding," Josef grumbled, chafing his hands together to rub feeling back into his fingertips. "How's business today?"

Mr Cohen's smile wilted as he gestured around the empty shop. "Between the weather and the air raids, nobody's out."

"Paper says the fog should clear by the weekend." Josef tied on his apron and stepped behind the polished wooden counter, dropping his satchel onto the floor next to the high stool. "No zeppelin forecast, I'm afraid."

"Balloons," Mr Cohen said, with a disbelieving shake of his head. "Who'd have thought they'd drop bombs from hot air balloons? It's fantastical, like something Mr Wells would have written."

Josef smiled but didn't comment. Seemed to him that there was nothing mankind could invent that they wouldn't turn into a weapon of war sooner or later. "Go and have your tea, sir," he said. "I'll watch the shop."

"You should have yours first. You look chilled."

"Don't worry about me—I'm alright. Besides, I prefer my tea stewed."

Mr Cohen made a face. "That's true. All right, lad, if you're sure. Call me if..." He glanced around the empty shop and sighed. "Never mind."

As he listened to Mr Cohen's footsteps climbing the stairs, Josef hopped up onto the stool and pulled his satchel onto his lap, keen to start work on the pamphlet May had promised to publish. Retrieving his notebook, he settled himself with pencil poised and stared at the blank paper.

Where to even start?

Unfortunately, he wasn't as good with words as he was with pictures: he preferred his photographs to speak for him. But this had to be written, and he had to write it himself, while his memories were crisp and his anger sharp. He couldn't give it over to May or one of her other scribblers to write up second-hand. There was so much he wanted to say, though. It was hard to know where to begin.

Well. Why not begin with the boy?

Josef pulled the disturbing image from the envelope in his bag and propped it up against a jar of nails on the counter, gazing at that ghostly face and the pale eyes staring right into the lens of the camera. At the time, when he'd taken the picture, he hadn't noticed that the boy's eyes were open. The distance had been too great, perhaps, or he'd been too focused on framing the shot. But as soon as he'd seen the photograph, he'd realised how that eerie gaze drew you in and became the rending heart of the image.

He wanted it seen. It had to be seen. The boy—all the men who'd suffered and died—deserved to be seen, and Josef would do everything in his power to make that happen. Starting with writing the pamphlet.

Sometime later, he was roused from deep concentration by the jangle of a bell as the shop door opened. Startled, Josef looked up to find a gentleman standing in the doorway.

Captain Winchester, no less.

No uniform, though. He was dressed in civvies: a well-made dark suit with an elegant overcoat and a black Homburg, which he lifted in greeting as he closed the door behind him.

Well, well, well.

Josef set down his pencil and sat up straighter. Neither man spoke.

Winchester glanced around the shop, a quick thorough inspection as befitted an agent of the Intelligence Corps. Then his eyes settled back on Josef, just as intent as he remembered, their deep blue as dark as a night sky. An attractive combination with the sleek black hair that had slid like heavy silk through Josef's fingers.

Irritated with himself for noticing such things, Josef said, "Can I help you, Captain Winchester? Or should I call you 'your lordship' today?"

After a beat, Winchester said, "Certainly not. The correct form of address is 'my lord' or 'Lord Ralph Beaumont'. But I'd rather you called me Alex."

"So many names to choose from," Josef said. "Must be hard to keep them all straight in your head."

Winchester—Alex—gave a flat smile. If Josef hadn't known better, he'd have called it rueful. "I owe you an apology."

"I'll say you do."

"It was...difficult to acknowledge you as I'd have liked yesterday evening." He hesitated. "But I was glad to see you returned safely."

Josef raised his eyebrows. "Well, that was bloody rude, but I don't expect politeness from your sort."

"My sort being the blood-soaked bourgeoisie, I suppose."

"Nah. You're one of the old, landed toffs still clinging onto power."

"I see."

Leaning forward on his elbows, Josef said, "You stole my camera."

Another pause. Alex hadn't moved from his position by the door, and Josef couldn't help but notice he looked less self-possessed than usual. Despite his dapper appearance, he had the air of a cat on hot tiles. "I did," he agreed. "And for your own good. They're forbidden at the front, as you well know. I'd have hated to see you shot as a spy."

"A spy?" Josef laughed, then lowered his voice. He didn't want Mr Cohen to hear them and come back downstairs. "You don't think I'm a spy."

"No. I think you're a photographic journalist who contributes to that socialist rag, the Daily Clarion, which is vehemently anti-war. And that would probably have been enough to get you shot had you been found in the line with your Box Brownie."

"It was an Autographic Vest Pocket Kodak. And it cost me a pound and ten shillings."

"It might have cost you your life, had you kept it."

"Bollocks." Slipping off the stool, Josef came around to the front of the counter. He wished he wasn't wearing his apron—didn't like how it put him in the subservient position—but he'd be buggered if he was going to untie it. "I was taking pictures of things you wanted to hide, wasn't I? That's why you nicked it."

Alex's face was studiously neutral. "I don't know what you were—"

"Come off it. It had something to do with that boy who clicked it at the dressing station. And with whatever caused his wounds." He held up a hand when Alex opened his mouth. "Don't even think of denying it."

"I wouldn't dare." He crossed the shop to the counter, setting down his hat and pulling off his gloves one finger at a time. Josef made himself look away from that little striptease. "I understand you were at St. Thomas's Hospital yesterday evening."

Startled, he said, "Are you *following* me?"

"Only a little." Alex smiled, again without humour. "You happened to run into a friend of mine—Lady Charlotte."

Lottie, the ambulance driver. "Bloody hell, are you lot everywhere?"

"Hardly." Setting his gloves in his hat, he turned to face Josef. "Let's chalk that up to serendipity, shall we? But the point is that you need to stop."

"Stop what?"

"Whatever it is you think you're doing."

Josef spread his hands. "I'm not doing anything."

"You're poking your nose into matters that don't concern you."

"And why don't they concern me? I've as much right as the next man to know if the government's unleashed killer rats or—"

"Killer rats?" This time, when Alex's lips twitched, it was with genuine amusement.

Josef felt his cheeks heat. "Not my theory," he said stiffly. "But if it's some kind of gas or...or infection—"

"No." Alex waved him silent. "It's not... I'm not..." He struggled inwardly, glancing up at the ceiling as if pleading for strength. "I don't work for the government."

"Riiiiiight." Josef folded his arms. "'Course you don't."

"I don't."

"According to Who's Who, 'Lord Beaumont' works for the War Office."

His eyebrows rose. "You...looked me up in Who's Who?"

"Dunno. You tell me. Are you Lord Beaumont, or are you Captain Winchester? Or someone else entirely?"

Silence.

"If you don't work for the War Office, then what were you doing in the salient?" Josef took a step closer. "Are you really with the RAMC? Are you even a doctor? What caused the wounds on that boy, and why is it killing men in London? Who's the man you—?"

Alex seized him abruptly by both shoulders. "Stop." His expression was cool, but his eyes flashed, his grip fierce. Josef felt his skin prickle all the way up the back of his neck, little electric jolts of awareness. "All right. You win. Yes, I work for the War Office. We're investigating a new..." His gaze flicked away and back. "...a new infection. It's broken out among the men."

"Oh yeah? What kind of infection?"

"A deadly one."

Josef frowned. "How come I never heard anything about it at the front?"

"Because we're trying not to cause panic." He took a deep breath and, more calmly, said, "Listen to me, Josef. This thing you're poking about in is dangerous."

"This 'infection'?"

"It could get you killed."

"It's already getting people killed."

Alex's grip eased, but he didn't let go. Josef wished he were less aware of the warm weight of his hands. "We're handling it."

"How?"

"You don't need to know that."

"Yes, I do. I have a bloody right to know that." Irritated, he shrugged out of Alex's grip. "The people have a right to know what their government is doing—here at home, in the war, and across the whole bloody Empire. You can't keep us in the dark no more. I won't let you."

Alex's jaw bunched, and he ran a frustrated hand through his hair. "I shouldn't have come here."

"No, you shouldn't."

Snatching up his hat and gloves, Alex snapped, "I was trying to protect you."

"You were trying to silence me."

"Funnily enough, in this instance, they amount to the same thing." He looked like he was about to leave, yet he remained standing by the counter—taut, aristocratic, and troubled. His gaze touched Josef's and held. And held. And held. Josef's heart started pounding against his ribs as if he'd been running or fighting. Or something else entirely. In a softer voice Alex said, "For what it's worth, I very much enjoyed our time together in Poperinge. I think back on it often, and with fondness."

So did Josef, which only irritated him further. He said, "You mean the time you seduced me and stole my camera?"

"I didn't..." He closed his eyes with a sweep of dark lashes and sighed. "Well, it was what it was, I suppose."

And what it was was bloody confusing.

Saying no more, Alex donned his Homburg and strode to the door. At the last moment, before he opened it, he turned back around. "If you value your life, Shepel, stay away from this business. No good can come of your involvement. And plenty of ill."

Without waiting for a response, he pulled open the door with a sharp jangle of bells and disappeared into the skulking fog.

Chapter Seven

Nothing was more likely to encourage Josef along any path of action than being told it was forbidden. Especially when the man doing the telling was a bona fide thieving aristocrat.

Which was why, the morning after Alex's visit, Josef found himself standing on a cold street with his notebook out, staring down into a hole in the ground.

"And it was Tuesday, when the body was found?" he asked the man warming his hands over the brazier. A breeze had got up in the night, shifting the fog enough that a pale sun was visible through the mist today. Not that it provided much heat.

"Tuesday, aye. First thing. Couldn't hardly miss it."

"And can you describe its position?"

"Flat on its face."

Josef looked up, saw a gleam in the man's eye. It was about all of his eye that was visible, the rest lost in the deep lines of a face used to outside work. "I mean its location in the tunnel," Josef explained. "Was it directly beneath the hole?"

"Nah." He jerked his head to the left. "About twenty yards that way."

"So..." That was interesting. "The fall didn't kill him outright, then?"

"If he fell."

"Do you doubt it?"

The man shrugged and said, "If he fell, and could walk twenty yards, why didn't he just climb out? Not like there ain't a ladder."

"Well, it would have been pitch black, I suppose..." He thought again of his father's story of the man who'd stumbled over the edge of the dock. "Perhaps he got disoriented?"

"And then happened to drop down dead?"

Josef chewed the end of his pencil. "What's your theory then?"

"Where did you say you was from?"

"The Daily Clarion."

"Only I told the other bloke all this."

"What other bloke? From another newspaper?"

"Army. The poor sod's commanding officer is investigating what happened to him." He snorted a laugh. "I said, 'It's a bit late to bring him up on charges for being drunk and disorderly.'"

Josef laughed politely. "True. What did you tell him?"

"That there's more going on beneath the streets of London than most people want to know about." A knowing look lit his eye, a challenge in his bright gaze. A question.

"I'd like to know."

"Aye, but would you believe it?"

"How about you tell me, and we'll see?"

After a long, measured gaze, the man said, "You ever heard of Queen Rat?"

A trolleybus trundled past on the other side of the road; a car horn bellowed. Josef said, "Queen Rat?"

The man's expression cooled. "If you ain't interested..."

"I am!" He hadn't meant his scepticism to show. "I've just never heard of it. Her." But his heart sank. Queen Rat, indeed. "So, who is she?"

"Well." The man still looked doubtful, but at the same time, he clearly wanted to spin his tale, and that overcame any reluctance. "The stories go back a couple of hundred years. Back then Toshers used to work the sewers looking for coins and jewellery and the like. But they delved deep, and it's said they woke Queen Rat, and she's haunted the sewers ever since, preying on men. Seducing them."

Josef felt his eyebrows creep up, despite his best intentions. "She's a...giant rat?" He couldn't imagine that being very seductive.

"She takes the form of a beautiful woman, but her eyes...they're like a rat's eyes, gleaming in the dark."

Josef suddenly found himself listening very sharply.

"It's said, if the man pleases her, she grants him great good fortune. And curses him if he doesn't. But also—" he put a hand to his neck, "—she bites him here, leaves her mark. Now, the man we found? His neck was all chewed up. His arm, too."

"The police think rats might have—"

"No rat did that, I'll tell you that for nothing. 'Least, no natural rat."

"I see." Josef closed his notebook. "Thank you."

"It ain't just that either. There's been queer goings-on down here for weeks. All the men know it, not just me. Stinks—and not the usual sort—and sounds. And..." He looked genuinely uneasy. "Eyes in the dark."

Josef's heart jumped. "What sort of eyes?"

"Bright. Like a rat's, reflecting the light. But...too tall for a rat." He held his hand at eye level. "Human size."

A chill ran up Josef's spine that had nothing to do with the weather. His encounter with Alex had pushed his odd experience at Blackfriars Underground out of his mind, but it came rushing back to him now. It was stupid, though, utterly ridiculous, and he certainly didn't believe in any queen of the rats. Nevertheless, he heard himself ask, "What colour eyes?"

"Blue. Pale as ice." He cocked his head, measuring Josef. "You've seen something like it, ain't you?"

"I don't know." A cold breeze tugged at his scarf, and he shivered. "I thought I did. In one of the tube tunnels."

"Aye. They do say she gets out and about. That's how she finds her men, see? Lures them back into the dark and..." He struck a match and put it to his pipe. "The men aren't happy. I'll tell you that much. Won't go anywhere down here except in pairs."

"Did you mention any of this to the police?"

"The coppers?" He snorted around the stem of his pipe as he sucked on it. "Wouldn't give me the time of day. Told the army bloke, though. He was interested."

Ah yes, the army officer. Josef said, "He wasn't called Captain Winchester by any chance, was he?"

"Nah, it was a funny name. Lieutenant Twisleton." He reached into his pocket and pulled out a dented card. "Told me to contact him if anything else happened. I liked him. He took us seriously. Told us to be careful down there."

"May I?" Josef took the card and scribbled down the address and telephone number. He didn't bother with the fake name; Alex would be good enough. "I can't say I believe in your Queen Rat," he said, returning the card. "But something queer is going on, and whatever it is it's dangerous. Lieutenant Twisleton is right—you should be careful." He dug out his own card. "If you could let me know if anything else happens, I'd be grateful."

"The lieutenant offered us ten bob for useful information," the man said, taking Josef's card and examining it.

"The lieutenant has deeper pockets than me." And wasn't it typical of a bloody toff to think he could buy anything he wanted? "But he plans to hush up whatever's going on. I want to warn the world. So..." He shrugged. "Make your choice when you decide who to speak to first."

"I'm telling you it's a story."

May regarded him across her desk, fingers steepled and eyes sceptical. "A Queen Rat seducing men in the sewers? The Daily Clarion's a newspaper, Joe, not a penny dreadful."

"Not that." He waved it aside with a flick of his hand. "That's a myth, obviously. But there is something going on. I've seen these men's wounds, May. Two in Flanders, one here. I've seen them with my own eyes. And I saw—" He hesitated about confessing the rest, but if he didn't tell May everything, she'd never believe him. "I saw something in the tunnel at Blackfriars yesterday. Eyes, blue eyes."

Her lips pressed together. "Eyes." Her tone was as flat as her Mancunian vowels.

"I know it sounds mad, but I swear I saw it. And... and I've seen it before, too. Back in Poperinge."

"Joe..." Her gaze slid sideways, and he realised she looked embarrassed. "You've not been back long—"

"I'm not imagining it! Look, I thought that too at first. That maybe my nerves were dinged or something, but the men working in the sewer saw the same thing." And that had to mean something, didn't it? It meant he wasn't imagining it, that his mind wasn't playing tricks.

"And you think it's a giant rat woman—?"

"Of course I bloody don't. But I do think it's something—and that this bloke, this Lord Beaumont, or Captain Winchester, or whoever he is, knows what it is." He hesitated again, although God knows why, and added, "Why else would he have come round the Cohens' shop yesterday to warn me off?"

That got her attention. "He warned you off?"

"Yep. Said if I didn't stop poking my nose into it, I'd get myself killed."

"Blimey, Joe." May sat forward over her desk, suddenly interested. "All right, that's something. And you think this Lord Beaumont is Intelligence Corps?"

"I do. He denied it, of course."

"Well, he would."

"Right. He did confess to working for the War Office, though. He said this thing's an infection, but I reckon that's bollocks. God knows what the bastards have cooked up, but my guess is it's some kind of weapon. Maybe a new gas they're testing in the sewers before they get the sappers to deploy it under no man's land. Maybe it...seeps up into the enemy trench? Something like that. Only...well, something must have gone wrong."

May let out a low whistle. "Who else knows about it?"

"You mean reporters? I haven't seen anyone asking questions but me. The copper had seen at least two cases. So had the girls on the ambulance crew. Oh, and one of them just happens to be pally with Alex. No coincidence, I reckon."

"Who's Alex?"

Damn. Josef's face heated. "Lord Beaumont."

"Oh, on a first-name basis, are you?"

"Not exactly." Her penetrating gaze didn't let up, and he sighed, giving in. "Alright, we had a tumble one night, is all. Back in Pops. That's when he stole my bloody camera."

May snorted a laugh. "Oh, so this is personal, too. Did he tweak your pride, Joe?"

"Something like that." He smiled, although faintly. Ridiculous as it was, he felt unreasonably hurt by the whole business. Perhaps because he'd enjoyed their time together so much—the fucking, yes, but also the lovely room and the cosy supper in front of the fire. And Alex's gentleness in bed. You didn't often find that in fleeting encounters, and Joe hadn't had anything but fleeting encounters in all his twenty-six years. "But the fact is the man's iffy as hell. And whatever's going on here stinks—in all meanings of the phrase."

"It would be quite a scoop," May mused. "Government testing deadly gas beneath the streets of London. What's your next move?"

Sitting back in his chair, he folded his arms and braced himself. May wouldn't like this, which was fair enough because he didn't like it either. "I reckon I've got two choices—track down Lord Beaumont and make him tell me the truth."

"Unlikely to work."

He inclined his head in agreement. "Or go down into the sewers and see what I can find out myself."

Chapter Eight

What had seemed like a bad idea sitting in the office of the Daily Clarion that afternoon felt like a bloody stupid one at eight o'clock in the evening. Nevertheless, Josef, armed with his army hand torch, snuck over the barriers around the sewage repair works and stared down into the deep dark pit.

"Fucking hell." He directed the thin beam of his torch into the dark, watching it glance off the iron rungs of the ladder and glint dully on what looked like water—or worse—below. He wished he owned galoshes. He wished he was sitting by the fire in his room. He wished bloody Alex had just told him the truth instead of forcing him to resort to this.

But if wishes were horses, beggars would ride.

Shoving his torch in his jacket pocket, its beam lancing awkwardly upward, Josef began his descent. The rungs of the ladder were rough and damp, cold biting into his fingers, but he moved slowly for fear of slipping. At least nobody was shooting at him, he consoled himself. No mortars were landing, and no machine guns were in range. It was a thin comfort as he descended into the dark.

He counted fifteen rungs before his foot scraped on brick and he found himself at the bottom. Looking up, he could see no light, only a faint square of lesser darkness. The recent air raids meant London was always semi-dark these days, and the fog had returned with nightfall to do the rest. Turning slowly, one hand still on the ladder for balance, Josef fished out his torch and flashed it around. His breath billowed in the thin beam of light, steamy in the dank air.

The first thing he saw were neat piles of bricks where the repairs to the damaged sewer were being made. Tools were left propped up against the wall: spades, a pickaxe, buckets, and trowels. From the dark he could hear the plink-plink of dripping water. The tunnel was narrow with an arched ceiling of pale brick, and it led off in both directions. To his right, the torch light illuminated a large iron door; to the left the tunnel ran at a gentle downward incline until it turned a corner. Beneath his feet, the ground was wet, but there were no puddles and nothing foul, thank God. He glanced back at the ladder, then along the tunnel, getting his bearings. That would be where the dead man had been found, and in all honesty, Josef could see how, if he'd fallen drunk into the hole, he might have been disoriented in the pitch black and wandered in that direction before succumbing to the effects of a blow to the head. No supernatural rat queen was required to explain that. It would be easy to get turned around down here, he realised with a pinch of anxiety. Perhaps he should have brought some breadcrumbs to mark his way.

Suddenly, his breathing sounded loud in the silence of the tunnel, harsh and rasping. Like he'd been running. And his fingers had a death grip on his torch. God, this was a bloody stupid idea, and he should have let May talk him out of it. But he hadn't, and he was here now. Damned if he was going to scarper. He'd go to the turn in the tunnel, at least; he couldn't get lost if he went so far and no further.

Keeping the torch aimed at the ground, so he could see where he was putting his feet, Josef started walking. His footsteps echoed loudly. If something sinister did lurk down here, it would certainly hear him coming—and he would hear it. That provided less comfort than anticipated.

Should he grab the pickaxe?

He briefly imagined trying to swing it at a giant rat woman in the confined space of the tunnel and dismissed the idea, of both the weapon and the woman. Easy, in the dark, to let your imagination run away with you.

By the time he reached the turn in the corridor, his heart was thumping louder than his boots. The sewer bent sharply, turning back on itself, and becoming a steep flight of stairs heading down. He flashed the light around, but there were no other turnings, no other ways to go. No way to get lost. If he carried on down, he'd be able to find his way back all right.

Swallowing dryly, breaths still rasping, he started down the stairs.

Down, down, deep down.

The air grew colder, but it wasn't still—there was movement, drafts of air circulating. And distantly, a long bass rumbling. He stopped dead at the sound, mind darting helplessly back to the front and the devastating mines laid in long tunnels beneath enemy trenches. Sometimes the explosives caught them in the blast. Sometimes the tunnels caved in around the sappers, burying them alive. He caught a panicky breath and dug his fingernails into his palm. "Not there," he whispered. "Not them."

The rumbling faded, then returned, and he realised with a giddy sense of relief that it was the sound of trains running through the Underground. The District Line wasn't far from here after all, and the sense that people and civilisation were so close comforted him. He flashed his torch around and found the bottom of the stairs, which ended in a sharp T-junction.

And that's when he heard it.

Footsteps. Slow, deliberate footsteps echoed through the tunnel, the sound bouncing off the walls and making it difficult to determine direction. They couldn't be behind him, though—there was nothing back that way.

Except the ladder.

Bloody idiot. His chest tightened as he stood frozen in place, the beam of his torch wavering in his suddenly shaking hand. Fuck. He scrambled to switch it off, plunging himself into impenetrable darkness. Instantly, he was disorientated, panic rising uncontrollably as he squeezed his eyes shut and pressed back against the cold brick.

Think.

Think!

You can't see them so they can't see you. With one hand he felt back along the wall the way he'd come, digging the pads of his fingers into the bricks. What was he going to do? Run at the first sign of company? Wasn't that why he'd come down here in the first place, to find out what the hell was going on? But walking on in the pitch black was beyond foolhardy, and standing there like a lemon, waiting to be discovered, felt just as stupid.

Meanwhile, the footsteps continued their slow progress. Were they getting closer? It was impossible to tell. But now he listened, he could hear that the footsteps were accompanied by a sibilant whisper. A voice. No, voices. More than one, he realised with a jolt, straining to listen over the rasp of his own breathing. He couldn't make out a word, and the rhythm of the language sounded off, too. Not English, perhaps.

Not human, a panicked part of his mind whispered.

He dismissed that thought irritably and opened his eyes. It made no difference in the suffocating dark, and he felt his chest cramp in claustrophobic panic.

Plenty of air. There was plenty of air.

His heaving lungs didn't believe it, though, and he found himself gasping. And just like that, he had to get out. He couldn't stay in the dark a moment longer. Groping along the wall, he stumbled back up the stairs. Fuck, how long were they? He was half running, his chest too tight with panic and his breaths short, making him dizzy. At last, thank fuck, he found the top and felt his way around the corner. But still the voices and slow, steady steps persisted. Were they following him? Could they see him? He should have grabbed that pickaxe. He still could. One hand on the wall, he felt the tunnel sloping upward beneath his feet and finally felt a blessed breath of air against his face.

His relief was immense and lasted less than half a second.

Because the breeze carried with it a dreadful stench. A dreadful, familiar stench of rotting flesh. And up ahead he heard someone breathing, a wet sucking sound like air through a punctured lung.

Josef froze, clamping his jaw. His fingers clenched around his dark torch, too stiff to move. Petrified as stone. The breathing moved closer, the stench overpowering. Josef's stomach rolled, rose into his throat.

I'm going to die here.

Never in all his months in Flanders had he been so certain, but alone in this black tunnel he knew death approached. It stalked him in the dark. And out of that breathing darkness two points of eerie iridescence appeared not six feet ahead of him. Eyes. Pale blue eyes, like ice.

Crying out, Josef stumbled back. There was nowhere to go but down and no time to run because, with a hiss, those eyes were rushing at him. Josef flung up his arm, shouting in horror and fear as a heavy weight crashed into him and knocked him back against the wall.

He could see nothing but those unnatural eyes, but Josef had grown up on rough streets and knew how to scrap. Hands, knees, feet—he punched and kicked and tore at his attacker, using his torch as a club. He drove it off, but not for long. It was circling him; Josef could hear the laboured hiss of its breath.

Dear God, what was it? A man. A fucking rat queen?

"Fuck off!" he yelled in fury and fear. "I'll fucking kill you!"

Whatever it was, his shouting didn't intimidate. With a wordless snarl it launched itself at him again, pushing him back against the wall, its hot breath horrifyingly close to his neck. He brought one knee up, rolled them both, and slammed the thing sideways into the tunnel wall. But it didn't let go. Strong, biting hands clenched on his arms, bearing him backwards. Josef's feet skidded on the steps, and suddenly, there was nothing behind him, the weight of his assailant pushing him back.

He fell. Hard. His head cracked on the steps, back jarring painfully, breath exploding from his lungs. And the fucking creature was on top of him. Slavering. Light sparked behind Josef's blind eyes, his ears rang, but he fought with all he had left. Shouting, punching, kicking. It wasn't enough. Not nearly enough.

This was the end. All of it over, and for nothing. For nothing. He screamed his fear and fury and—

Suddenly, there was light. Bright, blazing light dazzling his eyes. He caught a glimpse of a monstrous face above him—snarling, ravaged, human—before it twisted away to face its new enemy.

Someone shouted in a language Josef didn't understand, but he recognised the shout as a challenge. Struggling to move his rubbery limbs, he hauled himself up to rest his back against the wall, still sprawled halfway down the steps. His head spun viciously, vision blurring and ears ringing. His grip on consciousness slipped, and he sank helplessly down into the dark.

When he opened his eyes again, a shape crouched over him, tearing at the collar of his shirt and coat. Bright light shone in his eyes, and he lashed out wildly against the attack, forearm connecting with a firm shoulder.

"Stop!"

A warm hand gripped his wrist, and he found himself blinking up into a pair of very familiar, very pissed-off eyes.

"Did it bite you?" Alex said.

Josef stared. "What...?"

The fingers on his wrist hardened. "Were you bitten?"

"There's no time," said another voice, and Josef looked up into the hard gaze of another man. He stood over them with a lamp held aloft, its light casting shadows over his brown skin and scarlet turban. "It didn't go far. We should just leave—"

"No," Alex said sharply. "Absolutely not."

The other man suppressed a sigh. "What then?"

To Josef, Alex said, "Can you walk?"

God only knew the answer to that, but he was bloody well going to try. He pushed himself up, stomach roiling and head pounding. He put his hand to the back of his skull, and it came away wet. "Shit," he said, staring stupidly at his bloody fingers.

"Dutta, take his other arm," Alex ordered.

"Saint's going to love this."

"Then don't tell him."

Dutta grunted but did as Alex asked, and between them—barely fitting in the narrow tunnel—they frog-marched Josef back towards the ladder. His head throbbed, his vision swung violently, although that might just be the wildly dancing lantern light, and his whole body felt... Well, it felt like he'd just fallen down a flight of stone stairs with a monster riding him. Which he had. All of that, plus a stomach in revolt, kept his jaw locked and voice silent.

"You go first," Alex ordered when they reached the foot of the ladder, sounding every inch Captain Winchester. He didn't look at Josef but turned his back to keep watch along the tunnel. Dutta did the same, facing the other direction. Soldiers, Josef thought. No doubt about that.

Josef didn't object to leaving first; frankly he couldn't wait to get out. Besides, he had no energy to argue. All his effort went into gripping the cold, gritty rungs of the ladder and climbing. Excruciatingly slowly. The pain in the back of his skull was unbearable, and he focused on that instead of on the wild pounding of his heart, his fear and utter disbelief.

He couldn't begin to process what had just happened to him and so he concentrated on the physical sensations of his body, on the climb, and at last on the sweet, sweet smell of London's fog.

Crawling out on wobbly arms and legs, he celebrated his escape by vomiting. From the pain and shock. He'd seen soldiers do the same, and now he knew why. Had he been alone he might have cried with the sudden, abject misery of it all, kneeling there shaking and shivering in the cold night.

A warm hand landed on his shoulder, and he looked up to find Alex crouching next to him. His usually slick black hair was dishevelled, falling forward over his forehead in a way that tarnished his aristocratic polish, the scant city light turning his elegant features monochrome. He wore a Norfolk jacket and held a Webley revolver in the hand that wasn't squeezing Josef's shoulder. "Come on, old boy. Let's get you home."

Josef felt a powerful desire to lean into that warm touch, to feel the man's strong arms around him. Pathetic, and aggravating as hell.

"We need to make sure he wasn't bitten anywhere." Dutta appeared at the head of the ladder as if he'd hopped up in one elegant bound.

An irritated expression crossed Alex's face. "I know. I'll check."

"Yes." A lift of one eyebrow, not quite a smile. "I'm sure you will."

The two men exchanged a speaking look. "You'll fill him in?"

"He'll want to talk to you, too."

"Tomorrow."

"He'll expect you tonight."

"Tomorrow." Alex put a hand under Josef's arm. "Can you stand? We shouldn't stay here."

"To get away from that thing, I can fucking run," Josef said, letting Alex help him to his feet. After heaving his guts up, he felt marginally better and was highly motivated to get the hell away from the dark maw of the sewer. "But I'm not going anywhere until you tell me what the bloody hell is going on."

Dutta cocked his head, looking at Alex with an expression that said, I told you so.

Alex's face darkened. "I warned you to stay away," he told Josef. "You know I can't tell you—"

"Bollocks." Surprising how fury could sweep away all your aches and pains. "I nearly got fucking eaten by your little experiment down there. Now, you either start talking or I'm going straight to the Clarion and—"

"I told you we should have..." Dutta made a throat-slitting gesture.

Josef jolted in shock. "What?"

"He's joking." Alex's glare didn't leave Josef, his eyes dark shadows. "Although, right now, I'm reevaluating."

"Are you serious?" Josef stared between the two men in disbelief. "Who the bloody hell are you people?"

Dutta smiled. "The people who just saved your life, Mr Shepel."

"And who put it in danger in the first place! Don't try to pretend you were just taking an evening stroll through the fucking sewer. Whatever happened to that...that poor sod down there, you did it to him. And if you think I'm not going to tell the world about what this bloody government is doing to men—"

"Stop!" Alex barked.

Josef jumped. And he didn't miss the way Alex had lifted his pistol. It wasn't exactly pointed at Josef but was very clearly in play between them.

Grimly, Alex said, "I'm afraid I'm going to have to insist you come with us."

"Or what?"

Their eyes met, and Josef was surprised to see a flash of real discomfort in Alex's shadowed gaze, something pleading. "I asked you to trust me once—can you do so again?"

"Last time I trusted you, you stole my camera."

A pause. "That's not all that happened."

True, and Josef's treacherous heart gave an unwarranted flutter at the memory of Alex's soft lips on his skin, his smile, their cosy supper before the fire. The warm weight of his sleeping hand on Josef's back. But Alex's betrayal clouded the pleasure of all those memories, chilling them. He glanced at Dutta instead, dressed like Alex in a Norfolk jacket and boots, as if off to hunt grouse in the Highlands. His expression was studiously blank, a skill they clearly taught in the Intelligence Corps.

He didn't want to go with them.

However, it occurred to him that, from a journalistic point of view, he had no choice. Despite Alex's firm grip on the Webley, Josef doubted he was planning to off him. If he'd wanted him dead, why rescue him from ... from whatever Frankenstein creature lived in the sewer? Either way, he'd find out more by going with them than by nursing his bruises at home. Besides, he had a strong suspicion that, if he refused, Alex would order him into the car at the point of the gun. He realised he didn't want to put either of them in that position.

Swallowing, heart jumping about in his chest, he said, "Alright, I'll go with you."

It felt rather like strolling into the lion's den.

Chapter Nine

Josef had been expecting a faceless government building, or perhaps sinister army barracks. Certainly, an interrogation room. It was a surprise, then, when Alex parked outside the giant and rather ugly Queen Anne's Mansions in Westminster, opposite St James's Park.

"I'll walk from here," Dutta said, climbing out of the car. He rolled his right shoulder as if perhaps he was stiffening up after the fight. If so, Josef knew how he felt—which was about 110 years old. He staggered out of the back of Alex's motor, grimacing. Throbbing head aside, his bruised back was killing him. And his neck, where the creature—man?—had tried—

No, he wasn't thinking about that.

Meanwhile, Alex was speaking to Dutta in the low, familiar tone of long acquaintance. "Tell Saint I'll be there in the morning with a report."

A pause followed, and then Dutta spoke in another language. Impossible for Josef to know what he said, but he sounded serious and sent a couple of significant glances in Josef's direction while he spoke. If Josef had had to guess, he'd have said Dutta was issuing a warning. Be careful of this one. What a joke! The only one in danger here was Josef.

Alex replied curtly, in the same language, but then, perhaps without realising, slipped into English at the end. "...and I know what I'm doing."

Dutta cocked his head. "That's what you always say." With that, he touched his forehead in a casual salute and loped away into the night.

Alex watched him go, lost in thought.

"You're friends?" Josef asked. "Or is he your superior officer?"

That made Alex laugh, and he was still smiling when he turned back around. "A little of both, perhaps. We've known each other since Cambridge and spent a couple of years working together in Ambala. In the Punjab."

"For the Intelligence Corps?"

"No." He gestured for Josef to proceed him into the building. "As I've told you, repeatedly, I don't work for the Intelligence Corps."

"Well, you would say that."

Alex huffed a laugh. "One day you'll believe me."

"That'll be the day you give me a plausible alternative, Captain Winchester."

Alex didn't reply, but Josef saw an amused glint in his eyes that made his heart jump infuriatingly. For God's sake, the man had practically kidnapped him at gunpoint.

They were met in the foyer by a concierge who tipped his hat and said, "Good evening, my lord." His gaze alighted on Josef in his shabby coat and flat cap, more dishevelled than usual after this evening's events. He probably had blood on his collar.

"All right?" Josef said, injecting as much Spitalfields as possible into his accent.

"Sir." No inflection whatsoever in the concierge's voice. Perhaps he was used to Alex bringing home rough young men for the evening?

The thought didn't sit well, for reasons Josef chose not to consider.

"I'm on the fourth floor," Alex said, striding across the foyer toward a bank of lifts.

Josef followed, gazing around at the elegantly dressed men and women coming and going. He'd never been inside one before, but these modern mansion flats were all the rage among a certain class of toff. Half hotel, half lodging house, the place came with an army of servants to pamper its residents and, no doubt, all sorts of modern conveniences.

The only convenience Josef wanted as he stood in the lift was somewhere to lie down. As his tension subsided, his headache grew more severe, thumping in the back of his skull.

The lift slowed to a stop, and he felt Alex's hand on his arm. "Here we are."

Josef blinked open his eyes; he didn't remember closing them.

One hand keeping a firm grip on his bicep, Alex marched him out of the lift and down a short hallway to a door that he unlocked. It led into...well, had he been in less pain, Josef might have whistled in astonishment. As it was, he had a brief glimpse of opulence before Alex steered him toward a large bathroom. "Sit," he said.

Josef sat, knees folding as he collapsed onto the wicker chair in the corner. Half his brain thought 'fancy having a bathroom big enough for a chair'. The other half shut down, and he slumped forward, face in his hands, and concentrated on quelling the pain.

A gurgle of pipes and the splash of running water roused him, and he lifted one eyelid to see Alex leaning over the bath, testing the temperature of the water coming out of the taps.

Odd.

As he watched, Alex straightened and turned around, drying his hands on a fluffy towel. "Right," he said, with the air of a man meeting a challenge. "Let's have a look at you."

Josef said, "You are a doctor then?"

"Let's just say I've had some experience in field medicine." Which, like most of Alex's answers, was hardly an answer at all. He crouched down in front of Josef, took his face in both hands, and examined his eyes. Warm hands, large and comforting. Which was ridiculous, all things considered. But this close, Josef could see a livid bruise rising along Alex's jaw and a raw scrape over his high cheekbone. They made him more real, somehow, tarnishing his patrician polish. And it was impossible not to notice the flecks of green in his dark blue eyes. Or the fact that they were...gazing at each other.

Alex seemed to notice at the same time and cleared his throat. "Good," he said with a curt nod. Josef assumed that meant neither of his pupils were blown. Standing, Alex ran his fingers lightly through Josef's hair to the back of his skull. "Lean forward," he said quietly.

Josef leaned, refusing to acknowledge the electric sensation caused by Alex's fingers in his hair.

"Well, you've got a lump the size of an egg back here, but the cut isn't deep, and it's stopped bleeding. Devil of a headache, I imagine."

"And how."

"Possibly a trifle concussed." Alex's fingers lingered in Josef's hair, and after a hesitation, he added, "I need to know if it bit you."

Reluctantly, Josef sat up, dislodging Alex's hands. "Tell me what it was."

"Show me your neck first."

Too tired to argue, Josef unbuttoned his collar and pulled it aside, tipping his head to let Alex see. He jumped when Alex's warm fingers brushed his skin, probing into his hairline and down over his collarbone. Despite his aches and pains, Josef felt a powerful charge building inside his body. Entirely autonomic and completely beyond his conscious control. If Alex was the lightning, Josef was the copper wire electrified by his touch.

"Good," Alex said again, stepping back. His voice was a little throaty. "Now, take off your clothes and get in the bath."

Josef stared. "What?"

"I need to see—"

"You already saw."

Delightfully, a flush crept across those refined features. "I need to ensure there are no bites."

"It didn't bite my prick. I'll tell you that for nothing."

A twitch of Alex's mouth. "I need to see for myself. Not just your—" He gestured towards Alex's groin. "I need to check everywhere. I'm sorry, but to do otherwise would be reckless."

"I swear to fucking God," Josef said as he began unbuttoning his waistcoat, "if you don't tell me what the hell is going on, I'll drown you in your own bloody bathtub."

"I do understand your frustration," Alex assured him. "And if I could say more—"

"Oh, you will say more." Josef threw his coat and waistcoat onto the floor and started on his shirt buttons. "Because if you don't, I'm printing this whole bloody story."

"That would be unwise."

Josef smiled, angrily. "Why? Because your friend will finish me off?"

"Because nobody would believe you."

"They will when I publish the photographs."

Alex stared, eyes suddenly very wide and dark. Behind him the bath continued to run, filling the air with fragrant steam. "What photographs?"

Ah, so that was interesting. Josef felt the power shift between them and stopped his angry disrobing, letting his shirt hang open. "That's for me to know and you to find out when I publish them."

"You can't."

"It's a free country. Well, it used to be. But sod DORA—the people have a right to know." He paused, made a show of consideration. "Unless, that is, you want to give me a good reason not to."

Alex briefly closed his eyes. "Take off your clothes. I'm not doing anything until I'm certain you weren't bitten."

Although he was sure he'd have noticed if a chunk of him was missing, Josef hesitated before he carried on stripping. "What happens if I was?"

Alex looked grim, face colourless save the dark pits of his eyes. Eyes which flitted to the Webley now sitting atop a wicker laundry hamper.

"You've got to be fucking kidding me."

"I think we'd know by now if you were…infected."

"Would we? How?"

"You'd be dead. Or…worse."

There are worse things than death.

Josef had a vivid memory of Alex saying those precise words as he'd gazed down at the boy who'd breathed his last that morning in the dressing station. They took on a horrifying new meaning now.

In silence, Josef pulled off his shirt and sat to unlace his boots. They were filthy. He and Alex had both tramped dirt all the way through his fancy flat. Should have taken them off at the door instead of creating more work for the maids, not that Alex would ever consider the maids. His sort never did. Josef tugged off his boots, saw his big toe sticking through the end of his sock—he kept meaning to darn it—and glared up at Alex, daring him to judge. Alex watched him with that same stony expression, face like marble. No sign he was enjoying this humiliation, at least.

Josef wasn't shy about nakedness. True, he was scrawny and rather underfed, but after spending ten months at the front, he wasn't shy about anything. Besides, he swam—and did other things—in the bathhouse on a semi-regular basis. But under Alex's stern observation he was irritated to discover that he did feel self-conscious. Perhaps because, last time he'd been naked with the man, circumstances had been so very different. But, like most things in his life, he brazened his way through the discomfort. When he was down to his underwear, he got to his feet. "You really think he bit me on the arse?"

"I just have to see for myself."

"I bet that's what you tell all the boys," Josef said, unbuttoning his underwear and letting it slide down until he was stark bollock naked. "Want me to do a twirl?"

Alex drew closer, eyes running over Josef's body. A clinical examination, nothing intimate at all, as he circled him. At least, that was how it began. But when Alex walked behind him, Josef felt a gentle touch on his back, fingertips tracing down his spine. "You're bruised here."

Goosebumps rose across his skin, coaxed out by that soft touch. Naked as he was, his physical reaction was painfully obvious. Cursing silently, Josef closed his eyes and willed his prick to behave. "Tell me something I don't know."

No immediate answer, but Alex's hand didn't leave his back. After a silence filled only by the slow running of the bath, Alex said, "I wish you'd taken my advice and left this alone."

"I bet you do."

"For your sake, not mine."

Josef felt a different kind of goose bumps, and he tensed. "That sounds like a threat, Captain Winchester."

"It's not. I...regret that you've been hurt, that's all. And I'm afraid you'll be hurt again, or worse, before this is over."

"And why should you care about that?"

A huff of self-mocking laughter and Alex's hand withdrew. "A very good question to which I have no satisfactory answer."

"You don't have any satisfactory answers," Josef pointed out, turning around. He found Alex watching him, his once-ashy face now warm. Flushed. Their eyes met, locking in a complex tangle of desire and distrust. Despite his accelerating pulse, Josef made himself say, "I'm deadly serious. If you don't tell me the truth about what the hell's going on, I'm taking this straight to my editor."

After a considering pause, Alex said, "Has it ever occurred to you that you might not want to know the truth?"

"Like a child, you mean, protected from a harsh world by his elders and betters? No, it bloody well hasn't occurred to me. Ignorance is not bliss, Alex. Ignorance is a prison."

Shaking his head, Alex looked away. "You have no idea what you're talking about."

"If I don't, it's because your lot think the likes of me don't deserve to know the truth—"

"Deserve?" He scrubbed a hand through his hair, leaving it even more dishevelled. "Christ, do you think it's a privilege?"

"Of course it bloody well is! And the only reason you can't see it is because you've enjoyed that privilege your whole sodding life."

Alex opened his mouth on a retort, then snapped it shut so hard Josef heard his teeth click. After a pause, in a more moderate tone, he said, "Take a bath. I'll have your clothes laundered; they stink of—of the sewer." He grimaced, glancing down at himself. "As do I."

He headed for the door, but Josef grabbed his wrist and stopped him. "You have to tell me. And no more lies—"

"All right!" Alex yanked his arm away, retreating a step. "If that's what you want, I'll tell you. But I'm warning you, Shepel, there's no coming back from this. Once you know, you know. And you may live to regret that choice."

With that, he stalked out of the bathroom, steam billowing out after him and the cool air from the rest of the flat chilling Josef's bare skin.

Despite the strangeness of the situation, the luxurious bath was incredible—scented with flowers, and hot enough to turn him pink all over—and went a long way to easing Josef's bruised body and aching head.

At one point, while he lay up to his neck in water, Alex returned with a large towel and a pile of clean clothes. He left them on the wicker chair, scooped up Alex's filthy clothes, and disappeared without a word. Josef was somewhat surprised he didn't have 'a man' to do such things for him. Then again, perhaps having naked socialists in your bathtub tended to cause gossip 'Lord Beaumont' would rather avoid.

He mulled on that title as he lay in the warm water, gazing up at the ceiling. The doorman had used it, and Alex appeared to live openly as Lord Beaumont. If he were a fake, surely the real Lord Beaumont would notice?

Which suggested that Captain Winchester had been the fake name. Fake rank too, which Josef was quite certain was the sort of offence that could get a man shot at dawn. If—when—he wrote this whole bizarre story up for the Clarion, he'd perhaps avoid mentioning Alex's alias. After all, despite his highhanded arrogance, he had saved Josef's life down in the sewer.

Even if his secrecy and scheming had caused Josef to risk it in the first place.

As the water cooled, Josef reluctantly climbed out of the bathtub and dried himself with the largest, softest towel he'd ever seen. It felt like a cloud wrapped around him. How the other half lived, eh?

At some point in his life, it might have felt a little odd, wearing another man's underwear, but after the deprivations of the front, he barely gave that a second thought. Alex's clothes—trousers, a striped shirt with no collar, and a heavy woollen cardigan—were a little large, but not ridiculously so, and Josef left the bathroom feeling a good deal better than when he'd entered. He found himself in a pleasant room, with expensive-looking furniture, a thick carpet, and soft gas lights on the modern mantel. A dining table stood at one end, close to the night-black window.

Alex was nowhere in sight, so Josef wandered over to the window, cupped his hands around his eyes, and peered out into the dark. The fog had thinned—or perhaps it was thinner this high up—and he could see London's chimney pots and steeples poking up out of the mist, stretching away from them beneath a glitter of stars.

"The rent is cheaper up here," Alex said from behind him. "People think there's a fire risk, you see, but I took this one for the view. When it's clear, you can see as far as Highgate."

Josef turned from the window to find Alex on the other side of the room. Like him, his hair was wet, swept back neatly now, and he'd changed into clean clothes—a warm-looking roll-neck sweater and slim tweed trousers. He looked...good. Attractive. Appealing. Josef couldn't suppress a pang of want, which was distracting and counterproductive. Ignoring it, he said, "I think I forgot to thank you and your friend for coming to my assistance tonight."

"Not necessary." Alex strolled towards a sideboard that was set beneath a large mirror on the long wall of the room. "Drink? I've a rather wider selection here than in Poperinge."

"I'll take a whisky if you have it, with a splash of water."

"Of course." Alex busied himself fetching glasses and pouring their drinks, keeping his back turned. Procrastinating. When he was done, he indicated the chairs before the fire, and they sat, nursing their drinks. The warmth from the blaze felt good on Josef's feet, cosy in the warm wool socks Alex had given him. He was entirely too comfortable and was afraid that was the point, that he was being managed.

Lifting his drink, he said, "Thank you for saving my life. Now tell me what's going on."

Alex watched him in silence, firelight playing over his grave features. "If you leave now, your life will continue unaltered. Your world will continue unaltered. Nothing will change. If I tell you the truth, it will change everything."

That, Josef suspected, was an attempt to frighten him. But what men like Lord Beaumont failed to understand was that men like Josef didn't give a rat's arse for continuity. Your world will go on unaltered? What use was that to him? The world was on fire, and he was happy to let it burn. Burn to the ground. From the ashes, they'd build a new world, a better world where men couldn't be sent to war by governments they'd had no voice in electing. He was sick of this world, run by and for monied men who valued continuity over progress.

Leaning forward, elbows on knees, Josef said, "Changing the world is exactly what I intend to do, Lord Beaumont. So go on, change it for me."

Their eyes locked in a push-pull of challenge and response. Alex bit lightly at his lower lip, a minor tell of vulnerability that spiked Josef's pulse. Neither looked away, and, after a long pause, Alex said, "What attacked you in the tunnel this evening was not human."

"Meaning what?" His mind grabbed at possibilities. "An animal? No, it looked like a man." Not that he'd got a good look, but—

"It was a man, once, but it has been...altered."

Josef frowned, shaking his head. "Explain. It's an experiment? The government has..." Imagination faltered. "What?"

"The government has nothing to do with this."

"Bollocks. You already admitted you work for the War Office."

"Yes, well." Alex hesitated. "That was an untruth, and I apologise. I don't work for the War Office, or any branch of government. At least..." An odd smile touched his lips, secret and rueful. "Not this government. An...older one."

"What? What the bloody hell does that mean?"

A shake of his head, as if trying to find words. "This is difficult. I've never had to explain—"

"Try."

"I am." His eyes flashed in irritation, and he took a sip of his whisky. "Very well. The creature you encountered tonight was what we call a ghoul."

Josef stared. Alex stared back, his gaze steady. He didn't appear to be laughing, which was strange because this was clearly some kind of fucking joke. "For God's sake," Josef growled. "Is that meant to be funny?"

"Not in the slightest."

He shot to his feet, prowled to the sideboard, and set down his drink. "I don't even know what to say to you. This is some posh-boy joke, is it? Let's tell the oik it's a fucking goblin?"

"Not a goblin, a ghoul. Goblins are different."

"Oh, fuck off."

"You asked for the truth."

Anger surged, hot and wild. "This is not the fucking truth. It's bollocks. Why are you trying to—?" He shook his head. "God, this is what you think of me, is it? That you can ridicule me, or fob me off with a load of old crap? Well sod you, Lord Beaumont. And expect to see your name in the fucking newspaper next to a picture of the dead men that...that thing, whatever it is, killed!" He stalked towards the door, his head thumping again. "Where are my fucking boots?"

"Josef, stop." Alex was on his feet now. "Look, I know it's difficult to believe, but you did ask—"

"It's bollocks, is what it is. For God's sake, you lying piece of shit, yesterday you told me it was an 'infection'."

Alex's brow furrowed, embarrassed. "Yes. Well, I apologise for that dishonesty, but it was kindly meant. I was trying to protect you from—"

"For Christ's sake! There's a war on, man. Men are being slaughtered. The government is burning off their faces with mustard gas. Boys are dying in the mud screaming for their mothers. And you think—you think—" His voice hitched, rage choking him. "Is it all a joke to people like you?"

"Of course not, but this isn't about the war. Rather, it is about the war to the extent that the death and horror of it draws dark creatures—"

"Shut up!" Josef spat. "I don't want to hear it. God, I thought—" What? That they were friends? Hardly. "I thought you had more respect for me than this."

Fuck his boots. He'd leave barefoot rather than spend another minute in the company of this man. And he didn't know why he was so furious, why his eyes burned hot and stinging, except that he'd thought there'd been a connection that night in Poperinge. He'd thought it had been a mutual, equal connection. But all along Alex had looked down that straight, aristocratic nose of his and seen Josef as just another one of the ignorant, unwashed labouring masses. Good enough to fuck and stupid enough to believe any old shit their masters fed them.

Well sod that. Sod that to hell and back.

"Josef, wait." Alex followed him to the door. "Look, perhaps I could have broken this more gently. We don't—that is, I've never had to explain it to an outsider before. It's ... not encouraged." He gave a soft laugh. "To put it mildly."

But Josef had had enough. "Keep it. I'm not interested in your lies." He levelled a finger at Alex. "But I'm not letting this rest, Beaumont. I know what I saw tonight. I know what I saw at the front, and I've got the photographs to prove it. So tell your masters, whoever they are, that I'm on to them. I'll find out what you bastards are up to, and I'll blow it so wide open they'll think a fucking mine went off under their arses."

With that, he stalked to the front door and yanked it open.

He told himself the only thing he regretted leaving behind was his boots.

Chapter Ten

"You're telling me a man is living in the sewers?"

May was walking at a fast clip along Carmelite Street the following morning, Josef trotting at her heels. He'd spotted her leaving the station and pounced before they reached the office. "Not a man." He was breathless from running to catch up. "Well, he was a man once. But he's been changed, dehumanised. I don't know how—electric shock therapy, perhaps? Or poison gas? His brain must have been altered or—"

May turned abruptly, and Josef almost bumped into her. "Joe, stop." She put her hand out, touching his chest. Her expression was grim. "I think—Joe, perhaps you need to rest and stop thinking about everything you've seen. The photographs, the pamphlet. They can wait. You're—"

"They can't wait! It's down there right now. It attacked me last night, and it's killing people. Eating them, perhaps? I don't know. Beaumont knows, but he's not saying. Well, he's saying it's goblins. Or ghoulies. But—"

"Josef." Her cold hands cupped his face, and he was astonished to see her eyes shining overly bright. "Please, stop. You need to rest. Let me take you home." One thumb brushed his cheekbone. "When did you last sleep?"

"I've not gone mad," he said, pulling back. "Is that what you think? May, it's real. I know what I saw. I have bruises. My head—" He pulled off his cap, turned around so she could see the cut. "I hit it when the creature pushed me down the stairs."

"Oh, Joe, you hit your head?" She pulled him back around. "You should see a doctor."

"I can't afford a doctor."

"You could have a concussion."

"May—" He grabbed her by the shoulders. "Listen. The government is ... is altering men, turning them into monsters. Beaumont said so—he said it had been altered. They're turning men into weapons of war. Imagine an army of them tunnelling under no man's land."

She closed her eyes. "All right," she said. "All right, Joe. Listen. Go home, write it up, and bring it in tomorrow. We'll look at it together."

They wouldn't, though. He could see that in her face. Dropping his hands from her shoulders, he stepped back, dismayed. "You don't believe me."

"It's an extraordinary allegation."

It was—of course it was. He could hardly believe it himself, and he'd seen it with his own two eyes. "What if I get proof? A photograph."

"Well... all right. But, Joe, don't go back into the sewer. Promise me. Monsters aside, it's not safe down there."

"I promise." And he wasn't lying; the thought of returning to that claustrophobic darkness filled him with horror. But that didn't mean there weren't other ways to investigate. "I'm not letting this drop, though. I'll find the truth, and when I do, you'll have to publish it because it'll be the biggest story the Clarion's ever had. Or any paper."

She didn't respond, just watched him with sad and steady eyes until he turned and walked away.

Well, let her think he was shell-shocked or driven mad by the war. He knew better. What had happened last night would haunt him for the rest of his life if he didn't get to the bottom of it, Alex and his lies be damned.

Avoiding the tube—if he ever went underground again, it would be too soon—Josef took an omnibus to St. Thomas's hospital. Rattling along on the top deck gave him time to think, and his thoughts turned back to last night and the horror that had attacked him in the dark.

But then, irritatingly, he found his heart skipping as he remembered Alex and his friend coming to his rescue like knights of yore. No, not like knights; he refused to romanticise them like that. If anything, they were more like zookeepers desperately trying to keep their escaped tiger from mauling the visitors. Because Josef had no doubt that they were responsible for the man—if he was still a man—prowling the sewers.

Still, no amount of rationalisation could keep his mind from drifting back to Alex's mansion flat and those few moments of connection, even intimacy, they'd shared while Alex had tended his wounds.

Before he'd thrown it all away with his offensive lies.

Josef was still furious. Baffled, in fact. What had Alex been thinking? There must be a hundred plausible lies he could have spun. Why mock him with one so ridiculous? Although now he thought back on it, there had been no mocking in Alex's tone. For whatever reason, he'd delivered the lie with utter conviction—as if it had been a genuine attempt at deception.

As if Josef would ever believe such nonsense.

He considered, briefly, that Alex might believe it. Was he the sort of spiritualist fanatic who harboured delusions about ghosts and ghoulies? No, that couldn't be true. Alex had been at the front, actively involved with whatever the government was testing in the salient. And he'd stolen Josef's bloody camera to keep it secret.

He had, however, returned Josef's boots.

They'd been delivered early that morning, cleaned and polished, along with his laundered clothes. No note. Not that Josef had been expecting a note, nor wanting one either. But it meant he now had a set of Beaumont's clothes, including the rather cosy cardigan he was currently wearing, that he needed to return. That thought sent irritating silvery feelings fluttering through his chest. Not exactly anticipation, but something like it—an agitation he couldn't quell.

It was enough to make him jump to his feet to dislodge the thought and make his way along the swaying aisle to the stairs, trotting down to stand on the rear platform and gaze out as they crossed the foggy river.

The army had commandeered hundreds of LGOC buses, and their drivers, for the war effort and used them to transport men, ammunition, and casualties to and from the forward lines. Once, Josef had stumbled across the corpse of one lying half on its side in a muddy ditch by the side of a shelled-pocked road. All skin and bones, with its London General Omnibus Company name still displayed on the front. The poignancy had closed his throat and made him reach for his camera.

It was disorientating to be riding one back in London. Everything was disorientating, as if the world had been picked up and shaken and nothing was where it should be anymore.

When the bus slowed in heavy traffic just after Westminster Bridge, he jumped off and hurried to the hospital, hands sunk deep into his pockets. He tugged the long sleeves of his borrowed cardigan down over his hands too, for a little extra warmth.

St. Thomas's was quieter today than last time he'd been there. No Red Cross vehicles—hot cross buns, they'd called them in Flanders—queued up to unload their sorry cargo, and that suited him just fine.

He walked around the back of the old red-brick Victorian building, in the direction he'd seen Vi and Lottie drive when they'd taken their body to the mortuary. His new camera sat snugly in his coat pocket, and his plan was to look for the soldier who'd been found dead in the sewer. Vi had said that was Tuesday morning, so he hoped the poor bugger would still be there. With luck and daylight, he'd get a better picture. Proof—of what, he didn't yet know. But of something, at least.

Josef had never been inside a hospital until he'd reached the salient, and St Thomas's was quite different to a field hospital. Long hallways infused with the stinging scent of carbolic soap echoed with the sober clip-clip-clip of footsteps on tiles, occasionally the distant wailing of a child or the slamming of a heavy door.

Nothing like the organised urgency of medicine on the front line.

Pulling off his hat, he attempted to look like he was meant to be there as he strode along purposefully, casting discreet glances at the signs pointing him in the right direction. The mortuary was in the basement, down a set of chilly, poorly lit stairs. It was colder still below, and Josef was suddenly gripped by clammy panic, the hair on his arms and the back of his neck rising, heart thumping and legs less stable than he'd have liked. He was no coward whatever his father might think, but what had happened to him last night... Well, it had shocked him, no getting away from that fact.

Mouth dry, his boots scuffed on the stone floor at the bottom of the steps. A stark electric lightbulb illuminated the space, and ahead of him extended another long corridor, lights spaced at intervals along its institutional length. A small sign saying 'Mortuary' pointed down the corridor, and, about a quarter of the way along, he saw another sign jutting out from the wall.

Mortuary Services

Right. He clenched his fingers and found they were ice cold despite the added warmth of Alex's cardigan. Nerves, he supposed. His blood was pumping hard enough—his heart certainly was—but the blood didn't seem to be reaching the ends of his fingers and toes. Stupid, to feel this…frightened. What did he think would happen in the middle of the day, in the middle of a hospital? The creature from last night was hardly going to jump out from around the corner.

'Course it bloody wouldn't.

"Get a hold of yourself, Joe."

His voice echoed in the empty corridor, tense and rasping. It didn't reassure.

Still, he'd been in stickier situations than this. Last night was one, and ten months under the German guns, stealing photographs beneath the nose of the army, was another. He could bloody well walk along this corridor and into the mortuary without cringing like a schoolboy.

And so, he did. He forced his legs into motion just like he'd done on those endless, exhausted nights driving backward and forward from dressing station to clearing station.

When he reached the door to the mortuary, he found it cracked open. After a moment's hesitation, he pushed it wider and poked his head inside. It was a large space, again lit by glaring electric light.

A man in a white coat was rising from a desk next to the door, and he looked at Josef in surprise over the rims of his wire spectacles. "Can I help you?" he said shortly.

Josef felt a stupid rush of relief to find another living, breathing human being here. But what had he expected? A room full of dead bodies? However, it meant he now had to think on his feet. "The police sent me," he said, pulling out his camera. "I'm to photograph the body of the man brought in on Tuesday. Private Andrew Sykes."

"The police?" The doctor frowned down at his desk, shuffling papers. "I was expecting Inspector Lakeman in half an hour."

"Really?" Shit, that was a bit of luck. "That is—the inspector's been called away on, er, urgent business. But he asked me to come along instead. I hope it's not too inconvenient, me coming a tad early?"

The doctor pulled out his pocket watch and frowned at the time. "I'm afraid it is, rather. I've a meeting with Dr Collins in ten minutes, and my assistant is at lunch. Can you come back?"

"That would be difficult," Josef said, which had the benefit of being entirely true. Snapping his fingers, as if coming up with a splendid idea, he said, "Why don't you point me towards the unfortunate private? I'll get my photograph and be gone before you get back. How about that?"

The doctor hesitated. Josef could see his gaze darting to his watch.

"I've done this plenty of times," Josef assured him. "I don't need any help."

"Well, it's not exactly orthodox..."

Josef shrugged. "We're not living in orthodox times, are we?"

That provoked a brief smile. "No, I suppose we're not. All right. Sykes is in drawer thirty-two." Gesturing to the far end of the large room, he said, "I warn you, though, there's a...pungent odour. Don't keep the drawer open long."

Grimacing, Josef said, "Yes, I've been warned about that."

"Very well. I'll leave you to your business and get to mine."

Josef waited until the doctor had gone and then closed the door firmly behind him before walking around the desk and into the rest of the mortuary. There were drawers on either side of both long walls, a narrow window high up at the end—at street level, he supposed—and in the middle of the room sat two metal tables, each of which had a drain beneath.

A year ago, that might have turned Josef's stomach, but he was inured to gore these days. At least the bodies on those tables would already be dead. It was far worse when they were screaming.

His footsteps echoed as he paced to the end of the mortuary, looking for drawer number thirty-two. Before he opened it, he pulled out his camera and adjusted the aperture for the light levels. He wanted that drawer open for as little time as possible and took the precaution of wrapping his scarf around his mouth and nose to keep out as much of the stink as possible.

Death no longer shocked Josef. He did not fear the sight of a man's mortal remains—it was only so much meat, in the end—but opening that drawer and sliding out the shelf within had his pulse racing. Perhaps it was the fear of being caught, or the dread familiarity of the stench, or just the memory of last night's attack. Whatever the reason, his heart hammered, breath harsh in the silence of the mortuary as he walked to the head of the body beneath its shroud.

Vi had told him that the man's arm was chewed up, and there was no mistaking that stink. Worse, he could see a dark stain beneath the sheet, as if the rot had infected the white fabric even after the man's death. Was that usual? He didn't know, nor did he want to look. The very idea of pulling back that stained sheet filled him with horror.

Why, he couldn't explain, but his skin crawled as he reached out to draw back the shroud, dismayed to see a tremor in his hands as he plucked the sheet back to reveal the man beneath.

The first shock was that the body was naked. Death, in Josef's experience, always came uniformed. But here, the man's clothes had been removed. His nakedness revealed a narrow-chested, spare-bodied youth, white and waxy in death. Livid bruises marred his alabaster skin, and Josef might have thought the fall into the sewer explained them had he not seen the unmistakable evidence of shrapnel injuries radiating across the boy's torso. Not old wounds, either. Fresh lacerations. Inexplicably, it looked as if the lad had recently taken the brunt of a Rum Jar exploding at close range.

Which was impossible.

And then there was the black rot on the boy's arm, extending down to his curled, misshapen fingers and up across his bony shoulder. The stink was intense, and Josef gagged, but he swallowed hard and pulled out his camera—the distance provided by looking through the lens helped him cope with anything. Beneath the bright electric light, and as much misty daylight as the high basement windows admitted, he began to photograph that terrible wound. He had a new film in his camera, so he had eight shots, and he planned to use each one wisely.

He was concentrating so hard on the lad's rotting arm and the inexplicable shrapnel wounds that it wasn't until his fifth shot, when he stepped back to photograph the whole body, that he noticed the boy's face.

Slowly, Josef lowered his camera.

A boy's face with fine, mousy hair and cracked lips—sixteen or seventeen, perhaps. Josef's skin prickled, lungs seizing as he froze in soundless shock. Impossibly, inexplicably, he knew that face. Alone among all the dead men he'd seen, this one was burned into his memory. Because he'd stroked that fine hair back from his forehead, put his own canteen to those cracked, blue lips and offered what comfort he could as this boy breathed his last breath.

Unless he had a twin, this was the boy who'd died among the dead at a forward dressing station a mile behind the line in Flanders.

With his own eyes, he'd seen it, and now here he was, lacerated with shrapnel, having been discovered dead after apparently falling into a London sewer.

Distantly, he heard the echoing clang of a slamming door. The sound roused him, jolting him back to the moment and his mission. Bringing the camera back up, he photographed the boy's body, then focused more fully on his face. He clicked once more, rolled the film on, lifted it again and—

Stumbled back, almost dropping the camera in shock.

The boy's eyes were open, pale blue and ghastly. Breath rasped in Josef's throat, loud in the silent mortuary, heart thumping wildly.

Had his eyes been open before? They must have been. Josef just hadn't noticed, that was all. Only—how could he not have noticed? The eldritch light in those dead eyes was all he could look at.

The silence grew deeper, as if the room itself had stopped breathing. Every muscle in Josef's body tensed, poised as if frozen in a nightmare. He edged back a step, feet scraping over the tiled floor, his gaze never leaving the corpse. It didn't move.

Of course it didn't fucking move!

Another step back, another rasp of his boots. His camera, clenched in both hands, bit into his palms. He didn't care. He just wanted to run, to put time and distance between himself and that terrible, impossible body. But he dared not look away, dared not turn his back. Scarcely dared move.

Afraid to wake the dead.

He took another hesitant step backward, and a hand touched his shoulder.

"Fuck!" Josef leaped out of his skin, camera clattering to the floor as he spun around to face—

Alexander Beaumont, tall and elegant with his unsmiling gaze fixed on Josef.

"Son of a bitch!" Josef gasped, scrambling to pick up his camera. "What the fuck are you doing...?"

He trailed off as Alex's gaze slid past him to the corpse. Still rattled—well, that was an understatement; he felt more like someone had plugged him into an electrical socket—Josef turned to look as well. He wouldn't have been surprised to find the body sitting up, but it was still where he'd left it, staring up at the ceiling with its dead, uncanny gaze.

Alex moved past Josef, the broad shoulder of his overcoat brushing Josef's arm as he passed. Impossible that he should feel any warmth from that brief touch, nor draw any comfort from Alex's presence, so he ignored the brief fluttering in his chest and, cautiously, followed. "It's the same boy we saw die at the dressing station," he whispered as they approached the corpse.

After a heavy pause, Alex nodded. "Damn. I'd hoped he'd be spared this...indignity."

"Indignity? For God's sake, man, he died in a pile of corpses. How is this worse?"

"You wouldn't believe me if I told you."

That was true if he was going to start wittering on about ghosts and ghoulies again. "You'd better give me the real truth this time, or I'm going to the police."

And, from Josef, that was saying something.

Alex turned and met his gaze, dark eyes full of an emotion Josef couldn't place. "Please don't," he said. Then his eyes fluttered briefly shut, as if in impatience, and he added more forcefully, "It wouldn't end well, for either of us."

Something about the way he spoke sounded wrong, like an actor speaking lines he didn't believe. Josef wasn't sure what that meant, but he was certain it meant something. He said, "Then tell me the bloody truth. Did you bring his body back here? Is it part of some grotesque experiment to—"

"I warned you to stay out of this business."

Defiantly, Josef lifted his camera and took his final picture—Alex standing next to the body of the dead soldier. "And I warned you that I'd blow it right open. Don't think I won't."

"You're a damned fool if you believe—"

Behind them, the mortuary door opened. Josef spun around, alarmed, and found the doctor from earlier entering the room. He looked startled too, pausing in the doorway, and then visibly relaxed. "Oh, Inspector Lakeman. Mr Talbot said you'd been called away."

A moment of confusion, before Alex said, "Doctor Wildsmith, good afternoon." He exchanged a quick look with Josef, and there was no mistaking the gleam of amusement in his eyes. Josef felt it too, albeit unwillingly. "Yes, that's right," Alex went on. "Talbot kindly came on ahead to get started, but we're finished now. Am I right, Talbot?"

Josef held his gaze. "Oh yes," he said, "we're certainly finished. In fact, I'd better get these photographs developed. People are waiting for them."

"Hmm," Alex said. Then, with a flourish, he flicked the shroud back over poor Private Sykes, sliding his body into the drawer and closing the door. "Thank you for allowing us in, Wildsmith. I do hope you and the lady wife are well?"

"Very well, thank you. All things considered."

"Quite," Alex said, affably, striding toward the door. "Do give her my regards." Then, over his shoulder—and with a devilish look in his eye—he added, "Keep up, Talbot. We don't have all day."

Josef glared but didn't dare argue in front of the doctor. Neither did he feel comfortable leaving him with...with whatever Sykes might or might not have become. "I'd get rid of that body as soon as you can, Doc. He doesn't look right at all."

The doctor's eyebrows rose. "He's dead. How did you expect him to look?"

"He—"

A firm hand closed on Josef's bicep. "The poor fellow's past caring now," said Alex. "His journey's ended."

And what the hell did that mean?

Alex didn't loosen his grip as he hustled Josef out of the mortuary and back along the corridor to the stairs. When Josef tried to shake him off, Alex's fingers only tightened. Did he have his gun, too? Josef imagined he did.

"I'm not going to run," he hissed as they marched up the stairs together. "I have too many questions for you."

Grimly, Alex said, "Questions I won't be permitted to answer."

"You're such a government stooge."

"I'm not. There are things you don't—"

"Understand. Yes, you've made that clear." They were walking through the hospital corridors by then, but Alex quickly diverted them out through a small side door and into the cold November air.

Instinctively, Josef sucked in a deep breath and saw Alex do the same, dropping his grip on Josef's arm. For a moment, they both stood there, breath condensing like smoke. Above them a low, pale sun made a perfect disk in the thinning mist, and Josef could almost imagine its warmth on his face.

It was reassuring to know that the sun still shone despite the murk—both literal and metaphorical—swathing the earth below.

"Christ." Alex's heartfelt exclamation broke the silence between them. "What a bloody mess." He pulled out a packet of gaspers and, to Josef's surprise, offered him one.

They weren't friends, and he didn't want Alex thinking they were, but Josef wasn't one to look a gift horse in the mouth. "Ta," he said, helping himself. Bond Street—a cut above his usual brand.

When Alex lit a match and Josef leaned in to light his cigarette, their eyes met above the dancing flame. Met and held like they'd held a dozen times, as if magnetised. Alex had ridiculously beautiful eyes up close, dark as a midnight ocean but with a scattering of sea green around the pupils. Josef couldn't look away.

And, for God's sake, now he was waxing poetic. What the hell was wrong with him? "I liked you better in Poperinge," he said, for the benefit of them both. "Before you nicked my camera."

Alex's mouth ticked up at one corner, but he looked a little melancholy. "Yes, I expect you did. That was a charmed evening."

Charmed. Yes, it had felt charming, which only made the aftermath more deeply disappointing. Josef said, "I bet you say that to all the boys you seduce for purposes of larceny."

"That's not what I—" His cheeks pinkened beneath their wintery hue. "The two matters weren't linked."

Josef lifted a sceptical eyebrow. "Bollocks."

"There are easier ways to pinch a camera."

"But less pleasurable, I imagine."

Another twitch of his lips, eyes smiling too. "Damn it, Shepel, why do you have to be so...so—"

"Irritating? You're not the first to ask."

"I was going to say likeable. But, yes, also irritating. And stubborn."

Josef shrugged. "Born that way I suppose. Now tell me what I saw in there just now. The truth this time, no ghost stories. That boy... We watched him die two bloody months ago in Flanders—I swear we did."

"Yes, we did." Alex's humour vanished. "He died but not before—hell." He glanced around, as if expecting someone to be watching. "Come on. I don't know about you, but I need a bloody drink. Let's find a pub."

A drink wasn't a bad idea, all things considered; Josef was still feeling shaken, not that he'd admit it. "St. Stephen's Tavern isn't far from here."

Alex made a 'lead the way' gesture, and they started walking.

"You can forget about pinching my camera, if that's your plan," Josef said. "Or seducing me, come to that."

Alex cast him a sideways look. "As much as I should do the former, and should like to do the latter, I feel we've gone beyond the point of no return. There's only one thing left to do now."

"And what's that?" he said warily.

"Tell you the full, unabridged truth, of course."

"Which is exactly what I want to hear."

"Hmm," Alex said, hunching more deeply into his coat. "I very much doubt you will."

Chapter Eleven

St. Stephen's Tavern on the corner of Bridge Street was a smart stone building from the last century, with elegant, arched, floor-to-ceiling windows and a rather beautiful bar of dark wood, polished to a sheen and lit by tasteful gas lamps. A bright and welcoming refuge from the dreary day.

It wasn't a place Josef often frequented these days, but before the war, he'd sometimes had occasion to meet his fellow journalists there, as well as a couple of Labour MPs. Alex looked right at home, of course. His brother, the earl, would have a seat in the Lords, and the place was positively riddled with Right Honourable Members. Alex nodded to half a dozen of them as he made his way to the bar. No doubt friends from school or Cambridge, although Josef didn't miss the surprise in their expressions, nor the disapproving stares levelled Josef's way.

It didn't bother him; he was used to disapproval. Basked in it, in fact. Why should he give a toss for the good opinion of these overstuffed, indolent anachronisms? As far as he was concerned, they'd all benefit from a long stint in the firing line.

What surprised him, though, were the looks sent Alex's way, and he wondered what they meant. Maybe Lord Beaumont went about spouting his lunatic theories among his own sort too? Or, more likely, he'd been indiscreet with his choice of bed mates and had been exposed as an irredeemable invert.

Either way, Alex appeared as unconcerned as Josef by their disapprobation.

He found that irritatingly admirable.

They each bought their own drink—under DORA restrictions, 'treating' another man to a drink was prohibited—and then looked for a table.

"This'll do," Josef said, sliding onto the bench behind a small round table tucked into the back corner of the pub. Before he sat down, Alex removed his expensive-looking overcoat and laid it neatly over the back of an empty chair. Josef kept his jacket on, although he unbuttoned it, forgetting that he was wearing Alex's borrowed cardigan beneath until he saw the man's eyes drift over it.

"What?" Josef snapped, eyeing him suspiciously. "You're smiling."

"Am I?"

Josef pulled off his cap, releasing the lock of unruly hair that always flopped forward over his eyes. Irritably, he pushed it back and reached for his half pint of Mild. "Bloody hell," he groused, "it's like dishwater these days."

"Which is why I avoid it." Alex lifted his single shot of whisky and knocked his glass against Josef's. "Salut."

"Cheers." Josef swallowed another mouthful of watery beer, grimaced, and set down his glass. "Right then," he said. "Let's have it."

Despite the recent air raids, Londoners were uncowed, and the pub remained busy. The shortened wartime opening hours helped, too, cramming everyone in between midday and two-thirty. All of which meant the place was alive with noisy chatter, and in Josef's experience there was nowhere safer to talk about secrets than in plain sight amid a noisy crowd.

"I'm going to tell you the truth," Alex said, "but I ask you to let me finish before you tell me it's all nonsense."

Josef sat back in his seat, unhappy. "If it's more of this goblin bollocks—"

"What I'm going to tell you is the truth. Whether you choose to believe it is up to you." He held Josef's gaze and said, "You want to know how the body of the young man we both saw die in Flanders came to be found in a London sewer, and I think you'd like me to say he was brought here by the Intelligence Corps, and that his body was used for experimentation in the search for yet another terrible weapon of mass murder. As if the world doesn't have enough of those. It would be convenient for me to let you believe that, but unfortunately, it's not true."

"Isn't it?" Josef folded his arms over his chest. "Go on then—astonish me with the truth."

Alex appeared to consider that, swirling his whisky around in the bottom of his glass, watching it catch the light. "I hardly know where to begin."

"Most stories start at the beginning."

Alex smiled. He had a lovely smile; it quite transformed his face, taking Josef back sharply to that warm room in Poperinge. "That'll make for a long story."

Pushing all tender thoughts aside, Josef said, "Pub closes at half two." He took another sip of beer, watching Alex over the rim of his glass. "Better get a move on."

Alex met his challenge with a glitter in his eyes that excited Josef more than was reasonable. "Are you familiar with the Norman invasion? The Battle of Hastings?"

"1066 and all that? Yes, I'm not a complete ignoramus even if this country doesn't see fit to educate working men beyond the age of twelve." He tapped his breast pocket and said, with satisfaction, "I have a library card."

A fleeting smile touched Alex's lips, and Josef bristled, ready to take offence. Then he realised it wasn't derision he saw in Alex's eyes; it was something else. Something... warmer.

"Very well," Alex said, "then you're aware that William, Duke of Normandy, landed in England almost a thousand years ago, bringing with him a coterie of Norman aristocrats who set about colonising the country, building castles and—"

"Are you taking the piss?"

"Are you going to listen?"

Josef gave him a mutinous look. "When I said start at the beginning, I didn't mean the beginning of the bloody history book."

"It's pertinent."

"For God's sake." He huffed, slouching back in his seat, lips pursed. "I'm warning you: if you tell me a load of old crock, I'll punch you on the nose."

"I consider myself warned." Alex took a bracing sip of whisky. "William sent his knights about the country to catalogue his new territory—every square foot of land, every building, head of cattle, and so forth."

"The Domesday Book," Josef said. "Yes, I know about that."

Alex inclined his head. "What isn't known beyond a certain, very narrow set of people is that a second, secret book was commissioned—a book to catalogue all the unnatural threats William would face in his new kingdom."

Josef frowned. "Unnatural?"

"Boggarts, silkies, grindylows, pixies, wights, changelings, revenants... What we call supernatural creatures."

"What I call children's stories."

"Hardly that."

"Folklore, then."

"Yes, some of it—but not all. And so, the knights went out, and with the help of their Saxon hunters, tracked down every report of such creatures. Killed them, when necessary, made peace with those they could. Everything was recorded and brought back to Winchester—at the time, the greatest city in England." He hesitated, as if considering how much more to say. "Over the centuries that followed, the Knights Winchester and the Wild Hunters maintained their watch." He met Josef's sceptical gaze. "And we maintain it still, the knowledge and responsibility passed down to the second son in every generation of the knight's family."

Josef stared at him. "You expect me to believe this codswallop?"

"The man you saw today, in the mortuary, died in Flanders. His body was infected by a... a creature woken by the cacophony of war. A creature that feeds on horror and violence." He met Josef's gaze, serious as stone. "A ghoul. They're haunting the battlefields, the trenches, and foxholes of no man's land... The soldiers call them wild men. They believe they're deserters and suchlike who live beneath no man's land, creeping out from abandoned trenches and tunnels to scavenge iron rations from the dead. Or to cannibalise them. You must have heard the stories."

"I've heard them. I don't believe them."

"As with most myths, they're part invention and part truth."

"I'll tell you what I think. I think it's easier for soldiers to believe in wild men than to accept that the cries they hear at night are friends dying alone and in agony behind the wire."

Alex conceded that point with a nod. "It's certainly easier to tell ourselves stories when the truth is too difficult to believe."

"And which of us is doing that?"

"You saw the body today. You saw its eyes."

Having no answer to that, Josef remained silent.

Alex said, "What is true is that the ghoul have reached London. As to why they left the battlefield, I'm not sure. But something drew them away from their natural haunt. Something brought them here."

Josef glanced away, out onto the street. The fog had lifted a little, the other side of the road now visible through the mist, but his mind's eye was back in Poperinge. Should he tell Alex what he'd seen—what he thought he'd seen— outside the hotel that night?

Across the table, Alex sat up straighter. "What is it?"

Shaking his head, Josef lifted his beer and took a frowning sip. Once he'd set it back down, he said, "I don't believe any of this bollocks..."

"But?"

He scowled, shifting uncomfortably on his seat as he tugged on the long sleeves of Alex's cardigan, pulling them past the ends of his jacket and around his cold fingers. Reluctantly, he said, "I've seen him before."

"Who? Sykes?"

He nodded. "In Pops."

Alex's attention sharpened palpably. "What do you mean?"

"He was outside the hotel when we..." He cleared his throat. "I couldn't sleep, so I got up, and I saw him. I mean, at the time I thought my eyes were playing tricks. But I saw his eyes, that same uncanny blue. They almost glowed in the dark. He was watching the hotel."

"Christ alive," Beaumont breathed. "Why didn't you say?"

Josef laughed. "Why would I? I assumed it was... It probably was just a bloke smoking a fag."

"The photograph was still in your camera," Beaumont said. "Even undeveloped, it was powerful enough to draw the creature to you."

"The photograph?"

"There's a certain power in images." He cocked his head. "But you know that, don't you?"

"That I do, but it's nothing supernatural. The power of a photograph lies in the truth it tells."

Alex smiled. "Yes, correct. And the one you took of Sykes at the front would have captured the presence of a ghoul. You would have seen it had you developed it."

Josef made no answer to that, thinking about the strange ghostly image around Sykes's face in the photograph he had developed. A double exposure, he'd assumed…

Into his silence, Alex said, "I destroyed the photograph when I exposed your film later that night, but…" He cocked his head. "Sykes followed you to London, which means you have another photograph."

Josef laughed darkly. "You'd better believe I do."

"Then you must destroy it." Alex leaned forward across the table, jostling his whisky in his urgency. "No, give it to me. I'll destroy—"

"Give it to you?" Josef said. "And why's that?"

"I just told you why. A ghoul tracked you in Poperinge, and it tracked you to London. It's drawn to the photograph. And you're in danger while you have it."

"Sykes is dead," Josef snapped. "What danger can he pose now?"

Alex looked grim. "Yes, Sykes is at peace now, but he's not the only one. The ghoul…" He considered his words, brow drawn into a frown. "They're not separate creatures, like humans. They're… connected. We call it an infection, but it's more like a spiderweb of consciousness. If a body fails, it's discarded, and the infection moves to another, but the 'mind', if you can call it that—"

"Bloody hell!" Josef fisted a hand in his hair. "This is bollocks, Alex. I don't know why I'm even listening to it."

"Perhaps because you know the truth when you hear it."

Josef barked a hard laugh and didn't reply.

"Or perhaps because there's no other explanation for what you've seen. As the great man said, When you have eliminated the impossible, whatever remains, however improbable, must be the truth."

"Who said that? William the bloody Conqueror?"

"Sherlock Holmes."

"Don't tell me you think he's real an' all."

"No." Alex studied him. "I know it's difficult to believe. I was fifteen when I was told and... well, it made for a memorable birthday."

Josef studied him in return, his noble features and intelligent eyes. "The thing is," he said slowly, "you don't look like a looney."

"I'm not."

"But what you're saying..." He shrugged. "Look, maybe you're not a liar. Maybe you believe it—maybe you need to believe it. But me? I'm a factual man. I don't put much stock in spooks. I don't even believe in God. I believe what I can see with my own two eyes, and through the lens of my camera."

"And what did you see in Poperinge?" Alex said, looking as calm and reasonable as a man trying to convince a sceptic that the sky was blue. "Or in the sewer last night? Or on the mortuary slab this morning? Was none of that real enough for you?"

Josef was having none of it. He knew Alex was an accomplished liar; first, he'd been Captain Winchester of the RAMC, then Lord Beaumont of the War Office, and now this. And of course, he'd taken Josef in completely that night in Pops. What he couldn't understand was why Alex was trying to sell this load of old bollocks, but either way it was time to put an end to it.

"You and I," he said, "we've seen horrors, haven't we? Real horrors, I mean. We've seen hell, Alex. We met in hell. And all of it was created by men. Ordinary men. Bakers and bus drivers, fathers and sons. Good men, too, killing for King or Kaiser. So, I don't need your ghost stories to explain what I saw last night, because I know the most dangerous, malicious, evil creatures on this earth are men. And that's explanation enough for me." He pushed to his feet, looking down on Alex. "Fair warning, I will get answers to this. You haven't scared me off."

Alex's generous mouth compressed into a grim line. "I wasn't trying to scare you—but, Christ, can't you see you're in danger?"

"A threat?" Amused, Josef raised his eyebrows.

"A warning, for God's sake!" A couple of heads turned in their direction, and Alex lowered his voice. "Listen to me. Drop this. I'm not acting alone, and others will be less forgiving—the ghoul aren't the only danger you face. Do you understand? That photograph makes you a target. There's a great deal at stake here."

"That, I can believe."

Clearly frustrated, Alex reached into the breast pocket and withdrew his card, offering it to Josef. When he made no move to take it, Alex set the card on the table between them. "If you refuse to believe me, or to heed my warning, then there's nothing else I can do for you. But..." He stood and collected his coat and hat from the empty chair next to him. "Should anything untoward happen, you'll be able to reach me here."

After a hesitation, Josef reached down and drew the card toward him with one finger. In gold lettering on a cream background, it said The Winconian Society, and, beneath it, an address in Belgravia. Of course.

He glanced up and found Alex watching him with an expression caught halfway between frustration and...something else. Something heated. Or perhaps it was simply a different sort of frustration. Nevertheless, Josef's blood rose in response, as helpless as the tide responding to the moon.

He fought the swell of desire back down. For God's sake, Alex was either a lunatic or a liar, and there was no chance of them reprising their night in Poperinge. There had never been any chance of that because it would be a dreadful mistake.

Deliberately, he pushed the card back across the table. "Keep it," he said. "I can look after myself."

Alex's expression cooled, turning decidedly haughty. "So be it," he said. "I'd advise you to be careful, but I doubt you would listen."

"I dare say we'll run into each other again, Lord Beaumont." Josef infused the title with trenchant irony. "If not, keep an eye out for my piece in the Clarion. You spell it B-E-A-U-M-O-N-T, don't you?"

Snatching up his card, Alex left without further comment.

Chapter Twelve

The first thing Josef did when he got back to his room was to develop the film he'd used that morning in the morgue. It was already growing dark outside, the early November dusk falling like a curtain, so he didn't have to worry too much as he took the film from the camera and slid it into the wooden winding box. Once he'd wound it onto the drum, the light-proof apron automatically winding around to protect the film, he reopened the box and slipped the drum into the aluminium tank and poured over the developing fluid, and then the fixer.

Twenty minutes later, the film was washed and hanging up to dry.

While he was waiting, Josef went to his desk to find the photograph of Sykes he'd taken at the clearing station. It was still where he'd left it, in the drawer of his little desk, tucked inside the folded piece of paper with his first draft of the words for the pamphlet. He pulled them both out with a sense of relief. Not that he'd thought Alex would be able to reach the shop ahead of him and search his room, but he knew for sure he wasn't above theft.

Pulling up his chair, he lit the lamp on his desk and held the photograph under the light. Impossible as it was to believe, there was no doubt that the face in the photograph was the same face he'd seen that morning in the morgue.

No explaining that, unless the man had a twin.

And there, too, was the eerie double exposure around his lifeless body that Alex had described. Except, looking closer, Josef saw that it wasn't the shadow of Skyes's face. Hard to say what it was, because it was very blurred. Sykes's eyes, though, even in the monochrome image had that eerie glaze he'd seen gleaming blue outside the hotel in Pops. In the tube tunnel.

And in the sewer.

A chill ran through him at the memory of that night in the sewer, of the stench and ferocity of the man who had attacked him. If it was a man.

Altered, Alex had said, and it was about the only thing he'd said that Josef believed. The question of who had altered him, how, and for what purpose remained unanswered.

Or, rather, unproven. Because Josef had no doubt in his own mind that this was the work of the government's war machine.

"Josef?" Mrs. Cohen stood in the doorway to his room, wiping her hands on her apron. She smiled wearily as he turned. "There's a pot of tea in the parlour, love. And then would you mind helping Moss shut up? He won't say anything, of course, but his rheumatism's shocking in this weather."

Josef slipped the photograph back between the folded paper and into his breast pocket. "Of course," he said, rising and extinguishing the lamp.

Mrs Cohen was a well-built woman, strong and robust, her hair gathered in a neat old-fashioned bun at the nape of her neck. She had a maternal face, for all that she'd never been blessed with children, and her kindly features gathered into a concerned frown as Josef crossed the room towards her.

"Oh, you do look pale," she said, reaching up to touch his forehead. "Are you feeling poorly?"

"No," he assured her, taking her hand and squeezing. "Tired, that's all. I was...working late last night."

"You work too much," she scolded, shepherding him out of the room. "And here I am, asking you to do more."

"Don't be silly. I'm here to help," he said, following her to the little parlour above the shop. "And you feed me for my troubles."

She chuckled. Mrs Cohen loved to cook. "You need feeding up, Joe. There wasn't much to you when you went to the front, and there's even less now."

That was true, although he didn't like the reminder. Stupidly, it made him think of Alex's broad frame and how his own wiry body must have appeared to him that night in Pops. Not that he'd complained, but of course he'd had another agenda, hadn't he? He'd have fucked Josef whatever he looked like to distract him enough to steal his camera.

Mind you...

He was struck, suddenly, by a memory of the heat in Alex's eyes that night. Desire that had looked and felt real. If Alex had been acting, he'd missed his calling on the stage. And a man that accomplished at deception would surely have been able to concoct a more plausible story than the cock-and-bull tale he'd told Josef this afternoon.

It was a conundrum.

He found Mr Cohen in the parlour and noticed the swelling around his knuckles and finger joints. They looked red and hot and painful. "There you are," Mr Cohen said, sounding querulous as Josef came to sit on the footstool next to the fire. "I didn't think we'd see you today."

"Moss," Mrs Cohen scolded mildly from where she was pouring tea from the pot.

Josef only smiled. Mr Cohen was a good man, but pain could make anyone irritable. "I'm sorry I've been out so much," he said, accepting a warm mug of tea from Mrs Cohen. "But I'm here now, and I'll shut up the shop as soon as I've finished my tea. You put your feet up, Mr C."

Mr Cohen narrowed his eyes at the offer, and the nickname. "I'm not so feeble that I can't shut my own shop."

"But you're rude enough not to accept an offer of help with good grace," said his wife.

Josef smiled and swallowed a mouthful of tea. No sugar, but who had sugar these days? At least there was milk and the comfort of the hot mug in his hands, the warm fire, and the cosy familiar parlour. Together, they conspired to overwhelm him with a sudden wave of exhaustion. When had he last slept properly? Two nights ago? Yet this weight of exhaustion was more than just the aches of his tired, bruised body and his gritty, sleepless eyes.

Was it possible for a mind to be bruised?

He'd never imagined that the horrors he'd seen in the salient could follow him home to London, that they could be lurking beneath the very streets he walked. Yet Sykes had been in the mortuary this morning, as if fresh off the battlefield, and last night, he'd been attacked by something he couldn't explain.

Suddenly, it felt too much to bear. Would the whole world be infected by this bloody war? Would it grind on and on until nowhere and no one was safe from the horror?

Alarmingly, he felt his eyes prick with hot tears, his throat closing in despair.

"Josef?" Mr Cohen sounded concerned.

Blinking, he took a sip of tea and forced it past the lump in his throat. No room for despair, no room for panic; he had to fight. And he wouldn't stop fighting until he'd exposed all the government's dark secrets. Because, in the end, truth was the only way to end the suffering of millions.

"Think I need an early night," he said, offering Mr Cohen the best smile he could find. "I've been burning the candle at both ends a bit, I'm afraid."

"You haven't stopped since you got back from France," Mr Cohen scolded. "You've given yourself no time to recover."

"There are some things that can't wait."

Mr Cohen's huff said all that was necessary about that.

Josef pushed to his feet, setting down his empty mug and trying not to wince at the ache in his back. "And talking of things that can't wait, I'm going to start closing up. No—" Mr Cohen was attempting to rise. "—You stay there. I can do it myself, but I'll bring up the takings so you can do the books."

A compromise, enough to let Mr Cohen subside. "All right, this once. If you insist."

His easy surrender suggested that his hands were troubling him today and that he was in no position to be lugging around heavy ironmongery.

After Josef brought the takings up to the parlour, it took him about an hour to haul the goods on display outside back into the shop, and then another half hour to tidy everything away to the Cohens' exacting standards. By then, the weariness that had overtaken him in the parlour had become a heavy blanket of exhaustion. Even though it was barely six o'clock, all he could think about as he finally locked the shop door was his bed and the oblivion of sleep.

Tomorrow, he'd make prints from the photographs he'd taken in the mortuary and take them, and the photograph of Sykes, to May. She'd have no choice but to believe him then, especially with Alex standing next to the body. No chance she'd think him shellshocked into madness when she saw—

Sepulchral blue eyes.

He saw them through the glass door, staring at him from within the fog.

Josef's heart crashed into his ribs, fear dispelling his weariness as he jerked away from the door. "Fuck," he hissed. "Fuck."

It wants the photograph. It needs it. And you're in danger while you have it.

Alex's voice sounded as loud in his memory as if the man had been standing directly behind him. God, Josef wished he was there, longed for it, but tonight he was alone.

No, not alone.

The Cohens were upstairs, sipping their tea in the cosy parlour. And Josef had brought...something to their door. Something dangerous. That much he knew to be true.

He also knew that he couldn't let them come to harm. Whatever this was, it was Josef's business, and he would deal with it.

Pulling one of the iron pokers from the display, he edged closer to the door and peered out. The eyes were gone, but it was still out there. He could feel it, a lurking lingering presence in the fog.

Would it try to get into the shop?

He thought suddenly of the back door, rarely locked, and sprinted, poker in hand out the back of the shop, past the stairs and down the short hallway. The door was closed, and he rammed the bolt across with hands that shook.

"Josef?" Mrs Cohen appeared at the top of the stairs. "Whatever's going on?"

Back to the door, poker in hand, Josef was aware of the sight he must present. He thought quickly. "Ah, a couple of troublemakers outside."

Her face tensed. They didn't get a lot of trouble in this part of London, but occasionally, and especially after the recent Zeppelin raids, a few yobs would take Jewish names for German ones and come looking for trouble. Before Josef had gone to the front, back at the start of the war, someone had put a brick through the shop window.

"Don't worry," he told Mrs Cohen, trying to sound less terrified than he felt. "Nobody's getting past me. Go back into the parlour. I'll keep an eye out at the front, make sure they've gone."

Returning to the shop, he extinguished the lights and peered out through the dark glass of the window. Nothing looked back at him, but a crawling unease shifted beneath his skin. A watching, waiting sensation. Briefly, he considered making a run for it with the photo, leading the creature away from the shop and the Cohens. But where would he go? The Clarion's offices would be shut by now, and he could think of nowhere else.

Besides, the idea of going out alone into that dismal fog, knowing what lurked within it... He couldn't do it. The prospect turned his guts and knees watery.

No, better to wait for morning. Then he'd take all the photographs to the Clarion. They'd be safer there than here. Safer for the Cohens to have them gone.

Meanwhile, Josef tightened his grip on the poker and prepared for a long and anxious night.

Chapter Thirteen

Josef took the tube the next morning, finding comfort in the crush of people. Better that than face more time than absolutely necessary in the foggy morning which scarcely seemed brighter than the previous night.

He ran from the station along Carmelite Street. When he reached the brightly lit offices of the Clarion, it was with a huge sense of relief, and he raced up the stairs, two at a time, and into the office.

There he found a scene of devastation.

May stood amid it, sleeves rolled up to her elbows and fists planted on her hips, flyaway hair looking like she'd been tugging at it with both hands. All around her lay papers. The whole office appeared to have been ransacked, filing cabinets emptied, drawers turned out, her desk raided.

She looked up when he slid to a stop in the doorway, and their eyes met.

"I can only think it was the police," she said, gesturing around. "Looking for censored material. We've sailed close to the wind a couple of times, but I never thought…"

Not the police. Josef knew exactly who'd done this; it was too much of a coincidence to be anyone other than Alex. Hadn't he, only yesterday, demanded that Josef hand over the photograph of Sykes? Clearly, he hadn't taken no for an answer. Then there were the photographs Josef had taken at the morgue. Probably, Alex had imagined Josef would develop them at the newspaper offices and had come here searching for them.

Only he hadn't found them here, which meant...

Josef's heart gave a hard thump. Alex knew where he lived, and the negatives showing Alex with Sykes's body were hanging up in his room.

Stupid!

He'd been so afraid of those eerie blue eyes in the fog that he'd forgotten that the real threat came not from a fairytale monster but from Lord Alexander Beaumont and the government for which he worked. Had Alex been out there in the fog last night, waving blue lights about to frighten him? At this point, Josef could believe anything.

Including the fact that right at this moment Alex was probably searching his bloody room. The Cohens couldn't hold back a powerful man like him even if he'd come alone. If he'd brought a companion, as he had the night in the sewer, the Cohens would be utterly at their mercy.

"Shit," Josef said.

"I think it might be a warning," May said, righting her chair with a sigh. "So far, I can't see that anything's been taken. There's nothing here that breaches DORA, but–"

"They were after my photographs. The ones from the front."

"How would they even know about them?" May frowned. "Here, you haven't been flapping your mouth about them down the pub, have you, Joe?"

"No, of course not. Anyway, it's not the police."

"Who then?"

"Military Intelligence."

Her face set. "Joe..."

"May, listen to me. Yesterday, I found Sykes in the mortuary at St. Thomas's. He's the same boy I saw click it at the front. The one I photographed. He'd been fished out of the sewer right here in London, but his wounds looked fresh, and then Lord Beaumont showed up, and he said—"

He cut himself off when he saw May's pained expression. She didn't believe him. Of course she didn't, because he sounded like a madman. Until he understood what was happening himself, how could he try to convince anyone else?

"Did you bring your article, and the photographs for the pamphlet?" May said, sounding weary. "If you give us a hand tidying up, I'll take a look at them afterwards, and we can—"

"No, I'm sorry. I can't stay. I have to... I left something back in my room. I need to get it. If I can, I'll come back later."

She nodded, looking more relieved than anything else. No doubt he was one less thing she wanted to worry about today. "Listen," she said as he was turning to leave, "be careful, all right? I heard there were zeppelins and Gothas over Kent last night. No casualties, but even so..."

Death from the sky, death from beneath the earth. Was there no part of the world men wouldn't pollute with their weapons of war? "You too," Josef told her. Then added, "If there is a raid, and you shelter in the underground, stay with the crowd. Don't stray into the tunnels."

May regarded him for a long, bleak moment before she nodded.

With that they parted, and Josef plunged back into the fog.

He wasn't afraid now. Only embarrassed that he'd let Alex's story distract him from what was actually going on. Embarrassed and enraged.

When he got back to the Cohens' shop, breathless after running all the way from the tube, he was relieved to find no signs of disturbance. Mr Cohen looked up from behind the counter, eyebrows rising when Josef burst through the door.

"Good heavens," he said, "what on earth's the matter?"

It took Josef a moment to catch his breath before he said, "Has a man been here? A toff. Or maybe a man in uniform? An officer."

"Josef?" Mrs Cohen came in from the back of the shop. "You're back quickly. What's happened?"

Mr Cohen said, "He's asking if we've had an officer in the shop."

Instantly, Mrs Cohen beamed. "Do you mean your friend, Subadar Dutta?"

Josef stared blankly. "Who?" Then understanding crashed in with a jolt. "An Indian officer? Quite tall and very posh-sounding?"

"That's right," Mrs Cohen said. "Very proper, he was. Well, they are, aren't they?"

"How long ago?" Josef hurried across the shop, ducking under the counter. "Did he go upstairs?"

"Upstairs?" Mrs Cohen looked at her husband in bemusement. "Of course not. He came in for a door handle and asked if you was here. When I said you wasn't, he bought his handle, one of the expensive brass ones, and left. He was very polite, and quite talkative..."

"Of course he was." Racing past them, Josef hurried down the passage and took the narrow stairs two at a time. Shoving open the door to his room, he half expected—hoped?—to catch Alex with his sticky fingers in the desk drawer.

No such luck. All was silent and undisturbed in Josef's room, no sign of the frenzied search he'd seen at the Clarion. Relief washed over him, and then drained away like cold bath water when he saw the empty space where the negatives had been hanging.

Fuck.

Of course, there'd been no need to search; like an idiot, he'd left what Alex wanted right there in plain sight. It would have been the work of a moment for him to slip in the back door and up the stairs while his friend kept the Cohens talking in the shop.

Furious with himself, Josef went to his desk. Someone had evidently riffled through the photographs in the drawer, but nothing else was missing. In fact, something had been left behind.

Alex's card sat in the middle of his desk, gold letters gleaming, and on it he'd scribbled four words.

You are in danger.

The fury Josef had felt earlier rushed back, hotter than ever. How dare the man break into his room, into the Cohens' home, and issue threats? Who the hell did he think he was? There might be a war on, but Britain still had laws. An Englishman's home was still his castle. Even if his castle was one room above an ironmonger's. Alex had no bloody right to march in here, steal what he wanted, and leave behind intimidating notes for law-abiding citizens. How dare he—how dare the government—think they could get away with this?

"Well, they won't," he told the empty room. "I'll see to that."

Snatching up Alex's card, he shoved it into his pocket and headed for the door.

The Winconian Society was to be found on Wilton Crescent in Belgravia, which was not a part of town where men like Joe Shepel usually had business.

Too bad.

After consulting his map, Josef took the tube to Victoria. Now that the morning crowds had thinned, the vast station was quieter, and his footsteps echoed as he left the platform and trotted up the stairs.

A familiar unease dogged him. That same sense of being watched that he'd felt last night.

Glancing over his shoulder as he hurried through the empty station corridor, he saw nothing. If anyone was following him, he told himself firmly, it would most likely be Alex or his Indian accomplice. Subadar Dutta, Mrs Cohen had called him. Although, if the man was anything like Alex, that name could well be false. Nevertheless, if either man was following Josef now, it would only save him the trouble of hunting them down at their poncy club.

Emerging from the station, he found himself in the same November fog he'd left behind in Spitalfields. Its slightly metallic, smoggy tang felt fresh after the stale air of the Underground, and he realised he was grateful to be outside. Despite his anger at Alex, his fury at having been lied to and stolen from again, he couldn't shift the memory of his murderous encounter in the sewer. It would be a long time, he thought grimly, before he would be comfortable beneath the ground. Or alone in the dark.

Luckily, outside it was busier. Traffic rumbled past, the steady mix of omnibuses, motorcars, a few old-fashioned horsedrawn carts, and plenty of people on foot. Plenty of men in uniform, too, as always. Men on leave, loud and noisy, no doubt trying to drown out their dread of returning to the front. Or their glee. A couple of men stood smoking in the lee of the station wall. One poor sod, in a captain's uniform, wore a God-awful tin mask over his nose and mouth. It was what they gave to men whose faces had been so shredded by shrapnel, or bullets, or mustard gas that the sight was too disturbing for civilians to witness.

Hastily, Josef looked away before the man saw him staring. It boiled his blood, though, to see his wounds and to know that men like Alex were cooking up more weapons. Worse weapons, weapons that stripped away the last of man's humanity. As if the war hadn't done enough of that already.

He'd find the truth, though. He'd find the truth and expose it. Strip off the hideous masks of King and Country behind which men like Alex hid their own horrors.

Thoughts of that, and of what he'd say when he confronted Alex, occupied his thoughts as he strode away from the station and into the rarefied air of Belgravia. Tall, elegant buildings of the last century, or perhaps older, rose up on either side of the wide streets. White-painted, they might have gleamed in the sun on a bright summer's day if it weren't for the smoke and smuts that turned everything in the city grey.

Beautiful, understated, and quintessentially British: this was the heart of the establishment. A place where men like Lord Alexander Twisleton-Beaumont made decisions over luncheon that sent men like Private Andrew Sykes to their deaths in the meatgrinder of the salient.

He hated it.

Hated the elegance and the beauty, hated the wealth and the privilege. All of it built on the bent backs of labouring men and women.

There were no streetlights here, even though the fog made it feel more like dusk than noon. No streetlights anywhere in London, not with the recent zeppelin raids. Some windows blazed bright, though, their light pushing into the fog and turning it a murky mustard yellow.

Like gas.

He shivered, then jumped at the scrape of a footstep behind him. Turning, he was startled to find a man, a soldier, walking towards him along the street. Why that should startle him, he couldn't say. London was full of soldiers. Perhaps because of the fog, and his thoughts of gas. His nerves had been jangling ever since he'd got back from the front, May was right about that, and for good bloody reason. Now, though, his fists clenched, and he wished powerfully for the poker he'd cradled last night.

So much for his vaunted pacifism.

Good job he wasn't standing there wielding a fire poker like a lunatic, though, because it was just a man going about his business. An ordinary man among millions in the city. Nobody Josef recognised, and why should it be? Not in Belgravia where he didn't know–

Metal glinted beneath the peak of the officer's cap. A mask, like one worn by the man Josef had seen smoking at the station.

Was it him?

Unease prickled along Josef's spine, lifting the hair at the nape of his neck as he started walking again. He could feel the man's presence behind him, hear his footsteps echoing flatly in the deadening fog. Josef's nose twitched, his heart stumbling as he caught a cloying, deathly scent in the dank air. Imagination. Surely?

He glanced over his shoulder, and now the man was closer, walking steadily. Josef tried to swallow, but he found his throat too dry. Stupid, to be afraid. It was just a man. An officer.

Not looking where he was going, Josef stumbled over a crooked paving stone. He almost fell but caught himself in time. When he looked back again, the soldier was closer still.

And then the man lifted his head and looked at Josef.

Spectral blue eyes gleamed above the tin mask, through which a sound that no man had ever uttered snarled through the fog.

For a dreadful second, Josef froze solid, as in the grip of a nightmare. Or the rigour of death.

Then the man—the creature—leaped forward with a cry, and Josef fled.

Heedless of where he was going, he bolted into the fog. Weird shapes loomed ahead, resolving into lamp posts, trees, motorcars, and then, appearing out of nowhere, a park railing. Josef skidded, sliding to avoid crashing into it headfirst. His momentum slowed, he scrambled for speed as he darted right, sprinting along next to the railing.

Belgrave Square, he recalled from the map. This was Belgrave Square.

Behind him came the wet sucking sounds of inhuman breaths. Close. Closer.

Lungs labouring, Josef fought for more air, more speed. Wilton Crescent was nearby, just the other side of the park. If he could reach it, Alex would—

A hand grabbed the back of Josef's jacket, yanking him sideways, slamming him hard into the park railing. He staggered, stumbling, caught himself, and spun to face his attacker.

Through the shifting mist, he saw the cursed phosphorescent gleam of eyes, a dull glint of the tin mask, and an officer's khaki uniform. His boots and puttees were caked in mud.

"Who the fuck are you?" Josef shouted, backing up, his hands raised defensively. "What do you want?"

The man, if it was still a man, didn't answer. He only prowled closer. That dreadful, familiar stench came with him, and now that Josef looked, he could see that it wasn't mud on the man's legs but blood.

"My God," Josef said, pity vying with horror. "What have they done to you?"

No answer came to him, but the creature coiled, and from behind the tin mask came another snarl. It pounced, but Josef was ready, ducking under the creature and jamming his shoulder up into its ribs. The stench was unbearable, and Josef retched as he pushed up with his legs and vaulted the creature over his back. It was a move he'd made a dozen times in a dozen street fights as a boy. He could hardly believe it had worked, but the creature landed with a wet thud on the street behind him.

Josef didn't stop to see whether it got up again; he knew it would. He just ran.

Keeping the railing on his left so he didn't lose himself in the fog, he sprinted north. Some small analytical part of his mind, the part that had kept him alive for ten months in Flanders, tracked his location and alerted him when he reached the curving sweep of Wilton Crescent.

The man—the thing—was behind him still, gaining ground. Josef could hear its wet, rasping breaths, feel its relentless pursuit. Its relentless hunger.

He couldn't go much further, though—his lungs were on fire, legs burning, but if he stopped, it would kill him. Or worse.

There are worse things than death, Alex had warned him that first day among the dead.

In his desperation, he tried to shout. "Alex..." It came out a gasp, a breath squeezed from empty lungs. "Alex!" Louder this time. "ALEX!"

And then the thing had him again, its inhuman hands scrabbling at his arms, his back, his hair. Josef spun, fighting it off like a cornered cat, spitting and hissing, lashing out, screaming Alex's name with his last shreds of breath.

The officer lunged, and they went down together, rolling, Josef on top and then beneath, punching and kicking and gouging. In the fight, the creature's mask came loose and fell away, hanging from one ear, swaying as the creature glowered down at Josef through spectral eyes. The face beneath the mask was nothing but gore and white bone, half the jaw missing, his teeth sharp and bloody spikes.

Josef screamed his horror, hands locked on the creature's coat, arms shaking as he struggled to hold it at bay, the ravening ruined mouth lunging and snapping at Josef's throat...

Then, a sound.

A silver whisper, like a sniper's bullet, and something flashed past Josef's eyes.

The creature's head landed on Josef's chest, spattering his face with gore. Then it rolled off onto the pavement with a sickening thud and lay there staring at him with doused, disturbingly human eyes. A moment later, the rest of the creature's lifeless body collapsed on top of Josef, and he found himself staring up into the stern face of Lord Alexander Beaumont.

He wore a fashionable slim-fitting suit, and a fedora cocked at a rakish angle. A gentleman on his way to the office, except for the sodding great sword clutched in one hand.

"Well," Alex said, slightly breathless. "Perhaps this time you'll believe me."

Chapter Fourteen

"Get this fucking thing off me!"

Crawling with horror, Josef pushed at the corpse, the headless bloody corpse, that pinned him to the ground.

"Easy," Alex said, shoving the body with his foot until it rolled aside, flopping grotesquely onto its back. Then he reached down to offer Josef a hand up.

He glared at the strong, elegant hand stretched out towards him and ignored it, rolling onto his hands and knees, gasping for air. But the stench of the creature made him retch, and only his own bloody obstinacy saved him from vomiting.

Shakily, he tried to rise, but his legs were like jelly from running and his lungs still burned, so despite his fury at Alex, he didn't object when the other man took hold of his arm to haul him up.

"Steady on," Alex said quietly. Kindly, even.

Josef stared at him, at his handsome face creased into a concerned frown, at the stupid bloody sword. His head swam, and he heard a clatter of metal on stone before two strong arms wrapped around him, pulling him close and keeping him on his feet.

"Easy, now." Alex's voice was oddly shaky. "Take another breath."

Josef did; it didn't help because of the stench, and he retched again.

He was drenched in gore and the stench of the creature, his head a swirl of horror and fear and fury. He hardly knew which way was up, and the only thing keeping him anchored to the world were those sure arms about him. Somehow he remembered the feel of them, as if despite everything that had happened since, Josef's body recognised the embrace that, for one night, had brought him respite from the war and its horrors.

Helplessly, he sank into that embrace, his head dropping onto Alex's broad shoulder as those strong arms tightened their hold on him.

"For God's sake, Alex, get him inside," said a crisp voice Josef recognised as belonging to Subadar Dutta. "Saint's going to have your hide for this."

Alex's arms tightened again. His voice, when it came, sounded angry. "What else could I have done? Let it kill him?"

A speaking silence followed, and when Josef lifted his head from Alex's shoulder, he saw that the two men were locked in silent communication.

And then there came a flurry of movement and people around them. Josef glimpsed a stretcher, a young man crouching next to the decapitated corpse, examining it with interest, before a billowing white sheet came up to cover everything and the shrill blast of a policeman's whistle pierced the fog.

"Come on," Alex said, steering Josef away. "Inside, quickly now."

Instinct made Josef baulk at being dragged away, but when Alex looked at him, there was such an expression of concern, even fear, in his eyes that Josef startled. It was possibly the most honest expression he'd ever seen on the man's face outside the bedroom.

"Please," Alex said at last. "I'll answer all your questions, but we must get inside now."

Nodding, torn between curiosity and distrust, Josef let himself be helped up the stairs and into the discreet building that housed the Winconian Society.

It was like entering a beehive that had just been poked with a stick—when you were the offending stick.

The door opened onto a large entryway, a grand staircase sweeping up to an entresol overlooking the foyer, and myriad doors and hallways leading deeper into the building. Several knots of respectable-looking men had gathered in the hallways and doorways; others stood looking down from the landing at the top of the stairs. Everyone was silent, the hush so recent Josef could hear it falling as the door swung shut.

All eyes were on them.

Having recovered somewhat from the flight and the fight, Josef became acutely aware that Alex still had an arm around his waist and that his own arm was slung across Alex's shoulders. He had a mad urge to take a bow, but instead returned the cool, curious glances with one of his own.

So, this was the Winconian Society. According to Alex, a secret order dedicated to fighting supernatural beings. More likely a shadowy branch of the Intelligence Corps.

"Lord Beaumont." A man stepped forward with the dress and demeanour of a servant. He glanced briefly at Josef. "May I be of assistance?"

"Mr Shepel has been attacked by a ghoul," Beaumont said, as if such nonsense was unremarkable. His voice, Josef noticed, was pitched for the onlookers as well as the servant. "He barely escaped with his life. See that he can bathe and has clean clothes."

"Of course, my lord." The servant gave a slight bow. "I will see to it myself. Meanwhile, Mr Saint is waiting in the library." A weighted pause. "At your earliest convenience."

Josef felt Alex stiffen, the arm still around Josef's waist tightening.

"I'll go to him directly." To Josef, he said, "Go with Graves. Do exactly as he says." Their eyes met and held, and again Josef saw that shadow of fear in the other man's eyes. "You are safe here."

Alarmingly, Josef wasn't sure that Alex believed it.

"I'd rather stay with you," he said.

Alex's eyes widened, and then he smiled, a faint but true smile. "Would you?"

"Better the devil you know, and all that."

Something passed between them, then, an unexpected sense of comradeship in a tight spot. "You'll be all right with Graves," Alex promised. "Trust me."

There was a hint of a question at the end of those words, and Josef nodded. "All right," he said. Not that he had much choice, but Alex had just saved his life. Again.

"Mr Shepel?" Graves gestured towards a corridor leading to the back of the building. "This way please."

Alex dropped his arm from around Josef's waist, and as they separated Josef swayed somewhat.

"All right?" Alex said, reaching out to steady him. "Do you need help?"

"No, I'm fine." He braced his shoulders. "Or I will be, once I'm out of these disgusting clothes."

With a nod, and a serious, lingering look, Alex turned and strode off in the opposite direction.

Josef noticed with unease that all the eyes in the room followed Alex, several men turning to murmur quietly to each other as he left.

For the second time in a week, Josef found himself stripped bare and studied as if he were a medical specimen.

This time, however, it was not in the warm intimacy of Alex's bathroom but a tiled, utilitarian space that reminded him of the mortuary where he'd found Sykes. There was nothing admiring in Graves's gaze either, thank God, just a clinical appraisal followed by the application of iodine on several grazes on his back, shoulders, and arms.

A porcelain bathtub stood against one wall, with a contraption of pipes hanging over it, and a curtain on a rail. Graves said, "You can shower off in there. I'll have fresh clothes sent in."

"Shower off?"

"The water comes out at the top," he explained, pointing at the pipes. "You stand underneath it to wash. Like a rain shower."

It sounded odd, but Josef would have happily bathed in a duckpond to get the filth off him, so once Graves had left, he turned on the water, startled as it spurted out about six feet above the bath, and hurriedly drew the curtain to keep it from spraying everywhere.

Then he turned his attention back to his clothes, left in a gory pile in the centre of the room. With one eye on the door, he picked up his jacket, grimacing at the stench, and with his fingertips reached into his breast pocket to retrieve the photograph Alex was so desperate to get his hands on. Glancing around the bare room, he set it face down on the tiled windowsill and hoped that it wouldn't be noticed by whoever brought in the clean clothes Graves had promised.

Then he returned to the bath, fiddled about with the taps to get the right temperature, and finally climbed into the tub.

The hot water hammering down on his head didn't feel terrible. Nothing like as luxurious as the bath he'd had in

Alex's flat, but it did the job and washed away the blood and gore. He watched it swirling around his feet and down the plughole until the water began to run clear. Then he picked up a bar of sweet-smelling soap that had been left in the tub and used it to wash himself from head to toe.

By the time he stepped out of the bathtub, shivering in the chilly room, someone had left a towel, a comb, a pile of clean clothes, and a pair of shiny black shoes on a stall next to the sink. Josef glanced quickly at the window, relieved to see the photograph where he'd left it. There was no sign of Graves, and so Josef could dry himself and dress in privacy. The clothes fitted remarkably well—a shirt and a smart three-piece navy-blue suit. Finer than anything Josef had ever owned. He planned on keeping it, too, because his own clothes must be beyond salvation. He hoped Graves had burned them.

Once dressed, he examined himself in the mirror and tried to tame his dark curls with the comb. While damp, they slicked back neatly enough, but he knew they'd be all over the place once his hair dried. He scarcely recognised the well-dressed young man staring back at him from the mirror and wondered what Alex would make of him, looking so posh.

Then he wondered why he cared. It was hardly relevant, was it? Although there had been something in Alex's gaze today, a concern for him that had felt honest...

"He's a liar." Sternly, he stared down his own reflection. "Don't forget that, Joe. Alex Beaumont is a liar."

That much settled, he tucked the photograph into his jacket pocket and pushed open the bathroom door with the hope of doing a little exploring, only to find Graves sitting sentry outside.

He rose when Josef appeared, looking him over in apparent satisfaction. "This way, please, Mr Shepel."

Josef had the strong impression that he had no choice but to follow, that had he asked to leave he'd have been politely and entirely refused. Besides, now that he'd recovered from the shock of the attack, his journalistic nose had started twitching. Here he was, Joe Shepel, inside a secret society. He paid attention to his surroundings as Graves led him back along the corridor to the foyer. The wood-panelled walls held several portraits, stern men gazing down at him from centuries past with little plaques on the frames that read Lord this or Viscount that. August members of the Winconian Society, no doubt.

His fingers itched for his camera.

The foyer was quieter now that the excitement was over, and Graves led him across it quickly, footsteps clack-clacking on the parquet floor, and from there along another short corridor to a small sitting area. A waiting room, perhaps, because there was a second, closed, door on the far side of the room.

And staring out of the window stood Alex. He turned when Josef entered, a flash of relief, quickly covered, crossing his face. Then his eyes flicked subtly over Josef's body, making him newly aware of his fancy suit, before returning to settle on Josef's face.

If Graves noticed the telltale sparkle in Alex's eyes, he didn't react.

"Please wait here, Mr Shepel," Graves said, before backing out of the room and closing the door quietly behind him.

Josef didn't hear the turn of a key in the lock, but the effect of that closing door was the same. Alex turned back to the window, frowning, and Josef noticed a splatter of dried blood on the pristine white of his shirt cuff.

Presumably from when Beaumont had decapitated the...man.

How on earth had they explained it to the police? Clearly, Alex hadn't been arrested. Perhaps casual murder went unremarked upon among the upper classes. Maybe it happened all the time. God knew people like Alex were happy enough to step over men, women, and children starving on the streets...

He rubbed a hand across his face. No, that wasn't fair.

He remembered Alex drawing the blanket up over Sykes's face, that day at the clearing station. There had been compassion in the gesture, more than Josef had shown. And Alex had saved his life, twice. Josef had no doubt that he'd be dead on the street right now if Alex hadn't, by some miracle, intervened.

The certainty made him shiver, and despite the warm shower and dry clothes, he realised he was still cold. Or maybe it wasn't the cold making him tremble. Another shiver as he squeezed his eyes shut against a flash of memory, then opened them abruptly when the creature's ruined face and sharp teeth forced their way into his mind.

He found Alex watching him from the window.

"You look like you need a drink," he said, and moved to a cabinet near the room's inner door. "Whisky?"

Protest formed on Josef's lips—it wasn't even midday—but he found himself too weary to argue. More than weary, mentally exhausted, and when Alex approached and offered him a glass, he took it without comment and sat down.

Alex wasn't drinking, but he took the chair opposite Josef's and leaned forward, elbows on knees, fingers steepled. He looked anxious. "How are you?" he said. "Were you hurt?"

"A few scratches, that's all." He hesitated, then added, "It didn't bite me."

Alex nodded. "I know. If it had..."

He didn't finish the thought, but Josef remembered the gun on the laundry hamper in Alex's bathroom. It hadn't occurred to him before that Graves may have been armed during his inspection of Josef's body.

He swallowed a mouthful of whisky, the fiery burn settling warmth in the pit of his belly, instantly relaxing.

"Who are we waiting for?" he said.

Alex looked up. "What do you mean?"

He really was handsome, with those fine aristocratic features and silky dark hair flopping over his forehead. Josef remembered the weight of it running through his fingers. He said, "You look like you're waiting for the other shoe to drop."

Alex surprised him with a snort of laughter. "Very observant."

"Journalist, remember?"

Across the space between them, their eyes met, and Josef felt the same electric jolt of recognition, of connection, that he remembered from their first encounter in Pops. It made his stomach fizz.

Alex smiled, rather a sweet smile for his serious face. "Have you ever heard the expression, 'Curiosity killed the cat'?"

"Frequently. And I say it's a good job cats have nine lives."

Alex's smile broadened, warming his dark eyes. Then it fell away abruptly. "I'm afraid things are about to get a little...sticky."

"They were very sticky out on the street." He took another sip of whisky, washing away the taste of his terror. "How did you know? Did you hear me shouting?"

"Not exactly." Alex tapped his fingers against his lips. Soft lips, Josef remembered. Clever fingers. "The alarm was raised by the watch."

"Coppers?"

"Hunters. We keep watch on all avenues of approach. For security reasons."

"Ah. 'Security' reasons."

Alex shook his head. "You can't seriously still think this has anything to do with the Intelligence Corps."

"You can't seriously think I believe your fairytales."

"Why not?" Alex snapped. "Did you fail to notice the ghoul trying to eat your face? Or the fact that I decapitated it with an original Crusader sword? Does that seem, even remotely, like the work of the bloody government?"

Josef set his jaw. "I don't dispute that something was about to eat my face, but—"

The click of an opening door had Alex jumping to his feet and standing to attention. Subadar Dutta appeared at the inner door. His cool gaze travelled over Josef and landed on Alex. Then he nodded and stepped back into the room beyond. Shoulders braced, Alex headed for the door, pausing at the last moment to give Josef a serious look before he disappeared inside, and the door closed behind him.

Josef was alone.

After a moment, he rose and ambled over to the bookshelf next to the fireplace. A small blaze flickered in the grate, pleasant on a cold November day, but the books were nothing extraordinary. Encyclopaedias, atlases, a couple of Bibles. Reference books. Nothing to hint at the secret purpose of this place.

Hunters of supernatural creatures.

Ridiculous. Every fibre of Josef's rational mind rejected the notion. And yet the horror of the attack, of that ruined face and those awful teeth, was sharp in his mind... His chest tightened at the visceral memory, and he had to push it aside vigorously.

Supernatural or not, there had been nothing natural about the man who had attacked him.

And the answers to who or what he was lay in this place of secrets, lay with Alex and perhaps with the man on the other side of that door. Stepping closer to it, Josef realised he could hear the low murmur of voices coming from the other room. He leaned closer still until his ear pressed blatantly against the door.

One voice, rising in volume, was clearly Alex's. "...couldn't leave him to die in the street!"

"Many men have been sacrificed in this war," said another, waspish and older. "More than you can possibly imagine."

"But this man is a...friend. Of sorts."

"A friend?" The other man sounded incredulous. "We are Winconians, Lord Beaumont, and we are on the front line of this conflict. There is no room for sentiment."

Silence. After a long pause, Alex said, "To answer your question, he came here because I told him to. I gave him my card, and I told him the truth."

A thump followed that announcement, the sound of an angry fist hitting a table, and a garbled exclamation Josef couldn't make out even though the other man's voice was loud enough that Josef pulled his ear from the door. "An outsider!" he fumed. "The founding laws of our society—"

"Were written a thousand years ago!" Alex had raised his voice, too. "It's a different world now. People have a right to know what's lurking in their city. Who are we to say they don't?"

"Who are we?" The other man was shouting. "We are the people keeping them safe!"

"Maybe they don't need us to keep them safe anymore—"

"Oh, believe me, they do. People are worse than the damned ghoul. They twist the truth and abuse it for their own gain."

"But they're changing." Alex again, quieter now. "Surely we should change too?"

A snort, the sound of a chair pushing back. "People don't change, I can assure you of that. People are fearful, vain, cringing creatures no better now than they were when King William and your noble ancestor first set foot on our shores. And no better equipped to deal with the truth." Footsteps, and then the voice was closer. Crisp and precise. "They used to drown witches in the Thames, and the only reason they stopped is because they stopped believing the truth. We will not—will not—give it back to them."

Into the silence that followed came a third voice—Dutta—who said, "It appears to be too late for that. Shepel is—"

"Right here," Josef said, opening the door. Given that he was the subject of the conversation, he felt it was high time he joined in, and sod propriety. "Shepel is right here."

As he'd guessed, the room was an office, or perhaps a small library because bookshelves lined all its walls. A grand mahogany desk dominated one end, Dutta leaning casually against the shelves to its right. Alex, who stared at Josef with wide, startled eyes, stood toe to toe with another man in front of the door.

That man was short, slight, and wiry, with a curiously ageless face and a corona of silver-gold hair. Dressed in a velvet smoking jacket the colour of red wine, he turned hard pale eyes in Josef's direction.

"Wait until you are summoned," he snapped.

"I don't think I will." Josef let the door close behind him. "Seeing as how you're talking about me, I might as well be part of the conversation, don't you think?"

Silence filled the room, and Josef was acutely aware of Alex and Dutta watching him, or perhaps watching the other man.

Eventually, the stranger spoke again, his voice very clipped. "Very well. Since you are here..." He shot a baleful look at Alex and walked around to sit behind the desk.

Alex visibly relaxed, and Dutta moved from his position next to the desk to take a seat in front of the small fireplace, stretching out his long legs.

His gaze touched on Josef, then moved to Alex. "I assume he wasn't bitten."

"Graves checked him."

Their locked gaze held before Dutta nodded and Alex subsided into another chair with a sigh, pulling a packet of gaspers from his jacket pocket.

"He has a name," Josef said. "It's Joe Shepel. And you, I presume, are Subadar Dutta."

The other man's eyebrows rose in an expression of polite surprise so like Alex's that Josef wondered whether they taught it at Eton. "Mr Dutta will suffice."

"I see. 'Subadar' being a fraudulent rank, I suppose," Josef said. "Just like 'Captain' Winchester over there. That's a serious offence, by the way: impersonating an officer."

"Don't you ever stop?" Alex sighed, lighting his cigarette.

"No. Do you?"

Their eyes met, clashing. "You're in enough trouble as it is, you know."

"I'm in trouble? You just chopped a man's head off in the middle of bloody Belgravia!"

"You're quite right," Dutta interjected pleasantly. "Alex is in much more trouble than you, as you're about to find out. However, the degree of trouble is all relative. In truth, we're all up to our necks in it." He turned to Alex with an ironic smile. "I see what you mean about his spit and fire. Right up your alley, I should imagine."

"Put a sock in it, Dal. You don't—"

"Enough." The other man's voice cracked across the room, silencing them both. His gaze fixed on Josef, bright, inquisitive, and cold. "My name is Saint," he said. "And Mr Dutta is quite correct. You—we—are now in a difficult situation."

"Are we now?"

"You have a photograph of a ghoul—"

"So you say."

Saint blinked his cold eyes. "So I say?"

From his chair, Alex added, "I didn't have time to explain that Shepel doesn't believe a word I told him. He thinks I'm a liar and a fraud. And that I work for the Intelligence Corps."

"Which is what?" said Saint.

Josef laughed. "Oh, very good. Deny it even exists. Of course, why not?"

Saint stared at him, unblinking.

"No, he's serious," Alex told Josef, taking a drag on his cigarette. "Saint is focused on ... other matters. He doesn't pay much attention to the outside world."

The outside world...

Josef rubbed his forehead. "If you expect—"

"What I expect," Saint snapped, "is that you hand over the photograph of the ghoul before it's too late. What I expect is that you will never speak of what you have learned here and that you never again return to this place, that you never—"

"Or what?" This was bloody rich! "Will you have me arrested for telling ghost stories? Sent to prison?"

After a long silence, Saint said, "We have no prisons, Mr Shepel, but rest assured that if your silence cannot be ensured voluntarily, it will be enforced. By other means."

"Oh, it's threats now, is it?"

Alex grabbed Josef's arm, holding him back. "Saint, you can't mean—"

"I ain't scared of you!" Josef spoke over him, trying to pull free of Alex's grip. "None of you. And when my editor gets that picture—"

"Silence!" Saint held up his hand, and the room fell quiet. After a moment, and in a cool voice, Saint said, "Beaumont, this is your error, and I expect you to correct it. All of it." His gaze lingered, measuring. "Do I make myself clear?"

This close, Josef could hear Alex's harsh breaths. "As crystal," he said stiffly, his fingers tightening on Josef's arm.

"Very well." Saint retrieved a letter from his inbox, flicking it open with a flourish. "Get it done, Beaumont. No more blunders. Put a lid on the ghoul situation before London's overrun with the stinking bastards. And no loose ends."

With that, they were dismissed.

Alex turned and, before Josef could protest, frogmarched him out of the office, out of the waiting room, and out of the building.

Dutta followed on their heels. "I did warn you," he said, as they stopped in the darkening November afternoon. A breeze had picked up, needle sharp as it dispersed the fog, and Josef pulled his coat tightly around himself.

"Warned me about what?" Alex reached for his cigarettes and lit up, offering the packet to Josef. He took one, and leaned in to share Alex's light, close enough that he could feel his warmth through the chill air.

"I told you in Pops that he'd be trouble," Dutta said. "And now"—he pressed a hand to his chest— "you're entangled."

Alex met Josef's eye, unflinching and unrevealing. "Nonsense."

"Liar."

Turning away, Alex blew a stream of smoke into the cold air. In the dusky light, his eyes looked like chips of coal. "Well, it doesn't matter," he said. "I've got my orders, and I'll follow them. You know I will."

After a silence, Dutta put a hand to Alex's shoulder. "Yes, I do," he said, letting go as he turned back to the club. "That's what concerns me the most."

No loose ends, Josef thought with a shiver.

It was transparently obvious that he was the loose end in question.

Chapter Fifteen

"Well," Josef said, "this has been enlightening, but if you'll excuse me, I should be getting back to—"

"The Cohens?" Alex shook his head. "I don't think so. Not unless you want to bring this," he made an encompassing gesture with the hand holding his cigarette, "to their door."

"But you killed the..." He grimaced. "... the ghoul." It sounded ridiculous in his ears, but he had no better word for the creature that had attacked him; certainly, it had not been a man.

Alex lifted an eyebrow. "I killed a ghoul."

"There are more, then."

"Inevitably."

Josef folded his arms, shivering as the rising breeze cut through him. "What—fuck, I can hardly believe I'm asking this, but what are they, then? Ghosts or...?"

"Not ghosts, no." Alex's eyes met his, bright with something like satisfaction. Excitement, perhaps? "They're creatures of the Otherworld, ancient and slumbering, for the most part, in the deepest parts of the earth. But now we've woken them, and they're hungry."

"You've woken them? Your society? Why?"

Alex shook his head, took a drag on the remains of his gasper, and dropped the stub on the pavement. Crushing it out with the toe of his shoe, he said, "When I say 'we', I mean mankind." He looked up again, right into Josef's eyes. "This bloody war has woken them, the violence and blood and agony of it sinking into the earth. And not only them." Alex cocked his head. "You must have heard the stories at the front? Angels and ghosts in no man's land."

Josef had, of course. "Men staring death in the eye will inevitably imagine ghosts and angels."

"Maybe so, but do their imaginings often chase them through Belgravia?"

Josef had no answer to that. His mind was slowly rearranging itself around a reality too incredible to believe, and yet with no convincing alternative. Eventually, he said, "I have a lot of questions."

A smile tugged at Alex's lips. "I can try to answer them for you, but let's go somewhere warmer, shall we?"

Josef couldn't argue with that; he was bloody freezing. "Any decent pubs in this neck of the wood?"

Alex consulted his watch and said, "The pubs aren't open yet." After a hesitation, he added, "My flat isn't far."

The idea of returning to Alex's warm and sumptuous mansion flat, with its soft carpet and well-stocked drinks cabinet, was extremely appealing. Too appealing. And Joe Shepel was no fool; he remembered the revolver on the laundry basket, and Saint's warning about loose ends. "How about you treat me to a cup of tea, instead? There must be somewhere around here."

Alex's expression closed. "There's always Harrods, I suppose. It's not far."

Harrods? "I was thinking of something more like a Corner House."

"It's a tramp to Leicester Square," Alex said, "and in the circumstances, I'd rather avoid the Underground."

Josef couldn't help but agree. The very thought of those dark tunnels made him shiver with something worse than the cold. To distract himself from unwanted memories, he said, "Lord Beaumont takes the Underground, does he?"

"Only when his golden carriage is unavailable." Then, with an exaggerated sweep of one arm, Alex said, "Shall we go?"

Josef had no reason and, in all honesty, no will to argue further and so he let Alex lead him through the quiet streets of Belgravia towards the bustle of Knightsbridge. It was a comfort to have the other man's company, but even so, his ears were pricked for the sounds of footsteps behind him, and his nose twitched in dread of that death-stench.

Into the quiet, he said, "Tell me this, then. Are they...?" He thought back to Sykes's body in the morgue with its sepulchral blue gaze. "Are they reanimated dead men, or do they just look like them?"

Alex gave a slight nod, as if in approval of the question. "By nature, ghouls feed on the dead—in graveyards or plague pits, typically. But at the front, in no man's land..." His expression darkened. "There, they've started to feed on the dying, and sometimes their victims become infected, for want of a better word, before they pass."

"Bloody hell, is that—?" Josef stopped walking, staring at Alex, who also stopped. "The black rot on Sykes's arm?"

"Yes. We believe that men infected like Sykes can transform after death."

"Transform into a ghoul?" Josef almost laughed; the idea was preposterous. "Like... Like Count Dracula?"

Alex winced, but only said, "Different process, but yes. The same outcome."

"Fucking hell."

"That's what I said, or something like it."

Josef laughed, although it came out wobblier than he'd have liked. "So, what you're saying is any of these poor buggers who got bitten at the front could turn into a ghoul when they die?"

"That's about the sum of it. We're trying to weed them out before they leave the Continent, or at least when they reach the hospitals, but a few are slipping through. Clearly." He added, "I'd hoped that Sykes had been spared that fate."

"There are worse things than death," Josef said, staring into Alex's stark, pale face. "That's what you said at the clearing station. I thought you meant dishonour, or some crap like that."

Alex cocked his head. "And now you know better?"

Something in the man's direct, dark gaze made Josef admit, "I don't believe in ghosts or ghouls, but... I'm struggling to find another explanation."

Alex held his gaze, and there was a warmth in his eyes at odds with the subject. "Well, as the great man said, There are more things in heaven and Earth than are dreamt of in your philosophy."

"True, but Hamlet was doolally, wasn't he?" He grinned at Alex's look of surprise. "What? Didn't think I'd know my Shakespeare?"

"I've come to realise, Josef, that there are more things to you than one might dream of."

"Oh yeah? Dream about me, do you?"

With an unexpectedly self-conscious smile, Alex said, "If I did, I'd hardly confess."

There was no reason whatsoever for that smile to work its way into Josef's chest, and yet he felt an anticipatory flutter of wings beneath his sternum just the same. "Come on," he said, "I'm freezing my balls off out here."

"And we wouldn't want that," Alex observed mildly, and started walking again. But his smile was still there and, aggravatingly, Josef's lips also curved up as he fell into step next to him.

They were halfway along Piccadilly when Josef heard the first boom of a distant explosion, then a second. A moment later, whistles began to screech in warning, and everyone started to run.

"Air raid!"

A new, different fear seized Josef as he looked up to find the night sliced by searchlights. In the distance came the rat-a-tat-tat of antiaircraft guns, and below that the ominous drone of huge German Gotha aeroplanes.

"Damn it." Alex pulled Josef back against the side of a building, out of the path of the panicking crowds.

They'd almost reached Burlington Arcade, and its well-heeled clients were being directed to shelter by the stoic Beadles in their ridiculous top hats and frock coats.

"Dover Street tube," Josef said, grabbing Alex's arm, "that's the closest."

Alex hesitated. "Not underground."

"What? Come on—it's a fucking air raid!"

"You know what's down there."

Josef watched helplessly as people ran past them towards the tube station. "Well, what about them?" he said hoarsely.

"The ghoul aren't hunting them."

"Shit." He scanned the sky. Was that a shadow, moving beneath the clouds? "But surely in a crowd we'd be—"

An enormous detonation sucked all the noise out of the world. For an instant, he felt weightless, and then the pavement thumped him hard in the back, knocking the air from his lungs, and something warm and heavy covered him. No, not something, someone. Alex, shielding him from the pattering rain. Only there was no rain, just falling masonry, brick, and dust.

Josef didn't move—couldn't move—as he struggled to get air back into his lungs. On top of him, Alex was still, too. Breathing, though. Josef could feel his chest heaving, heart pounding, breath warm against Josef's neck. He could feel the ponding of Alex's heart against his chest. It helped him find his breath, even if he couldn't hear it over the ringing in his ears.

The brickwork rain stopped; the world held silent for a long moment. And then the shouting and screaming began, and Beaumont moved, pushing himself up enough that he could study Josef's face. Very close. He'd lost his hat, and his hair fell forward across his handsome face, his eyes dark in the dim light, lips parted as if about to...

"Are you all right?" Alex asked in a ragged voice, barely audible over the concussion in Josef's eardrums.

Josef wheezed out his reply. "Think so."

"Fuck," Alex said, in very un-lordly manner, "that was a squeaker."

Josef only nodded, and with a soft exhale, Beaumont leaned forward and rested his forehead against Josef's. Only for a moment, but despite everything, Josef felt his blood rise and sing. Clumsily, he lifted a hand and patted the man's shoulder in reassurance. "I think it was me doing the squeaking."

To his surprise, Alex chuckled and lifted his head to look Josef in the eye once more before pushing himself up and away. It was easier to breathe without the man's weight, but nevertheless, Josef found he missed his warmth. He shivered as he sat up too, gazing around at a world transformed. People were scrambling to their feet, or standing dazed, clutching friends or family, staring at the flames billowing out of the building not a hundred yards further down the road.

"Christ," Alex said. "That's the Royal Academy."

"I hope no one was working late."

Alex scrambled to his feet, pushing his hair back with one hand. He cast around for his lost hat, snatching it up. Stiffly, Josef also stood. No permanent damage, but he'd probably feel it in his back tomorrow.

As he rose, Josef realised that all around them people were panicking. This was nothing like the front, where men bent lower beneath the deadly barrage, hunkering down into the sodden earth of the trenches. For these people, these civilians, this single detonation was a catastrophe, and they were reacting like ants when you lifted a stone, running in all directions without thought.

Further up the road, the Beadles were shouting orders—they were old soldiers, after all—but few were paying attention. A woman hurried towards them, a bloodied handkerchief to her head, dragging a screaming child along by his hand.

Another huge explosion echoed across London, not far away, and a plume of flame and smoke rose up from the direction of the river.

The woman yelped, half turned and caught her foot on a piece of broken brickwork. She would have fallen had Alex not caught her arm and steadied her. "Careful," he said. "It's all right."

She grasped at him, dropping her handkerchief, and revealing the bloody gash on her forehead. "Oh God," she said, wobbling on her feet. "My son..."

"I've got him," said Josef, and scooped the squirming lad up onto his hip. As the eldest child, he was no stranger dealing with young children. "He's all right, aren't you, mister?"

The boy sniffled and shook his head. Josef didn't blame him.

Another explosion shook the city, and then a third, as fire rose into the sky, red and bloody. Josef met Alex's eyes through the flickering flamelight, and they came to a silent agreement.

"Let's get you to the Underground," Alex told the woman. "You'll be safe there."

By the time they'd made their way back to the packed Dover Street station, the bells of the ambulances and fire engines were ringing, and they were able to discharge their wards into the tender care of the women on duty. And not long after that, the first bugles sounded, announcing all clear. Thank God.

Obviously, the tubes weren't running; their platforms and tracks would still be crowded with frightened Londoners. And that left Josef with a long walk home.

"You've no choice, then," Alex said as they left the chaos and noise of the station. "You have to come back to my flat."

Josef shook his head. That was a bad idea for many reasons, not least of which being that he had to check that the Cohens were all right. And to tell them that he was, too. They'd imagine the worst if he didn't come home after an air raid.

"We'll send a messenger boy," Alex said when Josef explained. "And to your family, too, of course."

"Not to my family, no."

Alex said, lightly, "No?"

"We're not on terms," he said. "Not since the start of the war." Which was all he intended to say on the matter.

Alex didn't press, simply nodded. "Very well. When we get back, you can write a note to the Cohens. The boy can take it and bring back any reply."

"Oh, so it's all right for a boy on a bike to be making his way through London during an air raid, but not me?"

"For one thing, the air raid's over," Alex pointed out, lifting a finger to count. "For a second, the boy hasn't been attacked, grilled by The Society, and nearly blasted to Kingdom Come this evening. And for a third—I tip exceptionally well."

"Even so, I could easily—"

"For God's sake!" Alex snapped. "Can't you just let me—?" He gritted his teeth, glancing around them and then lowering his voice. "You nearly died today. Twice. Don't you think you might need a little...care tonight?"

Josef swallowed at the strange crack in Alex's voice. "That's not what—" After a moment, he rephrased, "I'm used to getting by on my own."

"Yes, I realise that." Alex ran a hand through his dishevelled hair, a disarmingly frustrated gesture. "I'm also aware that your perception of the world has been radically altered in the last few days, and that I may be able to help you...adjust. If, that is, you trust me enough."

Josef held his gaze, trying to see into the heart of the man. "That's the question, isn't it? Can I trust you?"

"If I meant you harm," Alex said, "I'd have let harm come to you."

That was true, as far as it went, but Josef hadn't survived as long as he had in the world by trusting easily. "I suppose you do keep saving my life," he conceded.

Alex's lips twitched into his wry half-smile. "Only because you keep putting it in danger." He inclined his head in the general direction of St. James's Park. "Come back with me and we'll talk. I'm too tired to save your life again tonight."

Josef made a show of considering, but in truth his decision had already been made. "I do have a lot of questions," he admitted. "And no other bugger is going to give me any answers."

Chapter Sixteen

Alex's flat was as luxurious as Josef remembered, brightly lit and warm.

Tonight, its elevation and distance from the streets where danger lurked came as an unexpected comfort. Even if, from the window, Josef could see the fires from the night's air raid turning the sky ruddy. Just like at the front.

He wondered how many had died tonight.

As he walked closer to the window, Josef was aware of Alex behind him—lighting lamps, setting the fire. Meanwhile, far below them, teemed a frightened population. Spooks and ghouls aside, it was horrors of man's invention that stalked the streets tonight.

"You'd think," he said into the room's quiet, "that having bombs dropped on you from aeroplanes would turn people against this bloody war. But it just makes them more gung-ho to 'stick it to the Hun'."

"It makes them afraid," Alex said from the fireplace. "Anger is a potent salve for fear." He rose and joined Josef at the window. "It's why we keep our work secret. Over the years, many of us have fallen victim to fear and anger."

Josef glanced at him, at his strong, serious profile and felt that peculiar shifting in his chest again. Carefully, feeling his way, he said, "Because people fear what they don't understand."

Turning his head, Alex met his eyes. "Naturally."

"Don't you think, in this modern era of scientific curiosity, there's scope for more understanding? Why hoard all this secret information to some hereditary society? It's the twentieth century, for God's sake. Share your knowledge with the people."

Alex gave a contained smile. "I don't entirely disagree. But look what happened when I tried to tell you the truth, and you'd seen evidence with your own eyes."

Josef had to concede the point.

"Besides, it's too dangerous to be more open." He gave a peculiar little nod, as if convincing himself. "It's worked like this for a thousand years, and it can work for a thousand more."

"Except now you have ghouls running around London."

Alex's eyes narrowed. "That is not our fault. This damned war is waking too many things best left sleeping."

"And do you think this war will be the last, or the worst? For God's sake, we're dropping bombs out of aeroplanes onto people's homes." He shook his head, staring out over the burning city. "It's only going to get worse from here—God knows what we'll disturb. And then what will you and your merry band of toffs do? Will there even be enough of you to deal with it?"

Alex didn't answer, but he looked troubled, and Josef suspected he'd hit a nerve. Good. Some nerves needed to be hit. After a moment's consideration, he said, "Let me publish the story. Let me tell people about the ghoul, about how the war is bringing evil into the world."

"Absolutely not." Alex had lost all colour, his reflection ghostlike in the window. "Under no circumstances are you to do that."

Josef's hackles rose as they always did when he met with closed doors. "You can't stop me, you know."

Alex's expression turned baleful. "Do you truly believe that?"

"Yes. Unless you're planning to do me in. We still have something like a free press in this country, despite DORA."

Alex turned from the window, holding Josef's gaze with an expression impossible to decipher. "Then let me be absolutely clear," he said. "It would very much not be in your interest to attempt to publish a story about the situation with the ghoul."

"That sounds like a threat."

"It is a threat." Taken aback, Josef retreated a step, and Alex's mouth tightened. "Not from me. Others...are less tolerant."

"You mean your boss, Saint."

Alex jerked his head in a nod. "Secrecy has kept The Society safe for close to a millennium. It won't change now. He won't change."

"And I'm a loose end," Josef said, quoting Saint's words. "To be dealt with."

Alex didn't answer, turning back to the window, and for a while they both stared out over the city.

"So, what's the plan?" Josef said. "Knock me over the head and dump me in the Thames? Or shoot me with that gun of yours—the one you keep in the bathroom?"

"If you truly thought I'd do any of that, you wouldn't be here."

"Wouldn't I? I went to the front to report the truth, and this isn't half so risky. Besides, you can't kill me; you want that photograph, and only I know where it is."

Alex turned his head, half his face in shadow cast by the flickering light of the gas lamps. He looked stern, and unfairly beautiful. Josef had to clench his teeth against a betraying twist of want. Alex said, "Destroy it, both the print and the negative. It puts you in danger, and not only from the ghoul."

His expression darkened further. "The Society goes to great lengths to keep its secrets."

Josef thought of the photograph, and of the pamphlet May had agreed to publish. "I can't destroy it. I need it. I'm trying to tell people the truth."

"No one will believe you about the ghoul—"

"About the war," Josef interrupted. "About working men like Sykes being forced to kill each other to satisfy the greed of their bourgeois, imperial masters. Your lot can't have a problem with that truth, can they?"

"They will if you publish a photograph of a man clearly infected by a ghoul."

Josef lifted his chin. "It's my best one."

"For God's sake!" Alex grabbed his shoulder, turning Josef to face him. "I'm not joking. They will do anything to protect their secrets. Do you understand?"

"Of course I understand," Josef said, shaking free. "That's what your lot always do: protect their secrets. Why do you think they've gagged all the war correspondents?"

Jaw clenched, Alex said, "This is different."

"Is it? How?"

"Because some truths are too dangerous to tell." His eyes met Josef's with a look he couldn't misinterpret. "As you well know."

That, he supposed was true, but what Alex was talking about was a private matter that hurt nobody. "In that case," he said, "secrecy protects a man's right to live as he chooses. In the case of your Society, it keeps the people in ignorance of their own danger."

"And, in both cases, it preserves the peace."

"Until ghouls start infecting people in London."

Alex lifted a brow. "And you think provoking mass panic would help?"

"I think, if people knew the truth about that, about the war, they wouldn't keep taking it. Not when they're being slaughtered in the millions. Mustard gas or fucking ghouls, what difference does it make in the end? They're still bloody dead. And for what? To keep their bourgeois masters in champagne and caviar. That's the real reason for all this bloody secrecy."

Alex's eyebrows rose. "I see you're an acolyte of Messrs Marx and Engels."

"Oh, fuck off." Josef added with a sarcastic smile, "Maybe you should read them. Then you'll know what's coming."

"What makes you think I haven't?" Alex spun from the window, heading for his drinks cabinet. "Meanwhile, while we await the proletarian revolution, I still have the pressing issue of a nest of flesh-eating ghouls somewhere in London." He set out two glasses and reached for a bottle of brandy. "Drink?"

On principle, Josef felt like he should refuse. Some socialist he was, drinking with Lord Beaumont in his fancy flat. Even so, it felt churlish to refuse—and after the day he'd had, he could really do with a drink. And Alex had a point about the ghoul. "What do you mean 'somewhere in London?' Don't you know where they are?"

"If I knew where they were, I'd have dealt with them by now." He poured two generous glasses and held one out for Josef. "What else did you think I'd been doing for the last few weeks? Following you around for fun?"

"It crossed my mind," Josef said, accepting the drink.

To his astonishment, a flush coloured Alex's refined features. He said, crisply, "I'm looking for the nest."

Which was a terrifying thought. "Are you saying they could be anywhere in London?"

"Pretty much. Anywhere dark and dank, with a ready supply of fresh corpses."

With a snort, Josef said, "Have you tried the House of Lords?"

Alex choked on his brandy, resulting in an extremely inelegant coughing fit which set Josef giggling—fucking giggling!—as he tried ineffectually to thump Alex on the back. He didn't even know why he was laughing; nothing in his life was remotely funny. But maybe that was the point. Maybe you couldn't be afraid and angry all the time. Maybe sometimes those worming dark emotions escaped. And better to laugh than to cry.

Seemed like Alex agreed, because his coughing and laughter were all mixed up as he doubled over, hands on his thighs, and wheezed, "God, but that's so true!" before collapsing again into laughter.

Eventually, the squall passed, and Josef got himself under control, wiping his eyes with the back of his hand. Alex leaned against the drinks cabinet, catching his breath, watching Josef. And Josef watched him back, taking in the elegant suit with the splash of blood on one cuff, the brick dust in his hair and streaking his face.

Out of nowhere, reality landed a stealthy right hook.

Josef had nearly died today. Twice. By rights, he should be in the mortuary right now. Cold and dead, or worse.

But he wasn't dead; by some miracle he was warm and breathing and very much alive. Blood rushed in his ears, his heart thumped in his chest, and his body sang with sudden, physical presence as if every nerve was fighting for a taste of life.

"Fuck," he said in a voice that shook as hard as his hand. He set his drink down before he spilled it. "Fucking hell. If we'd been a hundred yards closer to that bomb..."

Alex straightened, eyes locked with Josef's, a bolt of heat flashing between them. "We were lucky."

"Bloody lucky." Josef took a step closer, too close to be misconstrued. "How about we do something with that luck?"

Alex's eyebrows rose. "What did you have in mind?"

"I think you know."

"But you..." He faltered, looking uncertain for a moment, before scrambling on a wry expression. "It's not against your principles, then, to fuck an aristocrat?"

Josef smiled, grinning when he saw the same expression kindling in Alex's eyes. "Fucking the aristocracy is my mission in life, my lord."

"Is that so?" Alex lifted his hand to run a light, intentional finger along the line of Josef's jaw. "I suppose you'd like to see us on our knees."

"Fuck, yes," Josef said, rather more breathily that he'd hoped. "I'd bloody love that."

Alex drew his bottom lips between his teeth, biting gently, a gesture at once so knowing and vulnerable that Josef groaned. Fuck. Was he really going to risk this? Again?

Apparently, he was.

"Jesus," Alex hissed, one hand landing on Josef's hip and pulling them together. He was hard; so was Josef. It felt wonderful. "I didn't think you'd want—"

"Shut up," Josef growled, and silenced both their doubts with a fierce kiss, driving his fingers into Alex's silken hair and holding him just where he wanted him.

Groaning softly, Alex met the kiss with the eagerness of a famished man. Josef knew how he felt; they were kissing as if the bombs were about to fall, and perhaps they were.

Perhaps this night was all they'd have.

He got his hands beneath Alex's jacket and shoved it off his shoulders, and then they were undressing each other in a scramble of buttons and waistcoats. There were no more words, only touch and want, and fire burning away the terrors of the night.

Chapter Seventeen

Afterwards, they lay quietly together, Josef spooned against Alex's chest with his head resting on one of Alex's powerful arms.

For the first time in forever, he felt relaxed. Boneless. His mind drifting in a happy miasma of drowsy dreams.

Alex's warm breath ruffled his hair as he murmured, "I've thought about you a great deal over the past few months."

"Have you?"

"I know I shouldn't; I know this can't be more than it is. But I wanted you to know that the night we spent together in Pops was... real."

Josef twisted slightly in his arms, trying to see his face. "Was it? You were lying about everything that night. Even your name."

"Not true. I told you my name."

"Only half of it."

"The most important half." He kissed Josef's shoulder, then sighed, tightening his arm around Josef's waist. "I wish things could have been different, though."

"Different how?" Josef squirmed onto his side so that they were face to face. Alex's hand came to rest on the small of his back, warm and heavy.

"I wish we could have parted as friends."

Josef snorted. "Friends? That was hardly possible."

"It could have been," Alex objected. "If...if we'd had fewer secrets."

"And you weren't such a toff."

"And you weren't such a socialist oik."

Josef gasped in mock outrage. "Oik?" He turned his caress of Alex's chest into a poke in the ribs, making him yelp. And then fight back, which resulted in a ridiculous tickling match as they wrestled around in Alex's enormous bed. It only ended when Alex pinned Josef's arms to the bed, straddling him as he leaned down and thoroughly kissed him into submission.

And submit Josef did, giving up everything to that moment of untethered joy. And to Alex, to his body moving over Josef's, moving inside him, to the overwhelming rise of pleasure. When it broke over him, he let it wash everything away and leave him, for a few precious moments, pure and cleansed of troubles.

Much later, Josef woke from a deep sleep to the sound of a telephone ringing.

For a moment, he was confused—the Cohens didn't own a telephone. And then, with a complex rush of warmth and wariness, he remembered where he was: Alex Beamont's bed.

Propping himself up on his elbows, blinking sleep away, Josef watched through the bedroom door as Alex, half dressed, picked up the telephone handset.

"Yes, of course," he said after a moment. "Send him up—the long way, please."

Josef sat up straight. Send him up?

Bolting out of bed, he scrabbled around in the semi-dark looking for his clothes. He didn't know what the hell Alex was playing at, but he wasn't about to be found naked in his bed.

"You might want to—ah." Alex stood, well, lounged, in the doorway. His shirt was only partly fastened and revealed a slice of muscular chest that Josef might have found enticing had he not been searching for his underwear. "I take it you heard that we're expecting company?"

"Yes, I bloody well did. And I suppose you think I'll just hide in a cupboard or climb out the window. Well, think again, sunshine."

Alex looked amused. "You're welcome to any of my cupboards, but I wouldn't recommend trying to scale the building at this time of night." His amusement softened, and he smiled, holding out a hand to Josef. "Come here."

Reluctantly, but unable to stop himself, Josef took the offered hand. Warm, strong—he remembered the feel of it on his body, the dexterity and subtlety of those elegant fingers. Goosebumps rose along his arms, despite the warmth of the room.

"Don't worry," Alex said, tugging Josef against him, "we have time. I've no intention of exposing you to any danger."

"Ghouls aside?"

Alex's eyebrows rose. "You were the one poking about in that business. I tried to warn you off."

That was true, Josef supposed. "I'm not very biddable," he confessed.

"I know. It's one of the things I like most about you."

Josef's turn to smile, and although he tried to make it arch, he had a feeling it was embarrassingly eager. "You like me, do you?"

He was expecting a wry response, but Alex only said, "I do, rather."

It was silly that those three words sent Josef's heart knocking about in his chest, but there was no denying that they did. Or that Josef was, apparently, in extreme danger of being smitten by this toff.

Bollocks.

When he didn't respond, one corner of Alex's mouth lifted into an odd little smile. "You should get dressed," he said, letting Josef go. "Dutta will be here soon, and you might be interested in what he has to say."

"Which is what?" Josef said, pulling on his underpants and buttoning them hurriedly.

"That, I don't know. But he wouldn't be here if there wasn't trouble."

"What—?" Josef began, but he was cut off by an urgent rapping on the front door.

Alex grimaced. "No more questions. Get dressed and come through. Then we'll find out what this is about."

He didn't much like being ordered about, by Alex or anyone else, but he was curious. Obviously. So, he dressed quickly and hurried out of the bedroom, trying to appear nonchalant as he sauntered into the parlour. Trying not to look like a man sneaking out of another man's bed.

He needn't have worried what he looked like, though, because neither man was paying him the least bit of attention.

Dutta, in a red turban, sat on the green velvet settee, his back to Josef, facing the fireplace where Alex stood leaning against the mantel in his—thankfully, fully fastened—shirtsleeves. He looked utterly unruffled, a cigarette dangling from one languorous hand.

"...died of wounds," Dutta was saying in his cultured accent. "He was taken to the mortuary at Cemetery Station to be transported by train for burial at Brookwood tomorrow. If they get out of London..."

"Yes, very bad," Alex agreed. Then, noticing Josef, he smiled. "Ah, there you are."

Dutta turned his head, eyes narrowing sharply, and Josef tried to match Alex's sangfroid. "Mr Dutta," he said, with a slight nod.

"Mr Shepel. What a surprise to find you here so late at night."

"I could say the same to you."

With a warning look at Alex, Dutta said, "Is this wise?"

"Wise or not," Alex said, dropping into one of the armchairs next to the fire, "Shepel knows almost as much as we do about the ghoul situation. Although he probably wishes he didn't."

"I don't wish anything so bloody stupid." Josef crossed the room to take the empty chair on the other side of the fireplace. "Only an idiot would wish for ignorance."

Dutta gave a chilly smile. "Are you sure about that? Ignorance is bliss, so they say."

"They also say knowledge is power. And they're right."

Alex sighed. "If you've both quite finished, shall we return to the matter in hand? Dal, are we positive this Major Giles has been infected?"

"I haven't seen the body myself, but Withers, our man on the ambulance train, said Giles was feverish and raving so badly they had to tie him into his bunk. He was dead before they reached Waterloo, apparently."

Alex looked grim.

"You're talking about a man bitten by a ghoul?" Josef guessed.

In the firelight, the silver pin in Dutta's turban gleamed as he nodded. "He'd been stranded in no man's land overnight before the stretcher bearers could fetch him back behind the lines." His expression turned grim. "The ghoul had feasted on him."

"That's... I remember the screams at night." Josef shivered, his mind turning back to those bleak months in the salient. "You could hear them even from the reserve trench. It was horrible enough, but I never imagined they were..."

...being eaten alive, wounded, dying, and alone in the cold dark.

"How could you imagine?" Alex said softly, reaching over to set his hand on Josef's knee.

Startled out of his thoughts by Alex's carelessness, Josef threw a panicked look at Dutta. He didn't seem to have noticed the indiscretion, and Josef quickly crossed his legs, dislodging Alex's hand.

"We can't permit the body to leave London," Dutta was saying to Alex. "Good Lord, Saint would skin us alive! And the last thing we need is one of the blighters setting up a nest in Brookwood."

Alex looked up at that. "Is it? I can't help thinking that a huge cemetery in the country would be a more natural place for a ghoul. In the past—"

"That's your uncle talking," Dutta said sharply. "And we don't live in the past; there's no natural place for ghouls in the twentieth century."

Alex went quiet, his expression turned inward. Dutta lifted his chin in a way that suggested, *I regret nothing*.

Josef held his breath, waiting to see what would happen next.

After a moment, Alex said stiffly, "Well, there's certainly no place for a ghoul nest in the London sewer system. That's the salient point tonight."

"Quite." Dutta rose. "Come on, then. We'll have to be quick; the body will be on the train to Brookwood in the morning."

Alex nodded grimly. "All right."

He turned a regretful look on Josef, but before he could apologise for leaving, Josef said, "I'm coming too."

The words left his mouth almost without thought. But why not go? Somehow, he'd stumbled into the most incredible story of his life—of anyone's life. Secret societies, monsters lurking in the sewers? He'd be a right bloody idiot not to find out everything.

"Absolutely not," Dutta said.

Josef ignored him, but Alex was frowning too, shaking his head so hard a lock of dark hair tumbled over his forehead. Irritably, he pushed it back. "It's not safe. And this isn't your business, Josef. I can deal with—"

"Bollocks." Josef sat forward in his chair, elbows on knees, and fixed Alex with a serious look. "Those bastards nearly killed me, twice. And now they're skulking about in my city, under my streets, threatening my people. Not my business? Give over."

"What Beaumont means," Dutta said crisply, "is that you're not a member of The Society."

"Oh, piss off," Josef snapped. "These things are attacking ordinary men; they're infecting fucking soldiers at the front. They're turning them into monsters! And you're bothered about whether I'm in your bloody club?"

"He's absolutely right, you know." Alex looked up at Dutta. "This is his concern as much as ours. Of course it is."

Dutta's lips thinned, but he didn't argue. He didn't look pleased, either.

"In which case," Alex went on, flashing a breezy smile that Josef didn't buy for a moment, "we have an appointment with the London Necropolis Railway."

Chapter Eighteen

In the middle of the last century, London's boneyards had been filled to bursting. When he was a boy, Josef's father, who'd loved a gory tale, had terrified him with stories of rotting corpses falling through the walls into people's cellars, or being dug up by stray dogs, or just emerging, rotting, from the mud when it rained.

Something had needed to be done, and so a ring of huge cemeteries had been built beyond the city's edge—the most ambitious of which had been the London Necropolis in Brookwood, Surrey, miles away from London's sprawl and accessed from the city by the 'Stiffs Express' running from Cemetery Station.

These days, the gothic station entrance loomed over Westminster Bridge Road in a gloomy tribute to those twin Victorian obsessions: death and railways. Many times, Josef had walked past the ornate iron gates, not yet sacrificed to the war effort, which guarded a grand stone archway large enough to admit a hearse. But he'd never been inside.

Tonight, or rather, this morning, because it was already past one o'clock, the lightless station building looked eerie and forbidding. And Josef was starting to regret his impulsive decision to join Alex and Dutta on their little adventure. London was darker than ever these days, what with the lights being dimmed in case of air raids, and while the darkness would probably help their housebreaking endeavour, it only added to Josef's jitters. Every sound had him jumping out of his skin, expecting a ghoul to leap from the shadows at any moment.

"Let's cross," Alex said quietly, glancing along the empty street before heading over the road towards the station.

Dutta walked a pace ahead of Alex, and Josef followed behind, sticking close. "Do you know how to get in?"

"I have some ideas." Alex eyed the iron gates. "Can you climb?"

"Over the gate? I'm not sure that's a good idea. We'll be seen—" Josef's foot missed the kerb in the dark, and he stumbled over it.

Alex caught his arm, steadying him. "You do not have to come with us," he said quietly, pulling Josef to a halt. In the night, his face was all shadow save the gleam of his eyes. "Dutta and I are quite capable of—"

Dutta snapped something at Alex. Josef didn't understand the language, but he didn't need to because Dutta's meaning was clear: Stop fucking around.

Alex snapped something back at him, and they glared at each other.

Into the silence, Josef said, "I'm coming. Fuck's sake, why wouldn't I? This is the biggest story of my life."

"One you can never tell without risking the asylum."

Regrettably, that was probably true. Josef grinned. "Doesn't mean it's not a great story. Maybe I'll write a novel?"

Alex smiled at that, and Dutta sighed. "Hell, Beaumont, can't I simply shoot him?"

Gradually, Alex's smile faded, but his hand remained locked around Josef's arm, fingers warm through the sleeve of his coat, and the longer Alex gazed at him with those penetrating eyes, full of secrets, the faster Josef's heart raced.

At length, Alex looked away, dropping his hand from Josef's arm. He cleared his throat. "You're right," he said briskly. "There is a risk we'll be seen, so we'll have to climb quickly. Are you ready?"

Josef eyed the shadowy gates rising into the darkness. Above them, carved into the great stone arch, were the words Cemetery Station.

Swallowing, Josef said, "Let's do it."

The ornate gates were easy to scale, though the iron was icy beneath Josef's fingers, and to his ear it sounded like they made a hell of a racket as their boots struck iron and the gate squealed under their weight. He expected a police whistle at any moment, but none came, and they scrambled quickly over the top and down the other side. Josef jumped the last foot or two and landed with a soft huff of breath, Alex a moment behind him. Dutta was already disappearing into the darkness beneath the archway.

They turned to look at each other, and smiled, Alex's teeth a flash of ivory in the dark.

"Come on," he whispered, and they followed Dutta into the shadows.

Josef stuck close to the wall as the driveway led them into a tunnel that ran through the centre of the whole building. On the other side, the drive made a sharp left turn beneath a glass canopy built onto the back of the station. Glazed white brickwork gleamed ghostly on its wall, and the silhouettes of palm and bay trees lined the route.

"Fancy," Josef murmured. He could imagine it in daylight, modern and elegant. Fitting, people would say, for the passage of the dead. Dignified and respectful.

And then he thought of the dressing station where he'd first met Alex, of the dead and dying left to rot. Of the corpses sinking into the mud of no man's land. Where was their dignity? Where was their respect?

"Over here." A row of doors lined the wall, and Alex was trying the handle of the first. It was locked.

Josef came to join him. "Is that the mortuary?"

"Maybe." From his pocket, Alex produced something that jingled like a set of keys. Lock picks, Josef realised with surprise. Not that he should be surprised, but the idea of Lord Alexander Beaumont knowing how to jimmy a lock amused him.

There were a lot of doors, though, and it wasn't quick work. They'd be here all night if Alex had to try them all.

From his pocket, Josef retrieved his hand torch. Maybe it was a risk, but he reckoned it was worth taking if it could save them time. Switching it on, he flashed it over the door.

Dutta hissed. "Idiot, turn that off!"

Josef ignored him. "Storeroom One," he read on the small brass plate fixed to the wall next to the door.

Quickly, he moved onto the next door. "Storeroom Two."

And so on, until, about halfway along the building, he read, "Mortuary—third class." He stared. "Third class?"

"Giles was an officer," Dutta said, as though Josef was stupid. "He'll be in the first-class mortuary."

Josef kept staring at the little brass plaque, but in his mind's eye he was back at that dressing station again. There, the only distinction that mattered had been between the living and the dead. Third class? "Are they fucking joking?"

Alex touched his shoulder. "I know, but there's not much time. Come on."

As it turned out, the first-class mortuary was only one door along, and after about twenty minutes of muttered cursing, Alex got it open, and they slipped inside.

Black as pitch, once the door closed behind them, and Josef had to force back the sudden panicking clutch of claustrophobia. Scrabbling at his torch, he switched it on again and swept the beam across the room. Like the rest of the building, it was modern and gleaming. On the far side were the drawers which housed the dead, enough to store six bodies until the next train ran to the cemetery. And on a table in the middle of the room sat three coffins, closed. Presumably, they were for those taking their final journey in the morning.

"He must be in one of these," Dutta said, crossing the room quickly.

Josef followed, the hair on the back of his neck creeping up. Something was catching in his throat, a memory, or a hint of that dreadful death stench.

"What are you going to do?" he whispered.

Dutta glanced at him. "What must be done, of course." In the dark, something gleamed dully in his hand, and Josef realised the man had drawn a gun.

"Does that work?" he asked. "Against a ghoul?"

"No," Dutta said in that supercilious voice of his. "But it works against infected men, before they fully turn."

"With luck, it won't be necessary," Alex said as he fished in his pocket and pulled out a handful of change, sorting through it and pocketing everything but a sixpence. "If we're in time, a silver coin under the tongue will keep the infection from turning him."

Josef looked at him. "And if we're not in time?"

"Then we'll have a fight on our hands." He lifted his walking cane. "Hold this, will you?" he said and threw it to Josef.

It was heavier than Josef expected, a comforting weight in his hands. "All right then," he said. "Get on with it."

"Bring your torch," Alex said as he moved carefully towards the coffins.

Josef followed on legs heavy with dread. Suddenly, powerfully, he did not want Dutta to lift the lids on those coffins.

"Can't we just lock it inside?" he whispered as they drew nearer. "It'll be buried tomorrow."

"If burial could contain a ghoul, don't you think we'd have collapsed the tunnels under no man's land and dealt with the lot of them?" Dutta peered at the first coffin, his face oddly lit by the harsh electric light of the torch.

Alex said, more quietly, "Ghouls are at home underground—it would easily escape the coffin. And then it would thrive; cemeteries are their natural habitat."

"Natural habitat." Dutta gave a soft snort. "Shepel, bring the light closer."

Josef did so, playing the beam over the lid of the coffin Dutta was examining. An ornate brass plaque announced the name of the Honourable Eleanor Woolsey-Banks. The second belonged to Thomas James Milton, OBE.

Josef's heart kicked as he read the plaque on the third coffin: Major Anthony Asquith Giles. "That's him," he whispered.

Dutta only nodded, then bent over and pressed his ear to the top of the casket. Listening for sounds inside, Josef realised with a creeping horror. Straightening, Dutta circled the coffin, running his fingers beneath the lid, looking for the catch to unlock it.

Fuck.

The torchlight wobbled, and Josef realised he was shaking. He tried to take a steadying breath, but the death-stench was stronger now, and it caught in his throat, making him cough.

Alex looked over. "All right?"

Josef nodded, then realised Alex might not be able to see him properly, so he whispered, "Fine and dandy."

His only answer was the click of the locking mechanism releasing. Dutta moved to the foot of the casket, reached over, and swung the coffin lid open. It moved silently, without the eerie creak Josef had been expecting.

Nothing happened.

Only silence.

Then a hand landed on his wrist, and Josef yelped, yanking his arm away before he realised it was Alex.

"Shine the light inside," Alex whispered, guiding Josef's shaking arm down towards the coffin.

He did so, teeth gritted against the sight to come. The creature from that afternoon was fresh in his mind, and he was expecting a snarling, slathering monster, leaping up to tear off his face.

What he saw was a tall, well-dressed woman lying on her side, limbs twisted awkwardly as if she'd simply been dumped in the coffin.

"Christ," Alex cursed, spinning away from the casket.

Josef swung the light towards him. "I don't understand."

"It's out. It's in here somewhere."

"What?"

"Back to back," Dutta snapped. "Move. And give me the—"

"Beaumont..." A sibilant hiss crept through the dark. "We know you. We know your line."

Josef's hair stood on end as he spun to face the sound, sweeping his torch in wide arcs. Nothing.

"And I know you, ghoul," said Alex. "I cannot permit you to remain here."

A wet, wheezing sound—laughter?—filled the room and with it a wave of that dreadful, rotting stench. Josef gagged, burying his mouth and nose in the crook of his elbow.

"This is no place for you," Alex went on. "Leave, return to the dark places you have known."

"You cannot stop us; we are many."

"I will stop you. I have stopped you. One of your kind is already dead by my hand."

The ghoul hissed, the sound coming from Josef's left and...up? He swung the torch towards the ceiling, flashing its beam over a desk, a set of tall filing cabinets—and above them, a wet gleam in the dark.

"There!" Atop the cabinets, something monstrous crouched. Once human, dressed in uniform, but with a face that seemed to shift between that of a man and that of...something other. Teeth like talons, eyes that eerie blue. And everywhere the stench of rot and death.

Horrified, Josef staggered back a step, knocking into the casket behind him and sending its lid slamming shut with a thick dead thump.

He froze. The room froze.

And then, with an inhuman scream, the ghoul launched itself from its hiding place and flew at Alex. They went down in a tangle of thrashing limbs, and Josef could hardly keep track of them in the dark. Dropping his torch, he waded in with Alex's cane, hitting the creature—God, he hoped it was the ghoul—with the heavy weapon. It barely seemed to notice, and Josef realised in horror that it was intent on one thing only: biting Alex.

The shock of that lit a fire in Josef, fiercer than he'd ever known. With a yell, he launched himself at the ghoul, grabbing it by the shoulders and trying to haul it off Alex. Noticing him at last, the creature turned its snarling face on Josef.

Those teeth, like needles, bared, the sepulchral gleam of its eyes fixed on him. Josef scrambled backwards, too slow, and the ghoul was on him, bearing him down with a strength far beyond human. His head cracked against the floor, sending lights dancing across his vision.

"Josef!"

That was Alex, though Josef couldn't see him in the dark. Couldn't see anything but the creature. He punched and kicked. Somewhere along the way, he'd dropped the stick. Not that it mattered, it was too big in close quarters. Should have brought a fucking knife.

The creature lunged and clawed, jaws slavering, and Josef screamed as he tried to fight it off, jabbing his fingers at its inhuman eyes.

And then something whistled through the air, connecting with the side of the ghoul's head, and it let Josef go. Knocked sideways, it scrabbled away, hissing in fury.

"Leave him alone, you fucker!" Alex bellowed, wielding the stick, sounding wild and furious and utterly unlike himself.

Someone—Dutta—grabbed Josef's arm, and he scrambled to his feet, backing away from the ghoul.

His head thundered, vision tilting, and he staggered against one of the coffins.

In the dark, he was aware of Dutta watching Alex, who stood in a fighting stance, braced for attack, one shoulder of his jacket torn and bloody.

Shit. Josef's head swam in sudden dread.

Then the ghoul hissed where it crouched, an unnatural, venomous sound as it leaped for Alex. But he moved faster, spinning away from it. As he spun, he took hold of his stick with both hands. Josef didn't understand what was happening until half the stick went clattering to the ground and silver gleamed in Alex's hand.

A sword.

A fucking sword.

With the elegance of a dancer, Alex allowed momentum to carry him right around, sweeping the sword in a wide arc until it sliced cleanly through the ghoul's neck, sending his head tumbling across the mortuary floor to land in a grisly mess at Josef's feet.

In the sudden silence, Alex's breaths rasped. "Are you all right?"

Josef dropped his hand from the back of his head, ignoring the pain. "I—"

The unmistakable sound of a revolver being cocked stopped him. Looking to his left, he saw Dutta with his arm raised and his gun pointed squarely at Alex.

Josef stared. "What the fuck are you doing?"

"He's been bitten." Dutta sounded cold, emotionless.

Alex jolted in shock, staring down at his torn jacket as if he'd only just noticed. "No," he said airlessly, "it's not..."

"You have. I saw it bite you."

"Fuck." With a clatter, Alex's sword hit the stone floor as he scrabbled at the hole in his jacket. "Fuck!"

Josef's heart did something peculiar, twisting in panic and pain. "Alex...?" It was barely a whisper, the word trapped in his tightening throat.

Dutta said, "Alex, close your eyes."

"What?" Josef spun towards him again, his gaze fixing on that unshaking, unrelenting gun. "You can't just shoot him!"

"I'm sorry," Dutta said. "Truly. But he'd do the same if it were me."

Suddenly, Josef couldn't speak, or even breathe, his outrage overwhelming.

"He's right." Alex stood straight, stupidly brave, but Josef didn't miss the suppressed terror in his voice. "There's no choice."

"There's always a fucking choice," Josef snapped, and in two steps he stood between Alex and the gun. He raised his hands, staring at Dutta. "Here's your choice: let him go or see yourself named a murderer in the Clarion. I won't spare the details."

Behind him, Alex cursed, but Dutta didn't react at all, and the gun remained steady. "Alex is already dead," he said cooly. "His noble sacrifice will not be forgotten by The Society; don't make this harder for him."

"Harder for him?" Josef growled. "Fuck this and fuck his noble sacrifice." He spun around to face Alex, taking an angry step closer. "For God's sake, don't you want to live?"

Alex's dark eyes were agonised. "Of course I do," he said stiffly, voice rasping. "But I'm infected. I've been bitten..."

"Barely a couple of minutes ago." Josef kept walking closer, his gaze holding Alex's. "We must be able to do something."

It wasn't much of a reaction, but Josef didn't miss the tightening of Alex's mouth, the way his gaze turned evasive.

"We can," Josef breathed. "Fuck, we can, can't we?"

Alex shook his head, brow creasing. "It's not actually—"

"Step out of the way, Shepel. Do it now."

Dutta's voice came from right behind him. Josef stilled; he could almost feel the gun's muzzle between his shoulder blades. His eyes locked on Alex. "And if I don't?"

"I doubt anyone will miss you."

That was probably truer than Dutta knew. Still, stiffening his spine, in every sense, Josef said, "I'm not going to stand here and watch you murder him."

"Then leave."

"If I leave, I'll go straight to the Clarion. News of Lord Alexander Beaumont's gruesome murder at the hand of his friend will shift a few copies, no doubt."

"Josef, for God's sake," Alex growled.

Cooly, Dutta said, "You're not making this any easier on yourself."

"Or you, I hope." Josef turned and found Dutta only a couple of feet away, his gun aimed point-blank at Josef's head. In the gloom, the man's face was entirely in shadow, his expression impenetrable.

He'll do it, Josef realised with a thud of sick fear. He'll shoot me, then kill Alex.

And Alex won't stop him.

Heart hammering, his vision narrowed, the world going dark at the edges until all he could see was the blind eye of that gun.

He didn't want to die.

He didn't want Alex to die.

He didn't want to accept that those were his only fucking choices.

Fists curling at his sides, Josef prepared to fight. If he could duck beneath the gun, slam his head into Dutta's belly, maybe he could wrestle the gun from his hand before—

"Lower your weapon."

Josef spun around. Behind him, Alex stood with his Webley raised and pointed at Dutta.

"I mean it," Alex said. "Dal, put the gun down."

Dutta's astonishment was visible in the uncertain wobble of his arm. "What the devil are you doing? You've been bitten. We both know how this ends."

"For me, yes. Not for him."

"For God's sake, Beaumont, you heard what he said. He'll go to the press."

"I'll handle that."

Dutta didn't lower his weapon. "Didn't I tell you this would happen? I warned you in Poperinge. I told you he'd be trouble."

Alex didn't answer. "Josef," he said, "come here."

Josef didn't move, frozen by the unblinking gaze of Dutta's gun.

"Joe!" Alex barked. "Now."

With his gaze fixed on Dutta, Josef backed towards Alex. As soon as he was within range, Alex grabbed his arm and pulled Josef behind him. To Dutta, he said, "I'll handle this my own way."

"Which is what?"

Alex didn't answer, and Josef's stomach pitched in alarm. What the fuck was Alex planning? If he thought Josef would let him put a bullet in his own stupid head, he could bloody well think again.

After a long pause, Dutta said, "I'll have to tell Saint."

"I know."

Some silent communication passed between them before Dutta finally lowered his weapon. "Unfortunately, it will take time to clear up this mess." He gestured around the mortuary. "It may be several hours before I'm able to return to Belgrave Square."

Josef heard the controlled rush of breath leave Alex's body, saw his shoulders relax as he too lowered his gun. "Thank you."

With a curt nod, Dutta said, "Make what use you can of the time, but if it were me..." His gaze held Alex's, bleak and dark. "If it were me, I'd want a swift end while I was still myself."

Chapter Nineteen

By the time they reached Alex's flat, it was closer to morning than midnight. Grey-faced, Alex stumbled as they left the lift, catching himself on the door. How much of that was exhaustion, and how much something worse, Josef dared not imagine.

"Come on," he said, taking Alex by the elbow. "Let's go inside."

Glancing both ways down the dark corridor, Alex nodded and went to unlock the front door to his flat. "Christ," he said, "we stink of ghoul."

They did. It clogged Josef's nose so much he could only breathe through his mouth. In horror, he wondered whether the stench was coming from Alex, from the bite on his shoulder.

It was darker inside the flat, the winter sunrise still hours away. Alex moved to a narrow table in the hallway. Gas hissed, and the bright flare of a match bloomed and faded as Alex lit the hall lamp. Then the mellow light grew, chasing away the shadows.

They stared at each other across the hallway. Alex looked ghastly. Josef had seen that grim look before, in the faces of men in the firing line, waiting for the orders to advance. He knew the look of a man waiting for death. And seeing it on Alex's stoic, stupidly handsome face, turned him sick with dread. And rage. He refused, he absolutely refused, to allow something as stupid as a bite to put an end to this man's life.

"Come into the bathroom," he said. "Let's get you cleaned up."

"There's no cleaning this up. A dab of iodine isn't going to help."

"It can't hurt," Josef said, pushing open the bathroom door. "If nothing else, we can wash the ghoul stink off us."

Alex hesitated, and then complied, moving as though he wasn't quite there, as if his mind was already disengaging. That, too, he'd seen at the front. Dead men walking.

The bathroom was dark. Alex said tightly, "There's an electric light switch on the wall, next to the door."

After a moment of fumbling around for the switch, Josef found it, and glaring electrical light burst into the room, steady and cold. Like a morgue. As he looked about, his eyes strayed to the laundry hamper where Alex had set his Webley while he inspected Josef for bites. It wasn't there now, of course; Alex was wearing his gun.

And no doubt he was considering using it on himself.

Putting that thought to one side, he turned to Alex. He stood blinking in the brash light which washed out what little colour had been left in his face, leaving him a gruesome grey.

"I hate electric lights," Josef muttered, shucking off his coat and setting it on the laundry hamper. "I don't think they'll catch on."

Alex stared at him for a moment, as if in incomprehension, and then with a slight shake of his head, he made a soft sound. A laugh. "I thought you were all for progress."

"I am!" Josef said, helping Alex off with his coat. "I'm in favour of universal adult suffrage, but not these horrible bloody lights."

Alex winced as Josef eased his overcoat from the shoulder that had been bitten, sucking air through his teeth. Josef grimaced but said nothing. The fabric of Alex's jacket was torn and bloody, his white shirt crimson.

"This is all going to have to come off," Josef said.

"There's no point." Alex turned his head away from the wound. "Dal's right. There's only one way this—"

"Shut up," Josef snapped. "I don't want to hear it."

Alex looked at him. There were words on his lips, but whatever they were, he kept them to himself.

Carefully, Josef unbuttoned Alex's jacket and eased it off, then his waistcoat and shirt. The wound on his shoulder was becoming more visible with each layer that was stripped away, a clear bite-sized mark, flesh torn and ragged. A deep but not large wound. Already, though, Josef could see the signs of necrosis around its edges. Pursing his lips, he said, "I'm going to use iodine anyway. To prevent other infections. Where is it?"

Alex directed him to a cabinet next to the sink and dropped into the wicker chair Josef had used that first night. Retrieving the iodine and a dressing from Alex's alarmingly well-stocked medicine cabinet, Josef turned back around.

Alex sat with one elbow braced against his knee, head in his hand. The other arm, the injured one, lay in his lap. The wound looked raw and ugly, midway between his shoulder and neck, but the rest of his body was undamaged. Strong, muscular shoulders, a scattering of dark hair across his chest. Josef felt an instinctive, involuntary stab of attraction, reminded suddenly of last night.

Then, Alex had been so alive, so full of life, but now...

Josef swallowed, and Alex looked up, perhaps conscious of being studied. Smiling, feeling his cheeks heat, Josef nodded towards the medicine cabinet. "You've a small pharmacy in there."

"Necessary, in my line of work."

"I suppose so. Now, hold still. This will sting."

Josef was not a trained medic, but he'd helped patch up the walking wounded and knew his way about a bottle of iodine and a field dressing. Jaw clenched, the cords on Alex's neck stood when Josef started cleaning the wound, and then dressed it, but Alex didn't make a sound.

Maybe he was right and dressing the wound wouldn't help, but it made Josef feel better not to have to look at the bloody mess.

"Well done, soldier," he said, smiling as he patted Alex's bare shoulder. "Very brave."

Alex looked up at him. Their eyes met and somehow didn't let go. Just like Josef's hand somehow lingered on Alex's shoulder, the skin feeling smooth and warm beneath Josef's fingers.

"You should go now," Alex said softly. "Let me deal with this myself."

"And you should know me better than that."

In a shaking voice, Alex said, "I wish... Christ, I wish I had the chance to know you better."

Josef's heart twisted, cramping in his chest. "Shut up. You still do."

"No." Alex swallowed, his throat working. "No, this is the end for me. I'm—" He cut off abruptly, eyes going very bright. Too bright. He blinked rapidly, but to no avail. Tears slid from the corner of his eyes, clinging to his lashes. "God," he whispered, "I don't want to die."

And how the fuck do you respond to that? Josef's own eyes filled. "I'm not going to let you die," he promised. "I'll chop your fucking arm off and stop the infection that way if I must, but nobody, including you, is putting a bullet in your stupid head. So, you can just forget about that, all right?"

Alex covered Josef's hand where it still rested on his shoulder, squeezing hard, saying nothing save the silent plea in his eyes: help me.

With no answer to give, Josef didn't know what else to do but lean down and kiss him. Alex's lips tasted salty, like tears, but warm and inviting, and after a surprised moment, he surged to his feet, pulling Josef into his arms, fingers tangling in his hair as he kissed him back hungrily. Desperately.

Josef met his hunger and desperation in equal measure.

They were incandescent with life. It flowed between them, from one to the other in streams of fury and desire. Death hovered over them, an angel's dark wing, but its shadow only stoked their passion; it burned in defiance of death, in defiance of a world that would hate them for loving each other but love them for dying as heroes.

There were no words; what was there to say? There was only mouth against mouth, skin against skin, pricks straining as they drove each other towards a detonation as fierce as a thermite grenade, leaving them in ashes on the bathroom floor, the horror of Alex's fate no less stark.

Still gasping for breath, somehow both hot and chill, Josef held Alex in his arms. The tiled bathroom floor was cold against his bare back and arse, but he ignored the discomfort as Alex pressed his face into Josef's shoulder. He made no sound, but Josef could feel him shaking. Perhaps he was sobbing out his fear and rage, the very feelings Josef felt in his own heart.

"I won't let it happen," he promised, stroking Alex's shoulder and back, his eyes fixed on the white ceiling and the too-bright electric light. "I'm going to save you."

Alex drew in a shivery breath and said, "Why?"

There were many answers he could have given, plenty of glib remarks or half-truths. But now wasn't the time for that, so he said, "I suppose I want the chance to get to know you, too."

At that, Alex lifted his head. "Do you?"

Josef made a gesture with one hand, encompassing them both where they lay on the cold bathroom floor. "Apparently."

And then, like a miracle, a smile touched Alex's lips—a sad smile, but warm. Real. "I wish—"

"Shh." Josef touched a finger to Alex's lips, then brushed his damp cheeks, drying his tears. "We've wasted enough time on sentiment."

Alex's smile tilted sideways. "If I recall, you started it."

"Maybe so," Josef conceded, finding a smile of his own. "But now you need to tell me how I can help you. Don't pretend you don't know."

A long silence followed as Alex disentangled himself from Josef and sat up. The dressing on his shoulder looked brilliant white under the bathroom light. "There are ways..." he said carefully. "That is, I've heard of ways to counteract the bite of a ghoul. Certain remedies..."

Josef sat up too, hope tenuous as spiderweb. "What kind of remedies? Medicine? Where do we get it?"

Alex made an equivocating gesture with one hand. "I'm no expert. I'd need help, but defined loosely, yes. Medicine."

"How loosely?"

"More of a...potion."

Josef raised his eyebrows. "A magic potion?"

"You could call it that."

"Oh, fuck off."

"Yes," Alex said with something approaching amusement. "That's what I thought you'd say."

Josef frowned. "Hold on. If there's a cure for this, why the fuck weren't you giving it to the men at the front?"

This time, Alex looked uncomfortable when he met Josef's eyes. "The Society's policy is to eliminate the threat rather than attempt a cure that...carries some risks."

"By 'eliminate', you mean kill."

Without flinching, Alex said, "They believe it's more effective in controlling the infection."

"And they make no exceptions," Josef guessed. "Even for one of their own."

"Absolutely not."

"So, if you can't get help from The Society, who can help us?"

Alex's expression turned wry, one dark brow lifting. "How do you feel about witches?"

Chapter Twenty

"This is not somewhere I'd expect to find witches."

They were standing on the pavement outside the Natural History Museum at nine o'clock the following morning. Josef had been all for racing down there immediately, but they'd both been exhausted and filthy, and instead they'd bathed and collapsed into bed 'for a few minutes'. Three hours later, they'd woken up tangled together with the sun streaming in through the window.

Josef had cursed the wasted time, but he could see that Alex was better for the rest. They both were, although the stiff way Alex moved his arm suggested he was in pain. Neither of them mentioned it.

Taking the steps to the museum two at a time, Alex said, "You need to adjust your expectations; the days of blasted Scottish heaths are long gone. Dr Wolsey is a botanist."

Josef hurried after him. "The witch is a man?"

At the door, Alex turned with an amused lift of one brow. "The doctor is a woman."

"Right." Josef felt his cheeks heat. "Of course. Stupid."

"For your sake," Alex said as they went inside, "I'll keep that little slip between ourselves."

They were met on the other side of the door by an elderly museum guard, moustache bristling as he bustled over with one hand raised in protest. "Beg pardon, gentlemen, but the museum isn't open yet. Please—"

Alex dipped two fingers into the breast pocket of his coat and produced one of his cards, wafting it beneath the guard's eyes. "Yes, I'm afraid we are a little early," he explained with that infuriating self-assurance that wealth and privilege bought men of his class. "Lord Beaumont. Here to see Dr Wolsey." He pocketed his card and kept walking, Josef doing his best to remain unobtrusive at his side.

The guard hurried to keep up. "Yes, my lord, but I don't know whether she—"

"Don't trouble yourself to show us the way," Alex went on blithely, heading for the sweeping staircase in front of them. "I'm quite familiar with the route. Good morning."

And up he went, overcoat flaring out behind him. Josef touched his cap to the guard and followed, conscious that Alex was breathing harder than he should have been as he climbed the stairs. How long, he wondered, before it was too late to help him?

At the top, Alex paused, evidently catching his breath before leading Josef away from the public galleries and into a very ordinary corridor that wouldn't have been out of place in a tax office. Green-painted doors with frosted glass windows lined each side, and Alex stopped outside one, about halfway along the corridor. Taking off his hat, he smoothed down his hair and then knocked. Josef snatched off his own hat and waited.

He was about to meet a witch. It seemed incredible. It was incredible. In fact, everything that had happened to him since first meeting Alex had been incredible.

Logically, he should wish he'd never laid eyes on the man, that he'd never snuck away for a quick smoke that morning in the salient. Logically, he should wish he'd never heard of any of this supernatural nonsense.

But logic must have deserted him because as he glanced over at the man by his side, his determined, impatient gaze fixed on the door, Josef felt a betraying flutter in his chest. What did it mean that Alex had defied The Society to protect him from Dutta? What did it mean that all Josef could think about was saving Alex from his fate?

Something, surely. Something men like them weren't supposed to have.

A noise came from behind the door. It sounded like a chair being pushed back, voices, and the stomp of heavy feet. Then the door swung wide, and he was met by the sight of a red-headed woman, solidly built, dressed for an office. Her expression was pure disappointment.

"Rats, I thought it was the tea trolley." Then her expression changed. "Oh, beg pardon, m'lord." Her gaze slid sideways to Josef and narrowed. She recognised him, and he recognised her.

"Violet?" he said, putting the pieces together. "I thought you worked on the ambulances."

"I do. Some of the time." Over her shoulder, she called, "Lottie, it's Lord B and that bloke what was asking questions at St. Thomas's."

Josef was struggling to keep up, but then another woman appeared at Violet's shoulder, and he knew her too: Lady Charlotte Wolsey.

Dr Wolsey, he presumed.

"Mr Shepel," she said, eying him sharply. With a warning glance at Alex, she added, "He's a journalist, works for the Clarion."

"Yes, I know. May we come in? I need your advice about something... Society-related."

Her lips tightened. "I assumed as much." Her gaze flicked to Josef again and stayed there, astute and assessing. "Close the door behind you."

With that, she crossed the room—a reasonably sized office—to the bench on the far side where an assortment of jars and bottles held various plant specimens. The walls were lined with shelves crowded with similar bits and bobs, along with more books than Josef had seen outside of the library. "Find a seat," she called while she rummaged in a stack of papers, apparently found what she was looking for, and turned back around.

Meanwhile, Alex had pulled out a chair at the large table in the centre of the room. It was equally cluttered with papers and specimens and any number of things Josef couldn't identify. Josef did the same, sitting next to him.

Lady Charlotte—Lottie—took a seat kitty-corner to Alex. She wore her light brown hair piled up on top of her head, not cut short in the modern fashion, and had a narrow, inquisitive face. Intelligent eyes of a wishy-washy grey. "Well," she said, "my first question is what's happened to you? And my second is does The Society know you're here?"

Alex set his hat on the table, atop a pile of papers. "No, in answer to the second question. As to the first..."

He glanced at Violet, who'd stationed herself at the bench, leaning back against it with her arms folded. There was something of the guard dog about her, Josef thought.

"As to the first," Alex repeated doggedly, "I had the misfortune to be bitten by a ghoul last night."

"Bloody hell," Violet hissed, starting backwards, staring at Alex in alarm. "And you came here?"

"It's all right," Josef said. "He won't bite."

She gave him a dark look. "Yet."

"It was less than eight hours ago," Alex told Lottie. "Is there time?"

Her expression grew keen, eyes glittering. "You want a cure," she said, surprised. "That's against Society rules."

"I know."

"I can see why they don't know you're here." When Alex only inclined his head in agreement, she said, "You, of all people, know the risk of defying them. So why are you?"

Without looking at Josef, Alex said, "Mr Shepel is in some danger because of me. I intend to ensure his safety."

Josef didn't argue, however much he baulked at all the noblesse oblige crap; conveniently, it masked a more complex, dangerous truth.

"Laudable," Lottie said, her attention turning to Josef. He had a strong feeling that she was seeing more than was visible to the naked eye. "And surprising."

Alex gave a slight shrug. "Is it possible? Can you help me?"

After another moment of studying Josef, she turned back to Alex. "Show me the bite," she said, rising.

With obvious awkwardness at undressing in front of a lady—he was such a toff—Alex slipped off his jacket and unbuttoned his collar to reveal the wound at the juncture of his neck and shoulder.

"Usually," Lottie said, "living victims of ghoul bites are close to death, either wounded or ill. It's rare that they attack a healthy person. I assume you had it cornered?"

"We did. We had to stop it leaving London for Brookwood Cemetery."

Lottie's delicate fingers carefully peeled away the dressing Josef had placed over the wound. "Brookwood seems like a natural place for a ghoul."

"You know what The Society thinks."

Clearly, she did, because she didn't bother to respond. "The infection spreads more slowly in a healthy body," she said, probing the wound. Alex winced, jaw clenching. "That gives you more time."

"More time for what?" Josef said.

Lottie's grey eyes met his, sharp as steel. "To live," she said simply. "And to find a cure."

"Find a cure? Don't you have one?"

"Do we look like a pharmacy?" said Violet, her gaze still fixed on Alex. Ready to pounce, Josef supposed, if he showed any signs of ghoulishness.

Lottie was still inspecting the wound, tracing her fingers across Alex's skin. Josef realised that down his left arm and up his neck towards his jaw, radiating from the bite, ran faint tendrils of grey, like veins beneath his pale skin. His stomach turned.

"I have the formula," Lottie said, "but you'll need to provide the key ingredient."

Teeth gritted against the pain, Alex said, "Which is what?"

"Blood from the ghoul that bit you."

He visibly paled, nothing but red spots of colour left on his cheekbones. "I killed it," he said airlessly. "The body travels to Brookwood this morning..."

"I'll go back," Josef said immediately. "The train doesn't leave until gone eleven..."

But Alex looked grim, his eyes dark as midnight. "I don't think—"

"If the ghoul is dead, its blood is dead too," said Lottie. "No good."

With a vehement curse, Alex dropped his head into his hands, elbows on the table.

Josef stared at him, heart thudding so loud he thought the whole room must be able to hear it. Mouth dry, he said, "Is that the only way?"

Lottie lifted her eyes to his. "Not the only way. The ghoul Lord Beaumont killed had been bitten by another, and that one by yet another, and so on. There are... connections between them all."

"A spiderweb," Josef said, remembering Alex's description.

She nodded, mostly to herself. "Yes, I could use the blood of another. Less potent, the more distant the connection, but probably potent enough."

Alex jerked his head up from his hands. "How the devil are we supposed to find one in time?" he snapped. "Christ, they could be anywhere in London."

"You have one thing in your favour," Lottie said, leaving Alex and moving to one of her bookshelves, studying the spines and then pulling out a book. Opening it, she began flicking through the pages.

"What?" Josef said, impatiently. "What do we have in our favour?"

Lottie looked up. "Hmm? Oh. Well." She glanced over at Alex again with those too-bright, too-clever eyes. "You'll know it when one's close. You'll feel it. Feel drawn to it."

"Drawn to it?" Alex sounded sickened.

Nodding, still leafing through pages, she said, "Blood to blood, as the infection takes hold. Ah, here it is." Then, to Violet, "I'll need lunar caustic, yarrow, comfrey root, sage, and honey."

"You're making a poultice?" Violet asked, with clear unease.

Lottie nodded. To Alex, she said, "It'll slow the spread of the infection, and buy you more time."

"How much time?"

"Half again as much."

Clearly, that meant something to Alex because he gave a curt nod. Then, remembering his manners, added, "Thank you. Thank you for helping me."

"I'll need a vial of live blood," Lottie said, pulling open a drawer and starting to rummage. "Remember, the ghoul must still be living for the spell to work."

Josef let 'spell' go without comment. Frankly, it was the least of his concerns. "You're saying we have to track down a ghoul, which could be anywhere in London, and not kill it but ask nicely for a cup of its blood instead?"

"That's about the sum of it, yes." Lottie retrieved a small glass bottle with a cork stopper from the drawer and held it out. Josef took it. "Now, be quiet the pair of you. Vi and I have work to do."

As she and Violet began pulling jars and implements off shelves and out of drawers, Josef glanced over at Alex where he sat at the table. He looked ashy and exhausted, purpling shadows under his eyes, but he smiled when he caught Josef's eye and murmured, "Don't worry. It'll be a doddle."

Josef didn't believe him for a moment.

Chapter Twenty-one

In the end, Violet threw Josef out.

"You're getting under our feet," she said, "and we don't need an audience. Come back in an hour. And bring some tea and biscuits when you do."

Perhaps seeing Josef's unease at leaving, Alex said, "I'll be all right. We can trust them."

"More than you can trust each other," Vi muttered and closed the door in Josef's face.

He stood staring at the frosted glass for a few moments, considered spending the hour wandering the halls of the museum in search of tea and biscuits, and decided he could do something more useful with his time.

A few minutes later, he was crowding into a third-class carriage at South Kensington and heading straight for the Clarion. He had no idea what the day would bring, but he knew one thing for sure: if the ghoul didn't get them, The Society probably would. Which was why he needed to see May while he had the chance; he needed some insurance.

It was a long twenty minutes, but at last the train rattled into Blackfriars and Josef trotted up the stairs from the station, heading back into the bright morning. After weeks of grey skies, the day had dawned bright and clear. Once, that would have been welcome, but these days, clear skies promised more Gotha incursions. Odd, to think about that. The war felt very far away now that death was stalking him here in London, but the war couldn't be forgotten. Not by him, nor by anyone. Besides, in a way, this was all part of the war. The slaughter in Europe had woken the ghoul to gorge on the battlefields, and from there they'd spread to London and to who knew how many other cities across the continent.

If the people knew that...

He mulled over the idea as he pushed open the office door and climbed the stairs to the Clarion's newsroom. The disarray following The Society's raid had been cleared up, and only the organised chaos of a busy newspaper remained. May, as usual, sat at the heart of it with her head down, reading at her desk. The door to her office stood open, and so Josef didn't bother to knock.

"May?" he said, when she didn't immediately notice him. "Can I have a word?"

Her head shot up, eyes widening. "Good God, Joe, you look like something the cat dragged in. What happened?"

He opened his mouth to respond—I've got tangled up with a stupidly noble, lying toff, and we both might be dead by teatime—and said, "Had a close call with one of the Gothas last night."

"Bloody hell!" May had never been ladylike, nor wanted to be, and Josef relished that enormously. Her eyes narrowed. "Are you all right?" He had the strong impression she wasn't referring to bumps and bruises. May still thought he was shell-shocked, after all. Well, today he was, but not for the reasons she imagined.

"Knocked the stuffing out of me," he admitted, stepping further into her office, and closing the door behind him. "But no damage."

Her expression remained doubtful, but she waved him towards the visitor's chair. "Did you get any pictures?"

"Pictures?" Christ, he hadn't even thought about it. Some journalist he was. "Too dark," he said. "Sorry."

Her eyebrows rose. "What's going on, Joe?"

Too uncomfortable to hold her piercing gaze, he dropped his eyes to the desk instead. Papers sprawled everywhere, and under a sheaf of them, he saw the corner of a photograph poking out. One of his.

"I..." He hesitated over the lie, but the truth was impossible. She'd think he'd gone doolally, and he needed her to trust him. "I need you to publish this in the Clarion, not in a pamphlet that half a dozen people will see." Reaching into his pocket, he set before her the words he'd written. No mention of ghouls, only the mundane horrors of war. The truth people needed to see and hear. It was only a first draft, but it would have to be enough. "I know people won't like it, but what are we here for if it's not to tell people things they don't like?"

May looked at him, then pulled the paper across the table, unfolded it, and started reading. It wasn't elegant prose, but it was a heartfelt account of Sykes's death among the corpses at the dressing station. As vivid as Josef could paint it with his inadequate words, far less eloquent than the picture. But that, he knew she'd never publish.

"Joe..." May shook her head, but he could see the tremble in her lips as she gazed at his words. "It's... very distressing, and it definitely breaches DORA." She looked up at him. "They'd shut us down."

"Then we regroup, change the title of the paper, and start again." Leaning across the desk, he grabbed her hand. "This war is destroying us. Destroying our humanity. It's turning good men into animals. Worse than animals. If you knew—" He took a breath. "For God's sake, May, we've got to do something before there's nothing left of us but monsters."

May stared at him, slowly tugging her hand free. "I don't know," she said, raising her voice when Josef started protesting, "but I will consider what you've said. There's a lot at stake here. You know that."

He did know that, although following the rules had never seemed more pointless. He also knew that this was the best offer he'd get; May had her own priorities, and he'd said his piece. He'd done all that he could.

The clock on the wall above her desk read a quarter past ten. Josef pushed to his feet. "There's one more thing before I go."

May leaned back in her chair, looking up at him. "Are you resting, Joe? Taking care of yourself?"

Ignoring the questions, he said, "You remember that envelope I gave you before I went to the front? Have you still got it?"

May stilled. "You mean the one with your will in it? And your Post Office Savings book? Of course I have it, but Joe..." She sat up straight again. "For God's sake, what do you mean? Why are you asking?"

From his pocket, he produced his notebook. It contained all his notes about the ghoul and The Winconian Society, including names and the address of their Mayfair club. Holding it out to May, he said, "Put this with the rest, and read it if anything happens to me in the next couple of days—"

May shot to her feet. "Joe, what the hell's going on?"

"I can't tell you. I just need you to keep this safe." He set the notebook on her desk. "And if you read it, just...do what you think best. Every word of it is true. I swear."

Coming around from behind her desk, May glanced at the notebook, then back at him. "Joe, promise me you're not about to do something stupid."

He laughed; it sounded too harsh. "You know I could never promise that."

"I'm serious," she said. "You've not been right since you came back from the war, and I'm worried about you." She scanned his face, her eyes full of concern. "Please, Joe, we've lost too many good men."

He took both her hands in his and tried to be as honest as possible. "Look, it's not like that. I'm just in a spot of bother, that's all. With luck, it'll all be fine and dandy."

"What kind of bother? Let me help you."

"Keeping this safe is helping me. And if you do read it, believe it. That's all I ask."

To his surprise, she threw her arms around him in a swift, hard hug. "Be careful, Joe. I'll need you after they shut us down for publishing that bloody photo, so make sure you're here to help, all right?"

He nodded stiffly but refused to make any promises. "You take care of yourself, May. London might not know it, but she needs the Clarion now more than ever."

Then, settling his cap in place, he turned and walked out of the newsroom. Very possibly, for the last time.

Alex was waiting on the museum steps when Josef got back.

Either the cold air, or Lottie's treatment, had brought the colour back to his cheeks. When he spotted Josef, he lifted his hand in greeting and trotted down the stairs towards him.

Josef's heart performed a mortifying little somersault at the sight, which he chose to ignore. "You look better," he said when they were close enough to speak.

"I smell like a dish of potpourri," Alex grumbled, touching his shoulder to indicate the dressing beneath his coat. "But it seems to be helping. They gave me something for the pain as well."

"Morphine?" Josef frowned; the last thing he needed was Alex falling asleep on him in the middle of a fight. He studied his eyes, but there was no sign of pupil dilation.

Without breaking eye contact, Alex drew closer, lowering his voice. "Something better, I think. More, um, witchy."

Helplessly, Josef found himself smiling fondly at his seriousness. Fondly? Ugh. "As long as it's working, I suppose it don't matter."

"My feeling exactly." Alex cast a cautious glance up and down the busy street. "And now I'd better get to work."

Josef followed his gaze, darting from face to face in the crowd. There was no mistaking his wariness. "I suppose The Society will be looking for us?"

"If not now, soon. Dutta could only have delayed his report until this morning. Come on," he set off along Cromwell Road, "let's walk."

Falling in at his side, Josef said, "He'd really have shot you, wouldn't he?"

"Yes. And he'd have expected me to do the same for him had the situation been reversed."

Josef dug his hands deeper into the thin pockets of his coat. "Your lot don't half love a noble sacrifice. I'd have thought the war would have knocked that out of you."

He felt, rather than saw Alex look at him. "If by 'my lot' you mean the aristocracy, then I suspect the war will have knocked it out of us—or at least, some of us. But if you mean The Society, then no, the war won't make a jot of difference. They've been at war for a thousand years."

"They?" Josef said, catching his eye.

"We," he corrected, although without much conviction.

"Lottie and Vi aren't part of The Society, I take it."

Alex's mouth gave a wry twist. "Definitely not. The Society doesn't tolerate dabbling in the occult. It has a very black-and-white perspective on these things."

"But you don't."

After a pause, Alex said, "No, I was taught differently." Then, changing the subject, he added, "What I need to do now is find the damned nest. Dutta and I were looking for it that night we ran into you in the sewer."

Josef snorted. "You say that sentence as if it wasn't completely mad."

Catching his eye again, Alex smiled. "Oh, it is completely mad. I'm just used to this particular kind of madness, that's all." His humour faded. "I plan to start there, but there's no need for you to put yourself in any kind of danger—"

"Oh, shut up," Josef said. "We're in this together, aren't we?"

Alex frowned. "I didn't realise seeking a cure would involve this much risk. I have nothing to lose, but you —"

"I have you to lose."

His words drew them both to an abrupt halt next to the museum railings. Alex stared at him, wide-eyed. "You... Do you?"

Irritated and embarrassed, not quite meeting his eye, Josef said, "Don't I?"

"Well, yes. If that's..." Alex stumbled. "I mean, if our friendship is something you'd like to...to continue?"

"Apparently, I would," Josef said, lifting his chin defiantly only to find Alex watching him in smouldering delight. Josef's cheeks burned, despite the cold day, but he found himself smiling. "And that's even madder than the rest of this bloody nonsense."

Alex gave a short, startled laugh. "Yes," he agreed. "By far the most improbable."

Improbable didn't even begin to cover it. "So," Josef said, aware suddenly that they were standing on a street corner, grinning at each other like idiots, "do you have any idea where in the sewers this nest is?"

Alex shook his head, clearing his throat as he glanced around them. "Ah, no. We hadn't had any luck until we came across you."

Came across him fighting for his life.

"Because the ghoul found me," Josef said slowly. "I had Sykes's photograph in my pocket."

Their eyes met. "Do you have it still?"

Josef tapped his coat pocket. "Do we go back there? It was close to the surface, where the bomb had opened the sewer. I don't suppose they'd lurk anywhere that easy to find."

"No," Alex agreed, "their nest will be somewhere hidden, preferably disused. Normally, you'd only find them in abandoned graveyards, or crypts. Places like that."

"Normally?"

Alex looked grim. "The war has made a charnel house of Europe and a feast for the ghoul. As their numbers grow, so they become bolder."

"Like the trench rats," Josef said. They'd grown fat and bold too. Nature's opportunists.

Another memory stirred: Sykes's dying words at the dressing station.

They come for the dead.

Creeping out of the sapper tunnels that wormed beneath no man's land, skulking through abandoned trenches, and collapsed foxholes, to gorge themselves on slaughtered soldiers, heedless of rank or nation. Men had dug those tunnels and trenches, men had slaughtered men in the hundreds of thousands, and the ghoul were feasting on the carnage. Like rats, they were opportunists, clever, resourceful, and remorseless.

You'd find them anywhere you'd find rats.

"I saw one in a Tube tunnel," Josef said abruptly. "At least, I think I did. I saw its eyes in the dark."

"Tube tunnels would be too dangerous." Alex frowned. "Although easier to navigate, cleaner and dryer than sewers."

"And closer to potential prey."

Alex shrugged, conceding the point. "But they couldn't live there, could they? Not with all the trains."

"I suppose not. But are there parts of the Underground that aren't used? Like sidings or some such?" Truth was, Josef had no idea. His only real interest in trains was getting from A to B.

Alex looked thoughtful, though. "Yes," he said, "that's possible. But scouring the Underground for disused sidings is hardly practical."

"Obviously, we'd need a map."

"I don't suppose you happen to have one?"

Josef huffed. "No, but I do have a library card."

"As you've previously mentioned." An amused smile tugged at one corner of Alex's mouth. "Is that the sort of thing they'd have in a public library?"

"Oh, you can find anything at the library."

Alex's smile broadened for a moment, then failed. "Maybe so, but I think it would be more sensible to return to the sewer, somewhere we know they've been."

"You mean loiter about, wait for one to show up?" That sounded like a terrible plan.

"Tactically," Alex said, sounding slightly affronted, "It's the soundest option." Then he conceded, "But, truth be told, I'd rather not spend my last hours loitering in a sewer."

"Alex..." Josef trailed off. "Look, the point is, they won't be your last hours if we find a bloody ghoul."

"And get some of its blood, without killing it."

They both knew the odds of success were low, though neither spoke the thought aloud.

Alex rubbed a hand over his jaw, then reached into his coat pocket and pulled out a packet of gaspers. He offered one to Josef, and they both lit up. As the smoke curled into the still morning air, Alex said, "I don't like it, but I think it might be a good idea to divide our resources."

"I don't like it, either." Josef took a deep drag on his cigarette and blew out a stream of smoke. "What do you mean?"

"You try to find a useful map of the Underground, while I take the photograph and go back to the sewer."

"Alone? Come off it."

Alex's jaw set. "We've no choice. We need to cover as much ground as possible before I..." Perhaps unconsciously, he touched the place on his shoulder where he'd been bitten. And although it was hidden beneath his clothes, Josef felt as though he could see the festering wound clear as day. His skin prickled at the thought.

And it told him how much time they were looking at—don't buy any green bananas, as his dad might have said. Alex had hours, perhaps a day before things got sticky. Josef swallowed, his stomach griping painfully, and his thoughts shying away from what that end would mean. "Even so," he said, "splitting up is a crap idea."

Alex raised his eyebrows. "Tactically—"

"Don't give me tactics," Josef growled. "Tactics got 20,000 men killed at the Somme in one bloody day. Sod tactics. We need to stick together, not let some ghoul or your Society friends pick us off one at a time."

Alex's brow furrowed as he smoked, gazing down at the pavement. Thinking, thinking... Abruptly, he gave a curt nod and lifted his head. "Yes, you're right. It's safer if we stick together. Someone should keep a close eye on me." Then, to Josef's astonishment, he reached beneath his overcoat and jacket and pulled out his gun, offering it grip-first to Josef. "Do you know how to fire this?"

He did, as it happened; he'd learned all sorts of things back in his radical youth. Nonetheless, he lifted his hands in refusal. "I'm sure you're a better shot."

Alex's expression tightened as he offered the gun again. "A bullet through the head will stop a ghoul. Especially a...a newly minted ghoul."

Newly minted? Fucking hell. Josef's breath caught in horror. "You can't ask me to do that."

"I'm not asking," Alex said. "I'm begging. If we fail, if we run out of time, I might not be able to...to act for myself. I need to know that you'll act for me."

Josef shook his head, even as he took hold of the offered gun. Alex didn't let go. "Promise me," he said. "Swear you'll spare me that end."

Throat too tight to speak, Josef looked at him. The idea of taking this man's life was horrific, but the idea of seeing him turn into a monster was a thousand times worse. "All right," he said thickly, "I swear."

With a curt nod, Alex said, "Thank you."

"Let's just make bloody sure we don't get into that situation," Josef said, tucking the gun into the back of his belt to hide it from view. He didn't want to draw any attention from the coppers.

"Right then," Alex said, adjusting his coat. "Lead the way to the library..."

Chapter Twenty-two

It was a ten-minute walk from Blackfriars Station to the public library on Charles Street, and they were there within half an hour of leaving the museum.

Snatching off his cap, Josef pushed open the door and stepped inside. A familiar hush and the scent of books enveloped him, although today he didn't feel the customary swell of ease that he usually associated with this place. All he felt today was fear breathing down his neck.

Alex was on his heels, looking about curiously. No doubt this was nothing compared with the private or university libraries he must be used to, but Josef would bet ten shillings that none of those places had what they needed. Public libraries were for the interests and needs of the working man, not for toffs buried in their Latin and Greek.

In the middle of the morning, the library was quiet. Probably especially so, given the air raid last night. People tended to stay at home when they were frightened.

Behind the long wooden counter opposite the doorway stood Mr Peters, and Josef's spirits rose. Peters was an excellent librarian, keeper of an astounding volume of trivia and exactly the man for the job in hand. He was a fastidious man, rotund and balding, sporting an old-fashioned Imperial moustache meticulously groomed until its pointy tips aimed skyward.

"Mr Peters," Josef said in his hushed library voice. "Good morning."

Peters looked up from his work and smiled. He had a small mouth and small, neat teeth. "Mr Shepel, how do you do?" His curious gaze darted to Alex, who looked entirely too well dressed for the occasion.

"I'm very well," Josef said. "This is my colleague, um—"

"Mr Beaumont," Alex supplied. "How do you do?"

"We're on a bit of a tight deadline," Josef cut in. "You know how it is."

"That I do," Peters agreed. "How can I help you?"

Josef outlined what they were after—a map showing all the Underground lines, even the parts used for maintenance or anything else. Peters looked thoughtful, nodding, as Josef explained. Then he disappeared into the back room, returning a few minutes later with a stack of small books.

"As you know," he said, setting the map books on the counter, "each railway company produced its own maps in the last century. It was only in '08 that they were brought together into a single map."

Josef knew no such thing. "Each of these maps relates to different lines, do they?"

"That's right." Peters frowned. "I don't know how much detail they go into, but I should think this is a jolly good place to start."

Thanking him, they took the maps into the reading room and started examining them. They were old, some of them going back to the late '90s, but unfortunately, they weren't any bloody use. All they showed were station stops, no sidings or storage areas. Nothing helpful. Fuck, this had been a mistake. They were wasting time—time Alex didn't have.

"There's nothing," Josef said crossly, shoving his maps aside. "This is useless."

That earned him a disapproving rustle of the newspaper from the man sitting opposite them on the large reading-room table. Josef didn't care.

Alex still had his head down, though, studying an old City and South London Railway map.

"I'm going to see if Peters has any other ideas," Josef said. "If not, I think we should go. You were right. The sewer—"

"Wait." Alex grabbed his wrist, still staring at the map. "Look at this." His finger was on a station just north of London Bridge. "This. King William Street Station."

"That's—" Josef frowned. "I don't know it."

"Me neither."

They looked at each other. "It must have closed."

From across the table came an irritated, "Do you mind? There's no talking in the reading room."

"Come on," Josef said, grabbing the maps and heading back to the desk.

Peters watched their approach expectantly. "Any luck?"

"Perhaps," Josef said, spreading out the old C&SLR map on the desk. "Have you ever heard of King William Street station?"

After a moment's thought, Peters' moustache twitched as he smiled. "Oh, yes. Goodness me, that's been closed for a long time now. Must be nearly twenty years. I know my father was still alive because I remember he thought it a terrible waste of money to build a station and close it ten years later. Mind you, he had no time for electric railways." He smiled fondly. "Truth be told, he'd only grudgingly accepted locomotives."

"My pa was the same," Josef said, smiling. "Do you know what happened to the station after it closed?"

Peters blinked. "To the station? Nothing as far as I know. The building's still there, on King William Street. It used to be the terminus, you see, but when they opened the new line to Monument, it bypassed the line entirely."

"Wait," Alex said sharply. "Are you saying the station is in a disused tunnel?"

"I suppose it must be, sir, yes. Now I think about it, I remember something in the papers about the LCC using the tunnels for storage." His eyes lit up. "I could search our newspaper archive if you—"

"No, that won't be necessary," Alex said quickly. "You've been extremely helpful already. Thank you."

Hurriedly refolding the map, Josef said, "Yes, thank you, Mr Peters. You've proved to my friend here that you can find out anything in a public library."

Peters puffed up a little at that. "I'm gratified to have been of service, Mr Shepel." He cast another curious glance at Alex, who looked far too well-dressed to be a member of a public library. "Mr Beaumont."

Replacing his homburg, Alex touched the brim in salute, and then they were off, back out into the cold morning.

"What do you think?" Josef said as they hurried across Blackfriars Bridge.

"I think, if I were a ghoul..." Alex stopped abruptly. Clearing his throat, he said, "I think a disused Underground tunnel is exactly the sort of place that would suit them."

Josef nodded. "Then the next question is—how the bloody hell do we get down there?"

"Why not start with the most obvious? Through the old station." He smiled at whatever he saw in Josef's face. "You're not averse to a little breaking and entry, are you?"

"In broad daylight?"

"That's the best time."

When they finally found the corner of King William Street and Monument Street, Josef was astonished to find a rather ordinary building. If you looked hard, at the very top of its curved frontage, you could see where old letters had once spelled out King William St Station, and lower down City and South London Railway. But the building now appeared to be occupied by W.R. Renshaw Ltd, Boilermakers.

"I'd assumed it would be empty," Josef confessed as they stopped on the opposite corner. Given the station had closed nearly two decades ago, that had been a silly assumption. Nothing stayed unused for long in London. "I'll bet you can't get down to the station anymore."

Alex gave a distracted shake of his head and pulled out a silver card holder from his breast pocket. Opening it, he shuffled through the contents, and Josef realised that he kept several different cards in there, with several different names. Well, of course he did.

"Your man, Peters, said the tunnels have been used for storage. In which case there's probably still access from the premises above, don't you think?"

Which, yes, did make sense.

Considering two different cards, Alex muttered, "It's a pity I'm not in uniform." Then, selecting one, he slipped it into his coat pocket and turned to Josef. "Follow my lead."

"And who, exactly, am I following? Captain Winchester?"

"Colonel Piers Montague." Alex lowered his hat, giving Josef a steely look from beneath its brim. "Secret Service Bureau. We're looking into suspicious activity in the area."

"I suppose that much is true."

"Come along," Alex said, heading across the road. "Let's get this done."

Josef didn't hold out a great deal of hope that the ruse would work when Alex stepped into the offices of W.R. Renshaw. Two clerks were working at their desks and looked up as the door opened. One was stout and middle-aged, the other younger. Josef wondered why he wasn't at the front, and then kicked himself for wondering. What business was it of his? Good for him if he'd saved himself from the meatgrinder.

"Good morning, gentlemen," Alex said in the crisp tones of an officer. "My name is Montague, SSB. Colonel." From his pocket he produced his card and set it on the desk of the youngest. "Who is in charge of this establishment?"

The two clerks looked at each other, and the older one said, "Mr Martin Renshaw, but he ain't here today. Only Mr Brooke, upstairs. The manager."

"Brooke will do nicely," Alex said. "Please be so kind as to fetch him. It's a matter of national security."

After exchanging another glance, the younger man rose. "I'll go," he said, and as he came out from behind the desk Josef saw that he walked with a pronounced limp, his left foot clumping heavily on the wooden floor as he left the room.

That explained why he wasn't in uniform, and some part of Josef felt relieved for him. As if losing his foot or his leg was getting off lightly. It was, though, Josef knew that all too well. Ghouls aside, there were other wounds that could destroy a man's life forever. And not just wounds to the body.

While Josef ruminated, Alex wasn't wasting time. "You're aware of the tunnels beneath this property? The old electric railway line."

The older clerk nodded. "I am, sir, yes." He lowered his voice. "They've blocked the tunnels now and taken up the tracks. In case of infiltration by the Hun."

Josef nodded seriously, although he found it difficult to imagine the Germans skulking around the Underground. Mind you, until a couple of weeks ago, he'd have found it even harder to imagine an army of ghouls doing the same. Nothing was impossible.

"That's right," Alex said. "Nevertheless, we need to get down there, now."

A clumping on the stairs above heralded the arrival of Mr Brooke, a wiry man of middle years with round glasses perched on the end of his nose, and his shirtsleeves rolled up to the elbow.

"What's all this?" he said as he entered the room, the younger clerk following and then sliding hurriedly behind his desk. Mr Brooke, it seemed, was not pleased. "Who are you?"

"Ah, the man in charge," Alex said, shoulders going back and his accent, if possible, sounding even more aristocratic. "My name is Montague. Colonel Montague, Secret Service Bureau. I need your assistance."

Brooke's eyes widened. "My assistance?"

"On a security matter of utmost urgency."

Alex knew exactly what he was about because Brooke inflated like an officious little balloon. "At your service, sir." He glanced at his two clerks, both with their eyes down and ears pricked. "We can talk in the—er, in my office upstairs, if that's more convenient?"

"Thank you, but time is of the essence," Alex said. "We need access to the disused tunnels beneath this building. I understand it once served as a station."

"That's right," Brooke said. "This was part of the ticket hall, back in the day. Over there," he gestured towards the far end of the room where the wall appeared to be poorly patched, "used to be the hydraulic lift shaft. They took it out years ago, though. Before the war."

"That can't have been the only way down," Alex said tensely. "There must have been stairs in case the electricity failed..."

"Oh, aye, there's stairs. But we ain't opened them since war broke out. War Office orders."

Alex nodded gravely. "Your diligence is noted, sir. Unfortunately, we must enter the tunnels immediately, and I urge you to lock the door after us."

That sounded like a terrible idea to Josef. "Lock it?" he said aloud. "Won't we need to...?"

Escape?

Alex gave him a quick, quelling look. "Civilian security is paramount, Sergeant."

It took Josef a moment to register the false rank, and another to remember that he was meant to be under Alex's command. He answered only with a nod as Alex said, "Quick as you like, Mr Brooke."

Brooke all but clicked his heels in his eagerness to obey.

He led them out of the clerk's office into a larger room filled with machine parts that Josef assumed related to boiler making. Picking their way through them, they made their way towards a stout door of heavy, dark wood that lurked in the far corner of the echoing space. Two new bolts had been installed, top and bottom, and they gleamed in the daylight streaming in through the windows.

With obvious trepidation, and not a little excitement, Brooke slid back the top lock and then crouched to undo the one at the bottom of the door. It proved stiffer, and he ended up kicking it open with his foot. Then, from his pocket, he produced a set of keys and unlocked the brass lock at the centre of the door. The key turned with a portentous clunk, and Josef's pulse jumped over a beat or two.

They were really doing this.

"You have your electric torch?" Alex asked quietly, his gaze fixed on the heavy door as Brooke hauled it open.

Josef nodded, reaching into his coat pocket. "I hope the batteries last."

"Indeed."

Flicking on the light, Josef stepped forward, shining the beam through the door and over an iron staircase that spiralled down into the dark. On the walls, his torchlight flashed over decorative tiles of the kind used in Underground stations. Hairs rose on the back of his neck, alongside a powerful urge not to enter that dark stairwell.

But Alex crowded in at his shoulder, and what choice did they have? They had hours, perhaps less, to find what they needed to save Alex from a fate that was quite literally worse than death. And the thought of what Josef might be forced to do if they failed was enough to propel him forward. He'd do anything—anything—rather than that.

"Follow me," he said, stepping through the doorway into the narrow stairwell. "And watch your footing."

Behind him, Alex said, "Thank you for your help, Mr Brooke. Lock the door after us please, and don't open it again for anyone but Seargent Lake, here."

Brooke frowned at Josef, as if the order was somehow his fault. "But what about you, sir?"

"Nobody but Lake," Alex repeated severely. "And now the door, if you please?"

With a nod and an aborted hand gesture that may have wanted to be a salute, Brooke closed the door. Josef watched the disappearing sliver of daylight until it was gone, and the door shut with an ominous thud, plunging them into deeper darkness. The only light came from Josef's torch.

"What was all that about?" he said, glancing over at Alex. In the unblinking light of the electric torch, he looked quite different, his features casting shadows across his face and his dark blue eyes black as night. "Why only me?"

"You know why," Alex said, rolling his left shoulder. Josef's gaze fixed on it, and on the way that Alex was flexing his left hand.

"What is it?" he whispered. "Do you feel... worse?"

Alex responded by hefting his stick like a cudgel. "Let's go down. Quietly."

And what else could they do?

Despite his best efforts at stealth, Josef's boots clanged on the iron staircase, the light of his torch bobbing ahead of them. Not too far ahead, mind, just enough to reveal the next couple of steps. As they descended, the air grew dank with the scent of musty disuse.

Strange, how the old C&SLR tiles lifted the hairs on the back of his neck. Strange that this station was still here, buried beneath the city as the world above moved on. Not even the war had touched it.

Behind him, Alex suddenly stopped with a swift indrawn breath.

Josef turned, looking back at him. It was too dark to see his face now. "What?" Josef whispered.

A long pause followed before Alex whispered, "I can...sense them."

Shit. Josef's heart punched against his ribs as he sniffed the air. Nothing. And that wasn't a stink you could miss. "Are you sure? I can't smell them."

"Very sure," Alex said, stiffly. "They're down there. Not near, but we're on their trail."

Through a dry throat, Josef said, "Good. That's good." His words came out papery thin, though, because what did it mean that Alex could sense their presence so easily?

As if he needed to ask.

"I'll go first, now," Alex said, passing Josef on the narrow stairs. Close enough that he could smell the herbal aroma of Alex's poultice, and beneath that...

He almost choked on the faint sickly stench.

Unmistakable, though. The putrid rot he'd seen on Sykes and all the other victims was eating its way, even now, into Alex's body. And if Josef knew it, Alex bloody well knew it too.

At last, they reached the bottom of the spiral staircase, the air growing colder and damper with every turn of the stairs. A closed door greeted them. For a horrible moment, Josef feared—hoped?—it would be locked, but no. When Alex slowly turned the handle, the door moved with a grinding complaint that echoed, Josef was certain, through the whole bloody Underground network. They could probably hear it in Kentish Town.

Alex grimaced but kept pushing on the door until there was enough space to squeeze through. "Torch," he demanded, holding one hand back towards Josef.

Muttering a curse about overbearing aristocrats, Josef handed him his torch. Suddenly plunged into darkness, he hurried through the door after Alex. This was not a place to fall behind.

On the other side, he found himself standing in a cavern. At least, that's what it felt like, a large, cold, and echoing space that smelled like damp and decay. All he could see, though, were slashes of tiled walls and ceiling as Alex criss-crossed the torch beam around the huge space.

After a few moments, the fragmented images started to come together, and he realised they were standing in a station tunnel. Three dark passageways disappeared ahead of them, and Josef could just make out words saying Way Out. They must have led to the hydraulic lifts. To their right, the station platform opened.

"Come on," Alex whispered, heading towards the platform.

With a wary glance back at the dark and silent passageways behind them, Josef followed. As they walked, Alex skimmed the torch across the walls, finding an old advertising board full of peeling advertisements for mortgages and property sales, and down to the rubble-strewn space where railway lines would once have run. Gone now, like the clerk had told them.

At the far end of the long platform, the tunnel divided, twin black maws leading off into deeper darkness. This had been a terminus, Josef remembered, so the tunnels only went in one direction—south, beneath the Thames. Somewhere in the darkness, water dripped, conjuring unhappy thoughts of leaking tunnels and a rush of filthy river water.

"There," Alex whispered, stilling the roving torchlight on a crumpled pile of rags down in the track bed.

Josef stared in horror, chest tightening as his brain tried to make out a human form amid the rags. Was that a body? "What is it?" he rasped.

"Nest," Alex said curtly. "At least one of them has been sleeping here."

Josef's skin prickled, and he looked around nervously. The torch cast just enough ambient light that he could make out a few details: King William St. tiled into the wall opposite, the rusty turnstiles that, once, would have admitted thousands of travellers each day, the empty signal box near the mouth of the tunnel. All abandoned, left to rot.

"If it sleeps here," he whispered, "where is it now?"

The torchlight moved, shining towards the twin tunnel entrances. "You choose," Alex said. "Left, or right?"

Chapter Twenty-three

"If the tunnels have been blocked off," Josef said as they crept along the platform, "how did the ghoul get in here?"

"They've spent a thousand years worming into stone crypts. A few bricks won't stop them."

"Right." Josef immediately tried to wipe that image from his mind.

At the end of the platform, they passed the abandoned signal box, its levers still in place. It was impossible not to imagine the last time they were used, the signalman leaving the station at the end of his final shift, the doors closing behind him and everything going dark.

Sometimes, at the front, he'd felt as if the whole world was going dark, that civilization itself was dying in the mud. One day, might everywhere be like this silent, abandoned place?

Alex swept his torch down onto the empty railbed. Was it Josef's imagination, or did its light seem fainter?

"Good idea to get the gun out," Alex said mildly. "We don't know what we're going to run into."

"We've got an idea," Josef muttered as Alex crouched down and, with one hand braced on the platform edge, hopped down onto the railbed.

Rather less elegantly, Josef scrambled down after him and pulled the Webley from the back of his waistband. It felt clumsy in his hands, and he wished Alex would use it instead.

Cautiously, they crept along the tunnel until the brickwork ended. After that point, the tunnel split into two, both lined with heavy sections of grey cast iron—presumably installed one by one as the tunnel was dug. They looked reassuringly strong. The leftmost tunnel was lower and dipped steeply down, while the rightward remained level.

"Which way?" Josef asked softly.

Alex wavered, torchlight dithering between the two tunnels. God, it was quiet. All Josef could hear was Alex's breathing—too fast, too laboured—and the slow drip-drip-drip of water.

Fuck, he wanted to get out of there.

"The left," Alex decided, indicating the downward sloping tunnel. "That's where they are."

Picking their way through the rubble—whoever had ripped up the tracks had not taken much care—they headed left without discussion.

Inside the tunnel, the going was easier, with less debris from the platform underfoot. The ceiling grew lower though, the tunnel narrower, and the downward gradient steep. With each step, they were going deeper and deeper into the earth—into the subterranean world of the ghoul.

Suddenly, the ground began to tremble, and the tunnel filled with a loud, rumbling rattle.

"A train," Alex said softly. "We're not far from the other lines, here."

Josef glanced up into the darkness. It was hard to imagine that they were close to anything, let alone a well-lit train full of people. "There must be a way into the other tunnels," he guessed. "This place would be useless to the ghoul otherwise."

"Yes, although I imagine that access is somewhere beyond this point." Alex had stopped and was playing the torch over a solid wall of brick filling the tunnel before them.

Presumably, this was intended to stop German infiltrators, although why they'd need tunnels when they could simply drop bombs from the air, Josef couldn't imagine.

"Over here," Alex said, getting closer to one side of the blockade where it abutted the tunnel wall. When he shone the torchlight on it, Josef could see that several bricks at the bottom had been dislodged and torn away, leaving a narrow gap. A narrow, man-sized gap.

He groaned. "Don't tell me we're going through there."

"You've got nothing to worry about," Alex said, crouching down to examine the hole. "Think of me, and my shoulders."

"Hey, are you calling me scrawny?"

Alex flashed a look at him, all shadows in the dark, save the gleam of his eyes. "Not scrawny. Slender." He turned back to the hole, shining the light through it. "I happen to find slender men extremely appealing."

Despite the circumstances, Josef couldn't stop his smile. "Turns out I rather enjoy a set of broad shoulders."

All he heard from Alex was a huff of amusement before he said, "Hold the torch, will you? I'll go first."

Pulse thumping, he watched as Alex worked his head and shoulders awkwardly into the narrow gap, grimacing as he moved. Obviously in pain. Whatever Lottie and Violet had given him, his shoulder was obviously still bothering him. And perhaps getting worse.

As Alex's legs and feet disappeared, Josef crouched and shone the light through the hole after him. "All right?" he whispered.

"Yes, come through."

Shoving the torch ahead of him, Josef wormed his way through the gap headfirst, feeling the rough brick edges snag on his coat. The ground was wet beneath his hands, icy water seeping into the knees of his trousers as he scrambled through.

Alex took his arm, hauling him back to his feet. And he didn't let go. Josef was grateful for that and crowded closer, pressing his body firmly against Alex's, relishing his warmth. His sheer human presence. To his delight, Alex wrapped an arm firmly around Josef's shoulders and pulled him close. Josef went eagerly, sliding his arms around Alex's middle and holding him tight. In the pitch black, what did it matter? No one could see. In a strange way, down here, they were freer than in the daylight above.

They stood like that for a few long moments, both perhaps needing an anchor in the disorientating dark.

"Fuck," Josef whispered at last. "It's dark."

"How much longer will the batteries last?"

The torch was noticeably dimmer now, its electric brilliance turning honeyed yellow. "I don't know. Half an hour? Shit, I should have thought to buy spares."

Alex didn't answer, his breaths loud in the silence of the tunnel.

"Maybe we should turn back?" Josef suggested, half hopefully and half reluctantly. As much as he hated this fucking tunnel, he knew they were running out of time.

Nobly, Alex said, "You go back. I'll—"

"Oh, fuck off," Josef muttered, pressing himself closer, feeling Alex's arm tighten around him. He gave into it for a moment, closing his eyes and resting his forehead against Alex's shoulder. He could still smell the poultice and the infection beneath, but for that moment nothing mattered more than the comfort of this closeness, comfort he hoped he was returning.

Briefly, both Alex's arms went around him, squeezing tight. In an emotional voice, very unlike his usual aristocratic calm, he whispered, "Thank you. My God, I'm glad you're here even if I wish you were miles away, and safe."

"You're definitely going to owe me a pint," Josef muttered, smothering his suddenly riotous feelings. "A real one, too, not that dishwater piss they serve these days."

Still in that tremulous, emotional tone, Alex said, "I want nothing more from this world than to buy you a pint, Josef."

Smiling against his shoulder, Josef said, "You know, my friends call me Joe."

Alex shifted, and Josef felt his cold fingers touch his cheek, his jaw. He lifted his head.

"Joe," Alex murmured and touched his lips to Josef's. "My friend."

Josef kissed him back, urgently, hungrily and all too aware of time running out. And then they were just hugging, squeezing tight until the squall of emotion passed and they stood, breathing hard, in each other's arms.

"All right then," Alex said at last, pulling away. He looked sombre in the fading torch light. "I think we need to conserve the batteries. Besides, we don't want to advertise our presence."

Josef stared. "Are you...? Turn off the torch?" It felt like a lifeline, that narrow beam of light. "We'll be blind."

"Our eyes will adapt. There might be more light down here than we realise."

"Under the fucking Thames?"

Alex gave half a smile. "We're not under the river yet. Let's save the torch for our escape."

He was right, of course. Whatever happened next, they'd never get out of here if the torch failed. There was no faulting

Alex's logic, no matter how much the thought of losing the light terrified Josef.

He let out a breath, aware of its wobble. "All right," he said, pressing the button on the head of the torch.

Darkness consumed them, total and absolute. A thick, claustrophobic blanket of nothing.

But not quite nothing. Alex was still there, one arm tight around Josef. The wool of his coat brushed Josef's cheek where he pressed his face against Alex's shoulder. The only thing left in the world.

"We need to give it a few minutes," Alex said softly, "for our eyes to adapt."

Josef doubted any amount of time would allow his eyes to adapt to this utter blackness, but he nodded gamely. Then he remembered Alex couldn't see him, so he said, "Yes, all right." An unhappy thought struck him, and he added, more softly, "I assume the ghoul can see very well in the dark?"

"Much better than we can," Alex agreed. "You've seen their eyes?"

The sepulchral blue? As if he could forget. "They're still men, though, aren't they? I mean, their...bodies?"

"Perhaps. By that point... I don't know. They're something other. That's why—" His voice cracked, and he cleared his throat. "That's why you need to end this before I'm too far gone. You understand? I want to die a man."

Josef closed his eyes, as if even in the pitch dark it could keep the thought away. "I know," he said, trying to sound brave. "I understand. I won't let that happen to you."

Whatever it costs me.

Pulling Josef closer, Alex hugged him tightly, and Josef did the same. Astonishing the comfort of holding and being held, even in the foulest of places. Alex's breath felt warm against Josef's neck as he ducked his head against his shoulder, and

Josef let his fingers brush the hair at the nape of Alex's neck. As he ran his fingers through the soft strands, he felt Alex contort, a strange unstructured movement of jerks and jolts as the breath left his body in a hiss.

Josef froze. "Are you all right? What was that?"

After a long silence, Alex said, "I don't know. A...pain."

"Where?"

"Everywhere. It's gone now." He pulled out of Josef's arms. "Mostly." Chill fingers touched Josef's face, tracing his jaw. "See? I told you there'd be some light down here. I'm starting to see your face."

Josef blinked into the unremitting black, his heart racing. "Are you?"

"Just the outline." Then he said, "Look, along the tunnel there. Maybe 200 feet? I think it's the outline of a door."

The only way Josef knew which way to even look was by feeling for the brick wall behind them. Peering into the darkness, he thought maybe the blackness had some contours. If not light, a paling of the dark. "Yes," he said, hesitantly. "I think I see it."

"It must lead into one of the other tunnels. An access passage for maintenance perhaps? That would be why they blocked the tunnel here." Releasing Josef, he said, "Let's go that way—"

Suddenly alone in the dark, Josef hissed, "Wait!"

"What?"

He forced back his panic and said, "I, uh, think your eyes have adapted better than mine. You're going to have to guide me."

Alex was silent for a moment, then said, "Can you see the door? Tell me the truth."

"No," Josef admitted. "That is, perhaps something but... No, Alex, I can't see a bloody thing."

Another silence. Then Alex said, with painful bravado, "In that case, it appears my night vision is rather improved."

"I might not mean—"

"It obviously does," Alex cut in. "But no point looking a gift horse in the mouth, is there? Here, take my hand."

Alex clasped Josef's hand, and he was pathetically relieved to have that lifeline restored.

"Looks like we don't need the torch," Alex said lightly. "I'll be your guide for now."

For now.

Josef straightened his shoulders. "We'd better get going, then." Because God only knew how much time Alex had left.

They moved through the darkness quickly, too fast for Josef's comfort, but Alex seemed certain. And with every step, the air grew colder and danker, the silence broken now and then by a distant rattle of an underground train. And the constant dripping of water.

"It's probably just condensation," Alex said, when Josef mentioned it, "rather than the Thames breaking through."

"Probably?" Josef muttered. Still, Alex's patrician tones lent authority to everything he said, and, on this occasion, Josef chose to believe him.

"We're at the side of the tunnel," Alex said after a few more moments. "Reach out with your right hand and you'll touch it."

Gingerly, Josef did so, his fingers scratching across the damp, icy surface of the cast-iron tunnel wall. "How much further to the door?"

"We're close," Alex whispered, slowing them to a halt. He shifted, letting go of Josef's hand, leaving him adrift in the dark. "Stay here. I'm going to open it."

"What? Wait! They could be right behind it!"

Alex made a sound of impatience. "They're not."

"You don't know that!"

"Apparently, I do."

Josef swallowed. "Are you...? As Lottie said, are you feeling drawn to them?"

"No," he said crisply. "Not drawn, exactly. More a certain... impatience to find them."

"Well, I feel that too," Josef said, forcing a laugh.

Alex didn't reciprocate. "I suspect this is rather different."

There came the sound of a door handle turning, and Josef held his breath. With a rusty squeal, the door opened, dim light blooming into the tunnel. Alex hissed, taking a step back.

The relief Josef felt at the light was squashed by the sight of Alex shading his eyes as if someone had shoved a lamp in his face. "All right?" he asked.

"In a moment," Alex said stiffly, peering out from behind his hand. "Christ."

The light, wherever it came from, wasn't behind the door but somewhere further along the passage beyond. By no definition was it bright. "Your eyes are sensitive," Josef said worriedly.

"Obviously." Alex lowered his hand, blinking and squinting. "It's getting better."

Josef peered through the door. It led onto a much narrower tunnel, more like a corridor—an access passage for engineers and other workmen, most likely. It had never occurred to Josef that people needed to move about down here, but then he'd never given it much thought. Now that he did, it was obvious that workmen couldn't simply walk along the train tunnels. "There must be a whole network of maintenance passageways."

Alex joined him at the doorway, his eyes still narrowed but no longer in apparent pain. "Yes. This one doesn't look much used, but it appears to lead to more well-travelled areas."

"A convenient way for the ghoul to move around the city."

"Quite." He glanced at Josef. "Keep your weapon to hand."

With that, Alex set off into the tunnel, Josef following at his heels. It ran for a good few hundred yards before they saw another door on the left side of the passage, and opposite it, a set of stairs leading down deeper. Even in the dim light, Josef could see that the door stood ajar, something blocking it—wedging it open?

Alex slowed, sniffing the air. "They're here."

A moment later, Josef caught the scent too. Or rather the stench, the familiar putrid rot he'd first seen at the front. He stopped dead, catching Alex's arm to halt him too. "Now what?"

Shaking off his hand, Alex kept walking. "Come on."

Fuck. Josef hurried after him, the gun heavy in his hand.

When Alex reached the door, he crouched down to examine what blocked it, still sniffing the air. For Josef's part, he was trying not to breathe too deeply. As he came to join Alex, he stopped, flinching back. A man's leg lay wedged in the door. And only a man's leg. Even in the dim light, Josef could see that it had been...chewed.

His stomach churned, bile rising into his throat. He'd seen plenty of severed limbs at the front, but this...? "Fuck," he whispered, jaw clenched against a wave of nausea.

When Alex stood, he looked harrowed. "Sometimes, they will fight over the spoils."

Yet another image Josef could do without.

"This is fresh," Alex went on, his expression stiff, haunted. "They're not far."

Josef reached out a hand and squeezed his arm. "All right?" He swallowed another rise of bile. "The stink's getting to me, too."

Alex lifted his eyes to Josef. "God help me," he said thickly, "but I only feel..."

"Feel what?"

Eyes dark and full of horror, he rasped, "Hunger."

Josef's heart lurched. "Can you...?" His mouth had turned dry, like ash. "Can you control it?"

With a curt nod, Alex said, "Yes, for now. I don't know how long—" His gaze dropped to the gun Josef held.

It felt like a lead weight, big and ugly in his hand. He'd rather do anything than use it on Alex. Hell, he'd rather use it on himself. "Long enough," he said firmly. "Come on, they're nearby. Let's get this blood and scarper."

Neither of them touched the human leg, stepping over it as you might step over a pile of horse dung in the street. Once, at the field hospital in Pops, Josef had seen a mound of mangled limbs, left behind after the surgeons had finished their bloody work. The pile of discarded flesh had been covered in flies, and Josef had vomited at the sight. But that had been in the early days of his time at the front, and his stomach had soon grown stronger.

They lived in a world of death. In a country that gaily threw millions of men into the meatgrinder of the salient, was it any surprise that here, beneath the streets of London, human flesh had become food for monsters?

Mankind deserved no better.

Beyond the door rose a narrow flight of stairs, the light at the top growing brighter. They climbed, cautiously, jumping at the sudden thunder of a passing train—closer here, right above their heads. Stupidly, Josef found himself ducking.

At the top of the stairs, an electric light had been fastened to the wall, its yellow light illuminating dark streaks of blood on the stairs. Next to the light, stood another door, also open. Another train thundered nearby, and a draft of warm air pushed through the door. The sort of breeze you might feel standing on a station platform. Only this one was ripe with the foetid stench of rot.

Josef put an arm to his nose, tamping down the desire to puke.

At his side, Alex looked ghastly, pale as bone. As he breathed in, his nostrils flared, and he wet his lips with the tip of his tongue. His eyes were bright and horrified.

From the other side of the door came a soft scrabble of movement, a low hiss.

The hair rose on the back of Josef's neck as he turned, meeting Alex's too-bright gaze. And then the light went out.

Josef stumbled backwards, breath catching in horror, because all he could see in the pitch-black tunnel was the sepulchral gleam of Alex's eyes.

Chapter Twenty-four

"They're here," Alex said in a voice that was somehow his and yet other.

Josef couldn't speak. No words would come.

Those eyes, all he could see in the dark was those eyes. They moved closer. Josef stepped back, holding out his free hand to keep Alex away.

"What is it?" Alex's voice quivered strangely. "You look... You're afraid."

Swallowing, Josef said, "Your eyes..."

Another sound drowned his words, the screech of unoiled hinges. The door. Alex's eyes turned away, and Josef couldn't see a bloody thing.

He could hear, though, and he could smell as something shuffled through that door. Another pair of ghostly blue eyes turned on him with a throaty hiss.

In the dark, Josef was useless, and that was impossible. Shoving the gun into the waistband of his trousers, he yanked the torch from his coat pocket and switched it on.

Alex hissed, raising an arm against the light.

Arrested halfway through the open door, the ghoul stopped too. It was—or had been—a young soldier, and still wore the vestiges of its uniform, torn and bloody with a gaping, blackened wound in its belly. It snarled, mouth opening to reveal spikes of bloody, inhuman teeth.

Its head moved strangely from side to side, nostrils flaring as it sniffed the air before its gaze fixed on Josef. The initial bright flare of torchlight was dimming noticeably, the beam shaking in his hand.

For a few frozen moments, they stood there in a standoff.

Then the ghoul pounced, launching itself at Josef with a howl. And Alex barrelled into it, rugby-tackling the creature to the ground. They went down in a confusion of limbs, wrestling and rolling on the ground.

"Pin it down!" Josef yelled, dropping the torch, its light skimming across the cold concrete floor. He dove in, trying to grab the creature's legs and hold it still. Fuck, how the hell were they going to get blood from this thing?

The ghoul stench of rot filled the small passageway, thickening the air until Josef felt he could hardly breathe. His stomach revolted, but he ignored it. Alex had the upper hand now, rolling the creature onto its belly and sitting astride its back. Josef held onto its legs for all he was worth.

In the dim torchlight, the silver blade of a knife gleamed in Alex's hand. "Give me the vial," he barked in that strange, not-quite-him voice.

Easier said than done. The ghoul kicked and struggled, and it was all Josef could do to keep hold of its flailing legs.

"Now!" Alex barked. "Come on!"

Cursing, Josef got one arm around both the creature's shins and reached into his pocket for the glass vial Lottie had given them. Alex had his back to Josef, legs clamped around the ghoul's back. One of its arms was trapped at its side. The other Alex pinned down with one hand and with a flash of silver stabbed the blade into its flesh.

The creature screamed and bucked, nearly throwing Alex off. But not quite.

"Now!" Alex shouted, holding his hand back behind him. "Give it to me!"

Removing the cork stopper with his teeth, Josef slapped the vial into Alex's hand.

In the dim light, the ghoul's blood looked sluggish and black. Alex pressed the vial against the wound in its arm, and the creature's viscous blood crept into it.

Lying across its legs, Josef fought to keep the ghoul still long enough for Alex to finish. It snarled and hissed and howled, and to Josef's ears, it sounded like a wolf calling to its pack.

"Hurry up," he hissed.

"What do you think I'm bloody well doing?"

And then, echoing through the tunnels, came a second howl—an answer to the first. Then a third. A fourth.

Josef's hair stood on end. "We have to go!"

"Here!" Alex stuck his hand back again, his fingers bloody and the vial only half full. It would have to be enough.

After wedging the cork back in, Josef grabbed the vial and shoved it into his pocket.

"On three," he said. "Let it go and run for it. Back down the stairs."

Alex grunted in agreement and yanked the knife out of the creature's arm. "One," he said, fisting his hand into the ghoul's hair. "Two." He lifted its head. "Three!" And slammed the creature face-first into the concrete floor, then leapt off its back.

Josef released its legs, snatching up the torch as he rolled to his feet.

"Go!" Alex shoved Josef ahead of him towards the stairs.

He went, snatching a quick glimpse of the ghoul struggling to its feet before he was pelting downstairs, Alex on his heels.

And the ghoul at their backs...

Josef was flying, but it wasn't fast enough. He could hear the ghoul, smell it. Alex shoved his back. "Faster!"

Fuck.

He stumbled, missing a couple of steps, only keeping from falling by grabbing the handrail. His shoulder wrenched as he caught himself, momentum slamming him into the wall. He looked back, flashing the torchlight behind him, and caught the moment the ghoul launched itself at him.

Not at Alex, but at Josef.

In the madly dancing light, it appeared to fly like a demon, gored teeth and inhuman eyes flashing in the dark.

Yelling, Josef threw up his arms to protect his face, stumbling backward down the stairs.

And Alex launched himself forward, right into the path of the ghoul, taking the full brunt of its attack.

They went down together in a tangle of arms and legs, crashing past Josef and down the stairs. Alex gave a sharp cry as they tumbled arse over tit and slammed to the ground at the bottom of the stairwell.

By some miracle, Josef still had his hand torch. Neither Alex nor the ghoul moved beneath its dimming light. Alex lay beneath the ghoul which was splayed over his body. Torch in one hand, gun in the other, Josef hurried down the rest of the stairs. In the distance, he could hear the howls of other creatures. They didn't have long.

"Alex," he hissed, drawing closer. Alex lay sprawled on his back, head tilted to one side as if sleeping. Or worse. Josef shook his shoulder. "Alex!"

His eyes opened.

Josef recoiled from the pale eerie blue gaze looking up at him. "Go," Alex said roughly. "Run."

"Yes, come on!" He tugged at Alex's arm, trying to pull him out from beneath the ghoul's inert body. Fuck, was it dead? If it was, did that mean the blood was no good?

Alex hissed and shook Josef off. "I can't," he said in an odd, breathless voice. "Go."

Josef stared at him. "What?"

"I can't—"

"You bloody well can!" Josef dropped the torch and the gun, grabbing his shoulders with both hands and heaving.

Alex screamed.

"Fuck!" Josef all but jumped out of his skin. "What's wrong?"

For a moment, the only sounds were Alex's laboured breaths. Then he gasped. "Leg. Broken, I think."

Fuck. Fuck, fuck, fuck.

And then the ghoul began to stir.

Josef stopped breathing; the walls were closing in, the roof collapsing. All their options shutting down. Fists clenched in his hair, he screamed in silent, wordless despair.

Alex grabbed his leg. "Joe..." With the torch discarded on the floor, all he could see of Alex were those cursed eyes. "It's time."

Staring at him, Josef shook his head. "No." His voice sounded like rust.

"I can't walk," Alex ground out. "I can't escape."

"But I have the blood!"

"Too late." Alex's eyes closed, then opened again. "Please. You promised."

"Well, I shouldn't have!"

Alex stretched his arm out, fumbling for the gun which lay next to the torch. "Then give it to me. I'll do it myself."

"No!" Josef snatched it up, backing away. "Fuck, Alex, no. We have the blood; we can cure you!"

"There's no time!" Alex shouted, breaking off into another cry of pain.

"Fuck that." Stuffing the weapon back into his belt, Josef started dragging the semi-conscious ghoul off Alex.

Josef was hurting him, he knew, but it was better than letting him die. Or killing him. When Alex was free, Josef grabbed the torch to examine his leg. The broken one was obvious; a bloody rent in Alex's trousers revealed the tip of a bone poking through his skin, just below the right knee.

Half sitting up, Alex took one look and collapsed back down. "Christ," he said thinly.

"All the stuff you've seen, and that makes you faint?"

"Just give me the fucking gun," Alex growled.

"I'm not leaving you here."

"I can't move!"

"You've got one good leg," Josef said. "Use it."

With a great deal of struggle, Josef got Alex upright, one arm around his shoulders. He tried not to think of how far they had to walk.

At the foot of the stairs, the ghoul gave a low hiss, apparently waking up. "Come on," Josef hissed, pulling Alex towards the door.

They moved agonisingly slowly. Literally, in Alex's case. He couldn't put any weight on his broken leg, having to hop, his breathing very fast and leaning more and more heavily against Josef. He wasn't a small man, either. Taller than Josef, broader. Heavier.

They stumbled out of the stairwell and into the corridor beyond, shutting the door. There was nothing to wedge it shut with—it didn't even have a lock—and the corridor ahead looked endless.

"Joe," Alex said urgently, and then twisted away and threw up.

The pain, Josef knew. Shock.

It was hopeless, he saw that now. Couldn't deny it as he tried, as gently as he could, to help Alex to the ground, resting his back against the corridor wall. He sat there, very still, face damp with cold sweat and breathing slow, controlled breaths. In the torchlight, his skin glistened corpse white.

Throat thick, eyes blurring, Josef said, "I'm sorry. I don't know what to do."

Without opening his eyes, Alex said, "Yes, you do."

The gun in his waistband felt like a live thing, like a grenade with its pin pulled.

"Please," Alex said softly. "While there's still time."

Josef's heart pounded slow and heavy, every beat a moment lost. His fingers closed around the grip of the gun, and with a shaking hand, he pulled it free.

From behind the door came scrabbling sounds.

He lifted the shaking gun, bile rising in his throat, vision blurring. Tears fell hot on his cheek.

"It's all right," Alex said softly. "We gave it our best shot."

No, Josef wanted to scream. It's not all right. It's all fucking wrong.

The gun shook more violently, and he grabbed it with both hands to steady it. If he had to do this, he couldn't fuck it up.

Something heavy thumped against the door. Soon, the ghoul would come through and be on them.

On him.

It would have killed him already if Alex hadn't got in the way.

He stared at Alex, at his deathly skin, the slits of blue beneath his half-lidded eyes. The bone protruding from his leg.

The ghoul had attacked Josef, not Alex. Even though Alex had been closest, it had launched itself past Alex to reach Josef.

His mind cleared, sharpened, and he shot to his feet. "Stay here."

Alex's eyes flew open. "What?" he said. "For Christ's sake, Joe. End it!"

"No." He lowered the gun. "No. I can't do that. I can't kill you. I won't."

"Then let me do it myself." He reached out for the gun. "Come on, give it to me."

But Josef stepped backward. "I'm sorry, no."

Alex's face contorted in rage, barely recognisable. "You fucking coward!"

It punched the breath out of him.

You fucking coward! You're a bloody disgrace to your family!

His father's wrath echoed across the years, his contempt mirrored in Alex's furious face. *I'm not!* He wanted to scream it. *I'm not a coward!* But that would do as little good now as it had that awful day on Goulston Street.

"I'm coming back for you," he said instead, voice rasping with distress. "I'm going to save you."

"I won't be here!" Alex spat. "Don't you understand? I'm holding on by my fucking fingernails." He slammed one palm into the side of his own head. "I'll be gone!"

"You won't." Josef took another step backward. "You'll hold on. Fucking hold on, all right?"

"Josef..." Alex's voice shook, fury ebbing away. And that was worse; now he just sounded frightened. "I trusted you. Please, don't leave me like this..."

A squeal of door hinges rang through the tunnel.

They were out of time. Shoving the gun back into his waistband, Josef took one last look at Alex. "Hold on," he said.

And then he ran, Alex's furious curses chasing him into the dark.

Chapter Twenty-five

When he looked back, all Josef remembered of his endless flight was terror.

Terror of being attacked, yes, but far worse, the terror of failing. Of not getting out, of not getting back to Lottie and Vi. Of not saving Alex.

It propelled him along the rubble-strewn tunnel, pushed him back to his feet when he tripped and went sprawling, the torch rolling away from him. Its light was failing now, barely enough to show the ground one step ahead. He knew if the light died, he would die with it.

At last, though, he found himself crawling through the hole in the wall that blocked off the abandoned station at King William Street. There was no sign of pursuit—he tried not to think what might have slowed the ghoul down—but he proceeded carefully, nonetheless. Trying to silence his heaving breaths, he crept into the station. He knew a ghoul had been here, had nested here. He knew it could be hiding in the dark, watching him. Skin prickling, he drew his gun and scanned the blackness for the gleam of dead eyes.

At length, he reached the platform and heaved himself up. His knee stung as he climbed to his feet; so did the palms of his hands. He ignored it, edging along the platform in search of the door they'd entered through.

His torch glowed faintly now, almost useless. But he was nearly there. He felt the papery old advertisements under his fingers as he trailed his hand along the wall. The door was on the right, at the end.

Behind him, something hissed. He spun, caught the gleam of blue eyes and fired. Right between them.

The gunshot ricocheted through the empty station, bouncing off the walls, deafening him.

The ghoul fell backward into the darkness and lay still.

A gunshot to the head will kill a ghoul, Alex had said, especially a newly minted one.

Josef's heart failed. He dropped the gun, heard it clatter to the floor. "Alex?"

He fell to his knees next to the still body, the glowing ember of torchlight in his hand barely enough to show him what he couldn't bear to see. What he had to see. Hands shaking, he lifted the torch and let the last of its light play over the dead face—young, handsome, a bullet wound just above the left eye, a private's uniform, bloodied and gored. One arm was lost below the elbow. A man fresh from the battlefield.

And not Alex.

He felt ashamed by his flood of relief. That this poor boy's miserable death should bring anyone relief was abhorrent. But it wasn't Alex. Thank God.

Thank God.

Josef pushed his aching body back to its feet. The noise of the gunshot must have woken anything sleeping in these tunnels, and he had no desire to be here when they showed up. Staggering away from the dead man, feeling his way along the wall, he finally found the open door. Slipping through, he pulled it shut behind him, for all the good that would do. He just caught a glimpse of the patterned tiles on the wall before the torch went dark and all he could do was climb and hope.

He'd lost track of time in the dark. When he hammered on the door at the top of the stairs, he was afraid it might be evening, and the shop closed. "Open up!" he shouted. "Open the bloody door!"

Through the thick wood, a man said, "Lake?"

It took him a moment to remember. "Yes!" he shouted back. "Yes, it's me, Lake! Open the door!"

There followed a ridiculously slow turning of a key in the lock, the drawing back of bolts before the door cracked open and light flooded the stairwell. Josef threw an arm up to protect his eyes. "Hell," he cursed, pushing through the door and slamming it behind him. Squinting in the brightness—it was still broad daylight—he said, "Lock it. Brace it, too."

The man—Mr Brooke—looked uncertain. "Where's Colonel Montague?"

"In trouble," Josef said, and that was honest enough. "I'm off to get help."

Brooke looked alarmed. "Are there...? Is the Hun down there?"

Josef almost laughed, felt the hysteria rising and shoved it back down. "What's down there is dangerous," he said, "and can't be allowed to escape. Do you understand?"

"Sappers..."

The second voice came from the other side of the room, and Josef saw the younger clerk standing there on his tin leg. He looked very bleak. "No," Josef said straight away. "No, nothing like that. You're safe up here, mate. Don't you worry. Just keep that bloody door shut, all right? I'll be back with..." With what? "I'll be back as soon as I can."

With that, he left, racing out of the shop and into the bustle of London, surrounded by people who didn't know that Alex's life hung in the balance. He felt like screaming it as he ran, heedless of the occasional affronted 'I say!' as he pushed past people in his race for Monument Underground station.

Alex might be under his feet as he ran, he thought.

And then he stopped thinking about that because he couldn't bear to remember that he'd left him alone and frightened in the dark.

You fucking coward!

When he reached the station, a train was just rattling into the platform and Josef launched himself, breathless, into the third-class carriage. It wasn't full—there were plenty of seats—and he dropped down into one, bent forward, elbows on knees, catching his breath.

The train pulled away with agonising slowness, plunging back into the dark of the tube tunnels. Not far from Alex, he thought again, he might be able to hear the train. If he could hear anything, if he wasn't already—

He shot back to his feet, too agitated to sit, and paced towards the doors. In the mirror dark window, he caught a glimpse of himself—hatless and dishevelled. He didn't remember losing his cap; it must have come off somewhere in the tunnels. A woman, sitting close to the carriage door, stared at him in alarm, looking quickly away when he caught her eye. Glancing down at himself, he saw with surprise that one knee of his trousers was torn and bloody. As he looked, his knee began to sting, or at least he recognised its stinging. Same as his hands, and when he turned them over, he saw that they too were dirty and bloody where he'd skinned his palms. When he'd fallen, he supposed.

And then there was the gun tucked into the waistband of his trousers. Visible to all.

Good God, no wonder the woman looked alarmed.

Pulling his jacket tighter around himself, hiding the gun, he went and sat down again.

It was a half-hour journey to Kensington, and standing up wouldn't make the train go any faster. Arms wrapped around himself, he sat back, eyes closed and tried not to think.

By the time he reached Kensington, Josef ached all over. Given time to rest, his body had started screaming about every little injury. But never mind that, he had no time for aches and pains. Josef was off the train as soon as it pulled into the station and running up the steps to the street above.

The museum was open, visitors milling around its grand entrance as Josef took the steps two at a time and hurried into the entrance. Knowing how he must look, he didn't give the museum staff time to stop him, running across the vast hall and up the sweeping staircase.

There were more people in the ordinary corridor where Lottie's office was located too, and he kept his head down, ignoring their curious looks, as he hurried up to her door and rapped on it hard.

"Hold your horses!" Vi said, pulling open the door. Her expression changed the moment she saw him, eyebrows rising. "Lord above," she said and held the door wider, letting him in. Cautiously, she added, "Where's Lord B?"

"Hurt," Josef said as she shut the door behind him. "I couldn't get him out." He took the vial of blood from his coat pocket, holding it out to Violet. "Do what you must but do it fast. I'm going back for him."

Lottie stood at the table, examining a plate of sandwiches. She looked up at him, alarmed.

"Out of where? Where is he?"

"An abandoned Tube tunnel," Josef said. "He fell and broke his leg. The bone..." He shied away from the memory of Alex's injury. "Please, you've got to hurry. I need to get that potion to him before..." He couldn't finish the thought, but he didn't need to; Lottie's expression told him that she understood, probably better than he did.

"A potion ain't something you can rush," Violet said, exchanging a look with Lottie.

"I'll prepare things," Lottie said in response. "Can you get Mr Shepel cleaned up a little? That knee of his looks nasty."

"Never mind me," Josef said, "Alex needs—"

"I'll go as fast as I'm able," Lottie said, brooking no argument. "Vi, sort him out. I'll get everything else."

Josef felt like a fool sitting there while Violet dabbed his hands with iodine and, rolling up his trouser leg, bandaged his knee with professional speed. It felt wrong that he should be treated while Alex—

"I don't know how I'll get him out," he said, more to himself than Violet. "His leg is badly broken. I'd need a splint and dressing, but even then, he won't be able to put any weight on it. The bone's through the skin."

Violet looked up. "Which bone?"

"Tibia."

She grimaced. "No, he won't be walking on that. Were you a medic at the front?"

"Only a stretcher bearer. I've seen plenty of broken bodies, though, and patched a few up myself."

"Any chance of getting a stretcher down there?"

Josef shook his head. "Even if there was, how could I manage one on my own?"

"Oi, what do you think I am, chopped liver?"

"You?"

She sat back on her heels, affronted. "And why not? I'm good enough for the London Ambulance Service, aren't I?"

"Those tunnels are no place for a woman," Josef insisted. "And those things, they're dangerous and—"

From across the room, Lottie said, "Dangerous, yes. Driven by insatiable hunger, but essentially mindless." She smiled, a thin and rather dangerous expression. "Violet and I have subdued far stronger and more cunning creatures over the years."

"You... Have you?"

Her smile sharpened. "You've dipped your toe into a world you barely comprehend, Mr Shepel. We've lived in it our whole lives. Trust us."

Violet grunted, standing up. "Besides, Lord B's broken leg is the least of his worries. You won't have time to bring him back here."

"I wasn't planning to. I'll take the potion to him."

"Like cough medicine?" She shook her head, apparently amused by his naïveté.

His turn to feel affronted. "Why not?"

"Because Lottie will need to perform the enchantment."

He looked between the two of them. "The... what?"

"Magic spell," Lottie said, "in layman's terms. The potion must be enchanted. Otherwise it's simply an unpleasant mixture of inert ingredients. Enchantments only last a few moments, you understand."

He did not understand. Why should he? He didn't understand any of this. "I thought—if I'd known I couldn't just bring the potion back to him, I'd never have left him—" His voice cracked, and he stopped speaking.

"What would you have done?" Lottie said, not unkindly. "Slung him over one shoulder and run for it, fighting the ghoul with your free hand?"

He couldn't answer; his throat had seized up.

"You did the right thing. If you hadn't brought me this," she indicated the vial of blood, "all hope would have been lost. Now we must hope we reach him in time."

Thickly, Josef said, "He was already changing... He could see in the dark, and his eyes..." He shivered at the memory. "They had a... a blue cast to them."

Lotti's lips thinned. "Good."

"Good?"

"It means the ghoul will probably see him as one of their own. Not prey."

Josef's heart thumped with a lumpen kind of relief. "Really? God, that's what I hoped. They were ignoring him, going for me. That's why I—" His voice failed, and he had to clear his throat. "That's the only reason I left him."

"And all we can do now is work as fast as possible."

"I'll fetch the first aid kit," Violet said. "And we'll need a splint."

"We'll need light, too." Josef pulled out his useless hand torch. "This is dead, and you can't get batteries for love nor money these days."

But at that, Lottie smiled. "Light, I can provide. You should rest while you can, Mr Shepel." She gestured at the plate of sandwiches. "Eat something. We'll be off in under an hour."

Josef didn't want to eat. His stomach rebelled at the idea, but he'd learned at the front to eat whatever you could whenever you got the chance. He forced down a fishpaste sandwich, and then a second. They tasted of nothing, going claggy in his mouth, making it difficult to swallow.

Or maybe it was the guilt making it difficult to swallow, because how could he eat while Alex suffered?

If he'd brought Alex out, he'd be minutes away from a cure, not hours. Maybe he should have carried Alex out? He could have tried a fireman's lift, couldn't he? He'd seen men carry comrades on their backs from the firing line. Why hadn't he tried to do the same?

You fucking coward!

Alex's curse rang clear as a bell in his ears.

And perhaps he'd been right, too. Perhaps they'd all been right, everyone who'd called him a conchie coward, a yellow belly, a disgrace. Because dress it up how you liked, Josef had run away from the fight—be it for his country or for Alex. Oh, he had his reasons, and they were good reasons, but in the end maybe they'd just given him an excuse to run.

A better man would have carried Alex out or died trying. That's what Alex would have done.

"Chin up," Violet said, and he looked up to find her putting on her coat and hat, a large first aid satchel slung crosswise over her shoulder. "It might never happen."

"I'm afraid it already has," Josef said, rising too. His knee stung, and a deeper pain in his knee joint twinged—he'd stiffened up, sitting still for so long.

"No point thinking like that," Lottie said crisply. She too was dressed in her hat and coat and had a smaller bag slug across her body. "Today, we must all be jusqu'au boutistes, yes?"

She meant they should fight to the bitter end, accept no quarter from the enemy. Win at all costs.

And she was right. In this, at least, she was right.

"So," Violet said, eyebrows rising in query. "Where are we off to?"

Chapter Twenty-six

Afternoon was waning when they reached the corner of King William Street, and as Josef led them across the road towards W.R. Renshaw Ltd, a figure detached itself from the gathering shadows to intercept them.

Not a ghoul, but possibly worse.

"Mr Shepel," said Daljit Dutta. "Lady Charlotte—I suspected you might be mixed up in this."

"Mr Dutta." Lottie came to a halt next to Josef. "Charmed, as always."

Dutta smiled cooly. "Where is Lord Beaumont?"

There was a slight bulge beneath his coat which drew Josef's eye: a gun. Well, he had a gun too, and drew his own coat back far enough that Dutta could see he was armed.

Their eyes met, and Josef said, "We're on our way to help him. Don't get in our way."

"It's been over twelve hours since he was compromised." He glanced around at the people passing by. "It's too late to help him now."

Lottie said. "I treated his wound this morning to delay the progression of the infection. There's still time, though the longer we stand here in idle conversation, the more sand runs through the glass."

"For God's sake," Josef snapped. "Either help us or get out of the way."

Dutta's eyes widened, the only hint of feeling in his haughty features. "Saint has given his orders regarding Lord Beaumont, and I—"

"You what?" Josef said, stepping forward, close enough that he could see the subtle circles beneath Dutta's eyes, the lines of tension in his face. "You're going to be a good little soldier? Or are you going to help us save your friend?"

"Help you?"

"Alex is injured. He can't walk. We could use another man to help carry him out. Or to fight off pursuit."

Behind him, Violet snorted her disagreement.

Dutta's jaw set in dislike, and after a long look, he switched his attention from Josef to Lottie. "Is there a chance?"

"I'd hardly be here if there wasn't," she said. "Although I don't expect you to help us. Unlike Mr Shepel, I well know The Society's rules about associating with women of our ilk."

"Sod The Society's rules!" Josef cried. "And sod you, Dutta. Alex needs help. Now." With that, he pushed past the man. Or tried to, but Dutta grabbed his coat lapel and held him in place.

"You're taking an enormous risk with his life," Dutta hissed. "Bigger than you can possibly know. Even if he survives, don't think he will be the same man. And don't think he will thank you."

Josef wrenched himself free, shaken. "Alive is better than dead."

"For you, perhaps. But this has been about you from the start, hasn't it?"

"You don't know anything about it. Or me."

"I know what Alex—"

"Enough!" Violet pushed herself between them. "This bloody nonsense is why men never get anything done. Come on, Lottie, we might as well get to work while these two growl at each other."

Smiling in amusement, Lottie followed Violet towards the shop door.

Josef glared at Dutta; Dutta glared back. Then, with nothing resolved, they both turned and strode after the two women.

If possible, Mr Brooke looked more bemused than ever when Josef returned to his shop with Lottie, Violet, and Dutta in tow.

Well, the ladies weren't so much in tow as in the lead.

"Lady Charlotte Wolsey," Lottie said, standing primly before Mr Brookes. "Thank you for securing the door. We'll be going in now. Kindly close and lock it behind us."

Brooke looked from her to Josef and back again. "Beg your pardon, ma'am—"

"That's 'my lady' to you," Violet piped up.

Brooke's eyes widened. "Beg pardon, ma'am—uh, my lady—but it don't seem right for two ladies to be going in pursuit of the Hun."

"Maybe not," Lottie said, smiling. "But there's a war on, Mr Brooke. We all must play our part. And your part is to open that door. Now."

Maybe it was his imagination, but Josef thought he heard an odd little thrill of power in that word. Brooke must have done as well, because he turned immediately and began unlocking the door.

Dutta tutted, loudly. Lottie ignored him

When the ponderous door swung open, she glanced once into the dark stairwell before reaching into her bag and retrieving what looked to Josef like a Christmas tree bauble of delicate blue frosted glass. The sort they'd made on the Continent, before the war. Then she stepped boldly through the door, Violet on her heels. Josef glanced at Dutta, met the challenge in his eyes with one of his own, and followed.

"We'll need to get out again soon," he told Brooke. "Stay by the door until we're back, would you?"

Brooke looked uncertain. "Well, we close at five o'clock."

Josef stared. "You close?"

"I dare say ten pounds will make it worth your while to stay behind," Lottie said. "And to say nothing of this, to anyone."

Brooke's startled expression was comical. "Ah, yes, I dare say it would, your ladyship."

"My lady," Violet corrected again.

Lottie's smile was small and frosty. "Close the door, Mr Brooke."

He did so with alacrity, plunging them into abrupt and absolute darkness. Josef's breath caught, chest tightening in claustrophobic panic.

In the darkness, Lottie murmured something, a slippery word Josef couldn't quite catch, and then a soft blue light blossomed around them. It came, he saw in astonishment, from the Christmas bauble she held aloft.

"What on earth...?"

"Witch Light," Violet said with a wink. "I'd leave it at that, if I was you."

Josef fully intended to leave it at that—for now at least. "Come on," he said, hurrying down the stairs. "He's this way."

As the others followed, a stark electric beam joined Lottie's light. Josef glanced over his shoulder to see that Dutta held an army hand torch, the same as his own.

"I prefer manmade light," he said stiffly. "More reliable."

"Until the batteries run out."

He raised an eyebrow at Josef's, apparently, stupid comment. "I have spares."

Of course he bloody did.

Lottie said, "Times are changing, Mr Dutta. Soon, The Society will have no choice but to value the female sphere."

"Not in my lifetime," Dutta predicted, smugly in Josef's opinion.

"And that lifetime's going to be bloody short," Violet said, "if you don't stop yacking and start paying attention. Joe, I can see a door down there."

She was right. They were almost at the bottom of the stairs. "Be ready," he said. "One attacked me on the platform earlier. It's dead, but there could be others nearby."

Reluctantly, he pulled Alex's gun from his waistband as Dutta drew his own weapon. After rummaging in her large bag, Violet withdrew what looked very much like a filched policeman's truncheon. Lottie simply lifted her free hand, palm out, holding the Witch Light high in the other. She murmured something, and the light dimmed.

After a moment's hesitation, Dutta switched off his torch and slipped it into his coat pocket.

Josef gave them all a quick glance to make sure they were ready before he turned the handle, pushing open the door to the remains of King William Street station.

In the blue of the Witch Light, he saw that the body of the ghoul he'd killed was gone. "Someone's been here," he said, drawing to a halt near a splash of blood that marked the spot. "There was a body here, but it's gone."

Dutta said, "Are you certain it was dead?"

"I put a bullet through its head."

He considered that. "The ghoul do reclaim their dead."

"Reclaim them?" Josef asked faintly.

"Consume them," Dutta clarified. "Others are likely to be close."

For all that he'd seen at the front, Josef's stomach turned. If Alex didn't make it, the thought that his body might be...

But no, he wouldn't let that happen. He'd save him from that, at the very least. Whatever happened in the next few hours, Josef wouldn't leave these tunnels without Alex. Even if that meant hauling his body out over one shoulder.

That settled, he felt marginally better. "Come on," he said, moving down the platform. "Watch your footing. Some of the platform has given way."

"This is remarkably unnerving," Lottie said, sounding gleeful as she looked about. "I remember using this station as a child. My father brought me when it first opened—it was the first electrical railway. But to see it like this..." She shivered, clearly delighted. "Abandoned places have such a powerful presence, don't you find?"

Dutta said, "I'm more concerned with the presence of the ghoul."

Which, against his will, made Josef smile.

"The tunnel divides at the end of the platform," he explained softly. "We'll take the leftmost branch. It goes deeper, so it's a bugger of a descent." He glanced uncertainly at the women's footwear. "And rough going."

"He's worrying we're going to sprain an ankle," Violet said. It was too dark to see whether she rolled her eyes, but the expression was very clearly in her tone.

"Don't worry," Dutta said, with what might have been a laugh. "They're not your typical ladies; they're quite capable of looking after themselves."

"Whatever you may think of 'typical ladies'," Lottie said crisply, "I can assure you that most of us are capable of looking after ourselves."

"And looking after lazy husbands, brothers, and fathers while we're at it," Violet added, with vehemence. "We're only here because you lot buggered it up, aren't we?"

Josef didn't think that was fair, but then Dutta said, "You can't blame The Society for this. It's the war causing the trouble."

"Didn't say I blamed The Society."

"Who started the war?" Lottie added. "And who's keeping it going? Certainly not women."

Lottie, Josef thought, would get on rather well with May. Perhaps, once all this was over, he'd introduce them. For now, though, he had other things to think about.

"Leave the politics for later," he said, because they'd reached the end of the platform. "It's down here." He jumped onto the empty track bed and didn't dare offer a hand to Violet or Lottie as they scrambled down after him. Not that they needed any help, despite the inconvenience of long skirts.

Violet sniffed. "I can smell 'em," she said quietly. "Lottie?"

Lady Charlotte nodded. "Yes. I don't think they're far. Nightfall will bring them out; they hunt at night."

Another chilling thought.

Although the Witch Light wasn't as bright as a hand torch, its light diffused further, giving Josef a wider look at the tunnel as they started down towards the wall that blocked it off. The grey iron walls gleamed wetly, the tunnel itself not much wider than a train carriage, and from the ceiling he saw the stubby start of stalactites where the water drip, drip, dripped.

"What's that?" Violet asked, pointing to something on the ground close to the wall blocking the tunnel.

Josef's heart turned over uncomfortably when he recognised Alex's hat. He must have lost it, or left it behind, when they'd scrambled through the hole made by the ghoul. Crouching, he picked it up and turned it over in his hands. Expensive, well made. Very Alex. "We have to get through there," Josef said, standing. He didn't let go of the hat.

Dutta made a disapproving noise, crouching down to peer through the hole. "Risky," he said, as if they had a choice. "I'll go first." He glanced up at Josef and, after a slight pause, handed him his hand torch. "Hold this would you? Shine it through. I'd rather see what I'm getting into."

Between Alex's hat and his gun, Josef was running out of hands, so he settled the hat on his head to take the torch. Stupid, perhaps, but he wasn't leaving that hat behind.

When he shone the beam through the hole, Dutta poked his head through. "It looks clear," he said, doubtfully. "Clear enough." Then, keeping his gun ready, he slipped through the hole and reached back for the torch.

The rest of them followed, Josef taking the lead. His excitement was growing, fear and anticipation mingling queasily. Not far to the door and the passage where he'd left Alex.

How long had it been? Less than three hours. He'd be all right. There was still time. There had to be because any other outcome was... Well, he couldn't think about another outcome.

The door, when he found it, stood open. And this time, there was no light.

Wetting his dry mouth, heart thumping, Josef tried to remember whether he'd closed it behind him as he'd fled. Maybe he hadn't? Maybe he'd left it just like this.

Dutta flashed his torch along the corridor, nose flaring in disgust. Josef didn't blame him; the ghoul stench was powerful.

"Stay close," Violet murmured to Lottie.

Lottie's response was softer still. "You too."

Perhaps Dutta really was a Subadar, or perhaps it was simply his aristocratic assumption of authority, but he went first through the door. Josef didn't object. If toffs thought they had an inborn obligation to lead their men into the firing line, he was happy to let them do it. Especially happy in Dutta's case, who he didn't trust further than he could spit.

Lottie and Vi followed, side by side, and Josef brought up the rear. He kept one eye on the door behind them, belatedly wondering whether it would have been better to leave Dutta behind to guard their escape. He wasn't about to offer to stay behind, though; he had to be the one to find Alex. He wasn't leaving that to anyone else.

As they walked, the stench worsened. Josef's grip on the gun grew clammy, his stomach roiling with fear and disgust and a clinging, desperate hope that they'd find Alex. That he'd be exactly where Josef had left him...

You fucking coward!

...and that he'd be fine. Well, no worse at least. Alive and still himself.

"Alex?" he called softly. Surely, they were close now. "Alex?"

Dutta shushed him.

No other sound came back to him save the pounding of his own heart, hard as a sledgehammer against his ribs.

Dutta stopped suddenly, his flashlight playing over something discarded on the ground. A man's leg.

Violet swore creatively. Josef said, "It's not Alex. That was—it was here before."

He looked around, increasingly desperate in the soft glow of the Witch Light. "He should be here."

"This is where you left him?" Lottie asked.

He nodded, pointing. "Against that wall..."

He felt sick, suddenly, short of air. Alex was gone.

Dutta said, "There's a door here."

That's right. That led to the stairs Alex had tumbled down with the ghoul. The door was closed now, but Alex vividly remembered the sound of it opening as he fled...

Dutta leaned closer to it, listening, one hand up to silence the rest of them.

And then Josef heard it too, a wet slavering sound. Something—someone—eating.

God help me, I only feel...hunger.

Without thought, Josef reached for the door. Dutta grabbed his shoulder, stopping him. Silently, he raised his gun, readying himself, before nodding to Josef. He pulled on the door, wrenching it open on screeching hinges. Something crouched in the stairwell, bent over. When it lifted its head, gore dripped from its mouth, blue eyes like lamps in the dark.

Josef had half a second to process *not Alex* before the ghoul launched itself at Dutta. The gun fired, the bullet ricocheting into the stairwell but missing the ghoul, and the creature bore Dutta backwards and down. The Witch Light flared in Lottie's hand, suddenly, shockingly white, making the ghoul howl and rear back from Dutta. Violet swung her truncheon at the creature's head and sent it staggering sideways, time enough for Dutta to spring back to his feet. The ghoul howled again, a wet, hungry furious sound.

And Josef shot it between the eyes.

It crumpled and fell, and in the ringing silence, he was aware of everyone's eyes on him. Well, what did they think? The conchie didn't know how to fire a gun?

"Good shot," Dutta said, as if they were on a fucking grouse hunt.

Josef just said, "What was it eating?"

He couldn't bear to look, his heart a lead lump in his chest. The Witch Light had faded back to its soft purple, but it was still bright enough to see by. He heard someone turn back to the door, and then Violet said, "It's part of an arm. Can't say whose."

The tension in the pit of Josef's stomach tightened further, and he nodded. "At the top of the stairs, there's another door. I think that's where they are. We heard them through the door."

"Your light was a clever trick," Dutta told Lottie, sounding a little grudging. "Do that when we go through the next door, would you?"

"Yes, I had intended to." She exchanged a wry look with Violet. "Witch Light blinds them temporarily. Didn't you know that?"

Dutta didn't answer. He said, "We don't know how many we'll be facing. If Beaumont is up there, we're going to have to grab him fast and pull him out."

"He can't walk," Josef reminded them.

Lottie said, "And by now, he may well not be...quite himself. He may resist."

Josef closed his eyes. "I'll get him," he said, "if you lot can hold them off. I'll carry him out."

Like I should have done before.

Dutta frowned. "Beaumont is a large man, and you—"

"I can do it."

"We'll need to treat him as soon as possible," Lottie added. "Right there, if we can, though it will take a few moments to muster the enchantment."

"At least get a door shut between you and them first," Violet told her. To Josef and Dutta, she added, "She can't burn the Witch Light and cast an enchantment at the same time."

Which made sense to Josef. "Right," he said. "Me and Dutta get him through the door, then hold it while you two get to work." He looked at Dutta, expecting him to baulk at Josef giving orders. Dutta only nodded, though.

"Then let's get to it."

They stole quietly, quickly to the top of the stairs. Blood streaked the steps, as it had done last time Josef was there.

More blood? He couldn't tell. Didn't want to think about it. Just like he didn't want to think about how Alex could have climbed these stairs, or how he might have been dragged up instead, or whether he was still alive...

He didn't want to think about it, and yet it was all he could think about as they gathered around the door at the top of the stairs. Sounds bled through it, snarls, strange howls, shuffling movement. Josef felt sick with fear and desperation. He didn't want to go through that door, but the thought that Alex might be on the other side, alone with those monsters, made him want to rip it from its bloody hinges.

"Right," Dutta said grimly. "On three. One, two..."

Chapter Twenty-seven

"Three!"

They burst through the door in a blaze of Witch Light, so bright even Josef had to squint. Howls rose around them, and a desperate snarling, scrabbling. The space beyond the door may once have been used for storage, but it had obviously been abandoned for years. Pipes ran across its ceiling, some looking new, the walls Victorian brickwork. The floor...? God only knew, because it was covered now in vile, stinking rags. The whole place stank like a charnel house.

Or a dressing station.

Keeping the Witch Light so bright seemed to be costing Lottie because her face looked pinched, and Violet had one hand on her elbow, helping her keep the light aloft. It was working, though, making the ghouls cower, faces covered. But Josef guessed they didn't have much time.

Still squinting, he scanned the scabrous rags and writhing shapes of the ghouls in search of the only face he wanted to see. And dreaded seeing.

The glint of Witch Light on black hair drew his eye to a body slumped against the far wall.

Fear squeezed his voice down to a scratch. "There!" He tried again. "There. He's there!"

Two ghouls were near him, crouched and snarling, eyes hidden by their arms. Josef lifted the gun, but they were so close to Alex that he didn't dare fire. The light was dimming, though, Lottie struggling.

"Hurry," Violet snapped.

Turning the gun in his hands, holding the barrel, Josef waded in. "Get away from him!" he shouted, swinging the grip of the gun at the closest ghoul. It hissed at him through rotting teeth, staring around blindly. Josef swung the pistol in a savage arc, connecting with its head and sending the creature staggering sideways, away from Alex. Desperation must have given him strength. He'd heard of such things happening at the front.

But as the light dimmed further, the ghouls began to grow braver. He saw movement from the corner of his eye, heard the crack of a gunshot ricochet around the small room, but didn't have time to look. All his focus now was on Alex. He lay sprawled against the wall, eyes closed, his broken leg out in front of him. Unconscious? God in heaven, he hoped so.

Josef fell to his knees at Alex's side, shaking his shoulder. "Alex? Alex, wake up."

"Just grab him," Dutta yelled. He sounded breathless, pressed. "Now!"

Shoving the gun into his waistband, Josef scrambled up, getting his hands under Alex's arms. He was heavy, a dead weight, but Josef had spent months manhandling dead weights at the front. Grunting, he pulled Alex away from the wall and began to drag him towards the door. His head lolled back alarmingly; Josef didn't stop.

Movement in the growing shadows caught his eye, more graveyard-blue eyes staring at him from the dark. Crouched and poised. And then with a yell, Violet leaped in front of him, swinging her truncheon, warding them off. Dutta fired again, and one of the creatures dropped. As he reached the door, the Witch Light flared once more, bright and white, sending the remaining ghouls howling into the shadows long enough for him to pull Alex through the door. Lottie and Violet followed. Then came three measured gunshots before Dutta backed out of the room, slamming the door shut and leaning against it.

Violet gasped, "Lottie!" And everything went dark.

Crouching, Josef lowered Alex to the floor. "What happened? Is she all right?"

"I'm fine," Lottie said, sounding exhausted. "Don't fuss."

And then the electric light of Dutta's hand torch split the dark. He still stood with his back to the door, bracing it. Lottie sat on the floor next to Josef, Violet crouching at her side.

"She's exhausted," Violet said, with enough accusation in her voice to make it clear who she blamed for that.

"Is he alive?" Dutta said, cool and crisp as ever.

Josef put his hand to Alex's throat, feeling for a pulse. Something else he'd learned in Ypres. Alex's skin felt cool and clammy under his fingers, but after a nightmare couple of seconds, he found a faint, fluttering pulse. His own heart slammed into his ribs in relief. "Yes," he said over his shoulder. "Yes, he's alive."

Behind him, he heard a rustle of skirts as Lottie climbed to her feet. "Vi," she said, a little wobble in her voice, "see to his leg. I'll prepare the enchantment."

Violet began what sounded like a protest but swallowed whatever she was going to say. Instead, she began rummaging through her first aid bag. Josef let them get on with it, his attention fixed on Alex's face.

"Alex," he said gently, tapping his cheek. "Wake up. Come on, open your eyes." He looked like himself, at least, though his skin was deathly white.

"He'll need to swallow this," Lottie said. She knelt on the other side of Alex, holding a stoppered glass vial of dark liquid. "You'll have to sit him up."

Nodding, Josef scooted behind Alex and hauled him up so that he was resting against Josef's chest. He held him there, arms wrapped around Alex, pinning his arms to his sides.

Lottie noticed that with a nod. Violet, meanwhile, was tying off a professional-looking dressing on Alex's leg.

"You need to hurry," Dutta said tensely. When Josef looked over, he saw that Dutta was pressing hard against the door, which jumped under the assault from the other side. Violet scrambled up and went to join him, adding her weight to the door.

"Tip his head back," Lottie said. "And be ready."

Then she bent her head and began to murmur soft, slippery, impossible-to-grasp words, one hand holding the vial and her other hovering over it. For long seconds nothing happened, save the dull thuds on the door and Dutta and Violet's answering grunts of effort.

But then the vial began to glow, a deep iridescent thread of amethyst swirling through the liquid, growing brighter. Lottie looked up, and for a moment, Josef saw that same opalescent glow in her eyes. "Now," she said, lifting the vial.

Josef tipped back Alex's head, prizing open his jaw, and Lottie poured the potion—no other word for it—down his throat. She clamped his mouth shut, and Alex immediately began to struggle.

"Hold him still!"

Josef held on for dear life as Alex bucked and thrashed in his arms, purple liquid seeping from between his lips. Lottie had both hands on his jaw, holding his mouth shut until Alex convulsed one more time and began to cough.

Lottie fell back, triumphant. "He's swallowed it!"

"How long until it works?" Josef asked, still holding Alex, though his convulsions were weakening.

"Fully? Several hours. But we should know if it's worked sooner than that."

"We can't hold the door much longer," Dutta warned. "You're going to have to move. I'll hold them back as long as I can."

Lottie nodded, holding onto the wall as she slowly rose to her feet. She was exhausted. Violet would need to help her, which meant Josef had to carry Alex alone.

"Shepel," Dutta said, holding out one hand. "Your gun."

For a moment he hesitated, but if he was carrying Alex, he wouldn't be able to use it, and Dutta could use all the help he could get covering their retreat. With a nod, he pulled it free of his waistband and slid it across the floor to Dutta.

Then, squirming out from behind Alex, he lowered him to the ground. Purple liquid stained his lips; his eyes were half-lidded now, that vile cold blue seeping out from beneath his lids.

God, let us have been in time, he prayed. Please.

He'd been trained to use a fireman's lift, so he hurriedly rolled Alex onto his stomach and got his arms under Alex's armpits, hauling him almost upright, before wedging one leg between Alex's, hauling one arm over his shoulder and lifting him. He staggered for a moment, then caught his balance, settling Alex firmly across his shoulders.

"All right," he said. "Let's go."

It was agonisingly slow progress getting down the stairs, terrified with every step that he'd lose his footing and kill them both in the fall. Violet and Lottie came next, Violet with a supportive arm around Lottie's waist and Lottie holding the Witch Light aloft once more. Its glow was dim now, barely enough to light their way.

Behind them, he heard two gunshots in quick succession, then a third followed by the sounds of a scuffle. Dutta was doing what he could; Josef prayed it would be enough.

Josef's legs burned by the time he reached the bottom of the stairs, but his heart thumped in relief as he carried Alex through the door and into the corridor beyond. He was stirring, though, starting to move, making it harder for Josef to hold him. "Lie still," he snapped, readjusting his grip. "I've got you."

Violet and Lottie appeared next, Lottie seeming somewhat recovered. The Witch Light burned brighter, at least.

"Keep going," she told Josef. "We'll try to seal this door once Mr Dutta is through."

Another gunshot came from the stairwell, as if in answer.

Josef kept moving, walking as fast as he could under the weight of Alex's body. He'd got perhaps halfway along the corridor before Alex woke up properly. He felt the moment Alex came to awareness, limbs jerking in panicked confusion as he started to fight against Josef's grip.

"Alex, stop!" Josef shouted, but it was no good—he couldn't hold him. He fell to his knees, letting Alex slide backwards off his shoulders, trying to protect his splinted leg from a bigger fall.

Alex cried out in pain, and Josef twisted around, getting hold of his shoulders, trying to hold him still. "Alex, it's me. You're all right."

They were deep in the shadows, far from Lottie's light, but it was bright enough that he could make out Alex's pale features. And he almost cried, tears bulking his throat, at the sight of Alex's eyes—wide, afraid, and dark.

Devoid of the sepulchral blue.

"Alex?" he said thickly, fingers tightening on his shoulders.

Alex blinked, staring. In a rough, rasping voice, he said, "You're wearing my hat."

Tears did fall then, through Josef's smile. "You dropped it. I thought you'd want it back."

Back along the corridor came the sound of shouting, the door slamming. More shouting and scuffling. The Witch Light flared, dimming as Lottie shouted a few unintelligible words.

Josef said, "We need to move. I can carry you."

Woozily, Alex tried to sit up. Josef helped him. "I can walk," Alex said. Then, "Can't I?"

"Not really. You've broken your leg."

"Ah."

Josef's heart did another elated cartwheel at that little 'Ah' because it was so very Alex. So very human.

"Even so, I'd rather not be hauled about like a sack of potatoes," he said. "Help me up."

Reluctantly, Josef did, one eye on the others as he pulled Alex upright. They were hurrying towards him, the Witch Light bobbing and growing brighter. Behind them, a faint violet haze hovered over the closed door. No ghoul came through it.

When Josef looked back at Alex, he found they were standing face to face, hands still joined, Alex watching him intently. Then, very quietly, he said, "You came back."

Josef's throat closed again. "Told you I would."

Alex squeezed his hands, hard, but there was no time for more because the others had reached them.

"Lord Beaumont," Lottie said, smiling. "You look better."

Alex's eyebrows hit his hairline. "Lottie? What on earth—?"

"No time for that now," she said crisply.

Then Dutta joined them. He had one gun in his hand, the other tucked into the waistband of his trousers. "Beaumont," he said, as though they were meeting in Hyde Park.

Josef felt Alex stiffen in alarm. "What are you doing here?"

After a pause, Dutta said, "Saving your life, it appears." Another silence followed, sharp as a blade. Then he said, "That enchantment won't hold them for long. I suggest we make a run for it."

"Then help me with him," Josef said, looping one of Alex's arms over his shoulder and sliding his arm around Alex's waist. It felt good to have his warm body close, to feel the play of Alex's muscles as he moved, and Josef had to struggle to keep his relief from showing.

Dutta hesitated, but then nodded and came to support Alex's other side.

The women took the lead, Witch Light held high, and the three of them followed. It was faster this way, if more ungainly, with him and Dutta supporting Alex between them. They struggled along in silence for a few minutes until, in a low voice, Alex whispered, "The Society is involved with this?" He sounded doubtful.

Dutta said, "Not exactly."

"Meaning what?"

"Let's just concentrate on getting out in one piece, shall we?"

Josef agreed. Alex was breathing heavily, the effort of hobbling along costing him too much. "Save your breath for walking," he said. "We can talk later."

Alex pursed his lips and didn't answer.

From behind them came a dull thud, then another, as the ghoul tried to get through the door at the bottom of the stairs. For now, whatever Lottie had done to it seemed to be holding, and ahead Josef could see the door which would lead them back into the abandoned train tunnel and from there to King William Street station. The door stood ajar, just as they'd left it. Thank God.

"Perhaps I could try another enchantment?" Lottie suggested from up ahead. "Seal this door, too."

"Oh, give over," Vi said crossly. "You can't hardly walk straight, let alone cast an enchantment. We'll have to wedge this one shut."

It sounded like a good idea. There was plenty of debris in the tunnel that they could use, left over from where the tracks had been removed. All they needed was a little time to get Alex back to the old station, up the stairs—he grimaced at the thought of that spiral staircase—and out into the daylight.

If it was still daylight.

"Not far now," he told Alex when they reached the door. Lottie stopped to light the way while Violet pulled the door wider to let them pass. It was too narrow to fit three abreast, though, so Dutta slipped free and went ahead, leaving Josef to support Alex as they hobbled through the doorway and down onto the track bed.

Alex cursed softly as his leg was jostled, and Josef winced. "Sorry," he murmured, tightening his grip, trying to take more of the man's weight.

"Never be sorry," Alex whispered back, close enough that Josef could feel the warmth of his breath against his ear. He felt weak again with relief that Alex was here, still alive and himself.

Thank God. Thank you, God!

Behind them, Lottie and Violet stepped down and pulled the door shut behind them. In the hazy pool of Witch Light, Josef scanned the ground near his feet for something to use to brace the door. He spied a large piece of concrete and said, "How about—?"

Light flared from all angles, blinding electric torch beams slicing through the dark. And hiding behind them in the shadows gleamed blank saucer-like eyes and weird, distorted faces. Josef staggered back in fright, Alex swaying and grabbing onto him to keep his balance.

What the fuck was this?

Then, from the light stepped a slight, familiar figure. Neat, orderly, and pointing a gun. "We'll take him from here, Mr Shepel."

The creatures were all holding guns on them, Josef realised; he recognised their dull gunmetal gleam. A dozen of them, standing in an arc around the door. Waiting.

His gun, of course, was in Dutta's possession. Dutta, who walked calmly to stand at the newcomer's side. Fucking traitor.

"Saint," Alex said, struggling to stand upright, almost to attention.

"You disobeyed orders, Lord Beaumont."

"Orders to die!" Josef spat. "But now he's cured, so you can shove your orders up your—"

"Cured?" Saint scoffed. "You're talking about witchcraft." The word dripped with disdain. More than disdain, revulsion.

"I'm talking about—"

"Might I suggest," interrupted Lottie, "that you secure this door before you bicker? There are several rather angry ghouls on our heels."

Saint ignored her entirely, although he turned and murmured something to one of the creatures behind him. On a silent command, half of them detached themselves from the group and headed towards the door. Which was when, with sickening understanding, Josef realised that they weren't creatures at all but men. Men wearing gas masks, and laden with gas bombs.

"The ghoul are no longer your concern," Saint said, as his men filed through the door and closed it behind them.

"What are they going to do?" Josef asked in horror.

Saint stepped closer, small and harsh in the strange light. "You've been warned before, and this is your final warning. Stay away from that which you don't understand and about which you have no business knowing."

"No business knowing?" Josef laughed, incredulously. "You don't think this"—he gestured around them—"is my business? It's everyone's business!"

"Of course it isn't." Saint looked genuinely baffled. "It is Society business."

"Yeah? Well, we'll see about that when I tell the whole fucking world what's going on down here."

At his side, he felt Alex flinch and glanced over to see him shaking his head in warning.

"I doubt even your little newspaper would publish such an...outlandish story," said Saint. "And if it did, who would take it seriously? You'd be a laughingstock—or worse. They'd call you a shell shock case."

There was too much truth in that for comfort. Nonetheless, Josef said, "We'll see about that, won't we? Don't forget—I still have a photograph."

"Josef, stop," Alex hissed. "Please..."

Saint levelled an accusing finger, his face dark in the shadows. "Listen to me, Shepel. Thus far, I have been forbearing—at Lord Beaumont's request. But my patience has surpassed its limits. And so, I warn you: if you come to my notice again, it will be for the last time." Then, to Alex, he snapped, "You're with me. Now."

"What?" Josef held Alex tighter. "Fuck off. He can't walk. He's broken his leg."

Dutta said, "I'll help him." He lifted his weapon, aiming it lazily at Josef. "Step back, Mr Shepel."

Josef could see Alex's fucking gun tucked into Dutta's belt. The bastard must have known this was coming; it must have been the plan all along. And Josef had handed over Alex's weapon like a bloody idiot. Well, fuck Dutta. Josef wasn't letting Alex go. Not this time. "You can't just abduct him. Who the bloody hell do you people think you are? Even the government can't—"

But Alex pulled away from him. "It's all right," he said stiffly, loud enough for Saint to hear. "Stand down, Mr Shepel. And thank you for your assistance."

Josef stared. Thank you for your assistance?

Their eyes met, Alex's dark and human in the crisscross of torch beams. Pained. "I'll be all right," he said softly. "Don't worry."

"I don't trust them."

Alex gave a small, heartbreaking smile. "Then for God's sake, don't give them a reason to kill you."

That gave him pause, but of course, Alex was right. Saint wouldn't think twice before shoving Josef into that tunnel with the fucking gas bombs. Who would know? Another dead prole.

He felt a hand on his arm and jumped, but it was only Violet. She didn't speak, but her face echoed Alex's warning. They were outgunned, their position was precarious, and one way or another, Josef was going to lose Alex. If not to death, then to The Society.

Perhaps that had been inevitable from the start.

Reluctantly, with a spear of pain lodged in his breastbone, Josef let Alex go. Let Dutta and one of the other gas-masked men escort him along the tunnel like a prisoner. Alex didn't look back.

And then, from behind the door, the screaming started.

Chapter Twenty-eight

London, February 1918 – three months later

On the wall of May's office, behind her desk, she'd hung a framed copy of the front page of the Clarion. The one on which she'd printed a photograph, Josef's photograph of Sykes. The image which had brought the police down on them, closed the paper, and lost them their patron in Countess Sackville.

He stared at it now, as he waited for May to return from her meeting. Even in the black-and-white image, he recognised the faint light of a ghoul in the boy's dying eyes. The headline read End the Slaughter, and beneath it was Josef's painstaking description of the forward dressing station in Ypres where Sykes had died. Or, rather, not died.

He couldn't write about that, of course. Hard enough to make people see the truth about the war. Impossible to explain that the horror of the battlefield had followed him home, had crept through the city's tunnels and sewers. That men destroyed by war and contorted into monsters had been gassed beneath the streets of London.

Even so, he'd been proud of those words and that photograph. Publishing them not in a pamphlet but in the Clarion had felt like a small triumph in the dark days after losing Alex.

Not that it had done any good; the war still raged, and men still died. Well, what had he imagined? The country had been sending its men and boys to the slaughter for four long years. People were used to it, now. Maybe it would never end.

The door to May's office rattled open, and he turned in his seat as she entered. He could tell from the glint in her eye that the meeting had gone well. "So?" he said, smiling.

"Lady Charlotte is a diamond. We're back in business."

Josef grinned. He'd known May and Lottie would get on like a house on fire, although he hadn't been certain Lottie would have the appetite for a radical newspaper.

"The fight isn't over for women's suffrage," May was saying as she took off her hat and dropped into the chair behind her desk. "But now we've got a foot in the door it's even more important that we educate and shape the female vote. And the working-class vote, too."

It had only been two weeks since the Representation of the People Act had passed, expanding voting rights to working-class men like Josef and to some women—those over 30 who met the property qualification. Wealthy women, in other words. Still, it was a start.

And it was exciting.

Now that the men who were fighting at the front could vote, there was a chance that things could change. He had to believe that; he had to have hope for the future. Even if, on a personal level, the future had felt rather bleak since the day he'd emerged from King William Street station to see Alex loaded into the back of a black, unmarked ambulance and taken straight to Belgrave Square.

He only knew Alex was still alive because Lottie had told him so. She'd spoken briefly to Dutta, at a society event. That was society with a small 's', not The Society. Lottie was no more welcome there than Josef, and he'd tried—five times—to get in and see Alex.

Apparently, Lord Beaumont was not at home to Mr Shepel.

Maybe it was Saint keeping Josef out, but he feared the choice was Alex's. He was still haunted by that terrible moment in the tunnels when he'd refused to put a bullet in Alex's head, when he'd broken his promise and left him alone in the dark.

You fucking coward!

That betrayal, he feared, was the reason Alex refused to see him. Whatever the reason, though, the result was the same—their friendship was over. Realistically, he knew that had been inevitable from the start. Even so, he felt the loss. He felt the ache of it in his chest every day.

It grieved him.

"Well?" May said, and he had the awkward feeling she'd been waiting for an answer. "Are you in, Joe?"

"You know I am," he said. "I wouldn't be here otherwise."

She flashed a grin. "All right, then. First off, we need a new title for the paper—something forward-looking. What do you think of The People's Tribune? Or the Voter's Vanguard...?"

They discussed that for a while, eventually settling on a couple of options to put to Lottie. There was some work to do to design the look of the new paper, but essentially it would be the Daily Clarion under a different name, and so soon they fell into talking about stories to cover, and that led them back to the war.

"We can't tackle it head-on," May said. She indicated the framed front page behind her. "I'm proud of that piece. I think it had to be said, but..."

"But it hasn't changed anyone's mind," Josef finished. "I know. I thought if people saw the truth..."

May looked sympathetic. "I think some truths are too hard to believe, even when you see them with your own eyes. People aren't ready for it yet."

He understood that in a way May couldn't imagine. How long had it taken him to believe the incredible truth Alex had told him? It was still difficult to believe. He laughed, or tried to, but it sounded more bitter than amused. "The things I could tell people, if they'd only listen."

Ghouls, witches and who knew what else? The story of a lifetime at his fingertips, but not even May would believe that one.

She cocked her head, studying him. "You know, sometimes it's easier for people to hear the truth when they think it's fiction." She shrugged at whatever she saw in his expression. "A story about the trials and tribulations of a conchie working as a stretcher bearer, perhaps?"

Josef shook his head. "I'm no writer."

"You're not bad." She grinned. "Besides, there's no such thing as a good writer—only a good editor. And that's me."

"I don't know. I'm a photographer. I prefer to let my photographs do the talking." It was a thought, though. And his first thought was of a story about the ghouls living in the disused Underground tunnels...

Saint would not be happy. That idea should worry him, but in fact it fired him up. Saint thought he had all the power, that he could snatch Alex away and silence Josef. Well, sod that. Maybe there was another way for Josef to speak?

If he dared.

Rising, he said, "I'm happy for you, May. I'm glad Lady Charlotte could help and that you're back in business. The country needs your voice more than ever."

"Our voice," she corrected. "Like I said, Lady C is a diamond but—oh, wait a moment." She rummaged in her bag. "Here, this is for you."

She held out a small envelope, his name written on the front. Instantly, his heart leaped at the idea it could be from Alex, but it wasn't his hand. Frowning, he took the envelope from May. "What is it?"

She raised her brows. "I'm no expert, but it looks like a letter."

"Very amusing." He studied it for a moment, then shoved it into his pocket. "Thanks."

May's expression sharpened into keen interest. God knew what she thought was in the letter—a love note probably—but he didn't want to find out with an audience. Not one as quick as May.

Nonetheless, the note burned a hole in his pocket all the way back to the Underground and by the time he'd found a seat in the carriage, it had become impossible to wait any longer. Pulling the envelope out, he quickly tore it open.

It wasn't a note from Alex. Simply a few lines in the efficient hand of someone who wrote a great deal—such as an academic.

Dear Mr Shepel, Our friend has finally been released. He's at home, terribly morose and rather immobile thanks to his leg, which is healing but not yet usable. Naturally, he believes he's unfit for company, but I rather think the opposite is true. If asked, he'll refuse to see you, so I suggest not asking. Yours in friendship, Lady Charlotte Wolsey.

Released? He suspected that was exactly the right word. It had looked like nothing more than an arrest that evening on King William Street. Had they punished Alex in other ways, too? God only knew what The Society might do; they clearly believed themselves above the law.

Anger, relief, and something he could only call excitement swelled his heart. Did he want to see Alex? Of course he bloody did. But he was afraid. Not of Saint, not of any consequences in that direction, but of Alex. Of rejection.

Truth was, he'd come to feel something for the man. More than something, if he was being honest. And why shouldn't he feel more? Alex had saved his life, and he'd saved Alex's. That alone would have forged a bond difficult to break, even without the...other things.

And the other things lived as bright memories beneath his skin. Each tender touch and forbidden caress more precious for being fleeting. For being secret, and theirs alone.

If he saw Alex again and was dismissed, those memories would tarnish and spoil. But that was the argument of a man who'd choose blissful ignorance over painful truth, and Josef was nothing if not an advocate for the truth.

Which meant his decision was made.

Chapter Twenty-nine

Josef was startled, although not surprised, to find Daljeet Dutta leaning casually against the looming bulk of Queen Anne's Mansion Flats, smoking a cigarette. Dutta's bright red turban gave a splash of colour to the grey February morning and suggested he wasn't trying to be inconspicuous.

Well, neither was Josef. Shoulders back, he headed straight for the stairs leading up to the entrance. Dutta moved easily to intercept. "Shepel," he said cordially. "I hoped I might run into you."

Josef considered punching him in the face, rejected the idea, and said, "Can't say I feel the same."

"I imagine not." Dutta took a drag on his gasper, blew out an elegant stream of smoke, and said, "Nevertheless, I want to warn you."

"Oh, fuck off," Josef said, folding his arms. "I'm not afraid of you, or your bloody Society. Tell Saint to shove his warning where the sun don't shine."

Dutta's eyebrows rose. "I'm not here on behalf of The Society." In a different voice, he said, "I'm here as a friend."

"You're not my friend."

"No. I am Alex's friend, however."

"All evidence to the contrary."

Dutta's eyelids fluttered, the only sign of an emotional reaction. "You may think what you wish, but I came here to warn you that Alex is... not what he was." His expression darkened. "You should prepare yourself."

Despite his distrust of Dutta, Josef's heart gave an unpleasant kick. "Meaning what?"

"Meaning that, if you're going to run scared, it would be better if you left him alone."

Josef's cheeks heated. "I'm not going to run scared. I'm no coward."

"No?" Dutta regarded him cooly, dropped his cigarette stub on the pavement, and ground it out with the toe of his shoe. "I told him from the outset that you'd be trouble, and I was right. This is where you've brought him. Remember that, when you go inside."

"Where I've brought him?" Josef hissed. "If it was up to you, he'd be dead."

"True. Judge for yourself which of us is the better friend."

With that he turned and stalked away, leaving Josef to watch him go with a sickening lurch in the pit of his stomach. He glanced up at the faceless windows of the mansion flats, and his scalp prickled. What the hell was he going to find inside?

Well, there was only one way to find out.

Bracing his shoulders, Josef headed up the steps. As he'd expected, the doorman took one look at him and stepped forward. "Tradesman's entrance is to the side, mate."

"And I'll be sure to tell any tradesmen I meet," Josef said with a smile. "But I'm here to see Lord Alexander Beaumont. I've an appointment at twelve o'clock. For luncheon."

The doorman looked sceptical.

Fishing in his pocket, Josef said, "I know the way," and slipped the man half a crown. "No need to bother the concierge. He looks busy."

With that, he walked quickly into the foyer and headed straight for the lift. Happily, the concierge was indeed busy placating a tall woman wearing an enormous hat and unfashionably long skirts and carrying a small dog tucked under one arm. Her strident demands for assistance with her luggage echoed around the lobby.

Stepping smartly into the hydraulic lift, Josef pulled the lever and let it whisk him up to the fourth floor. The last time he'd been here it had been dark, but this morning, the February light, still wintery but with a hint of spring strength, spilled into the corridor and lit his way to Alex's door.

There, he hesitated. He'd told himself that truth, or the quest for it, had brought him here but as he stared at the black, polished door, he realised that hope was the true culprit. Hope that all was not lost, that something could be salvaged of his friendship with Alex.

As improbable and impossible as it had been, the bond they'd forged meant something. He wanted it to continue; Alex might not. If Dutta was right, Alex might not even be capable of friendship. His heart shrank from that, from what he might find behind the door, but he'd told Dutta the truth: he was no coward. He'd never been a coward, no matter what anyone thought, and he'd never run away from the truth.

Lifting his hand, Josef rapped on the door. Stomach clenching, pulse accelerating, he waited. And waited. His mouth went dry. He wet his lips, hesitated, and knocked again.

Rap, rap, rap.

A sound came from behind the door, the rattle of a key in the lock, a muffled curse. Josef's adrenaline surged, a quicksilver flare in his chest, and the door opened.

"I didn't order any bloody tea—" Alex broke off abruptly. His eyes went wide and, for the briefest moment, astonished.

"Pity," Josef said, pulse racing, "I could do with a cuppa."

Alex scowled. He leaned heavily on a black cane, his face pale and pinched, overgrown hair on the unkempt side of tousled. Shadows gathered beneath his eyes, and stubble darkened his jawline. Frankly, he looked awful. But he looked human, and Josef felt weak-kneed with relief.

"How did you get in?" Alex growled. "I said no visitors."

"The usual way—I bribed the doorman. And since I am here, can I come in?"

"No." He wasn't looking at Josef, gaze lowered, half hidden by his too-long hair. "I don't want to see you." He started to shut the door, but Josef got his foot in the way.

"I want to see you," he said. "I want to see how you are, that's all. You look..." He studied Alex's eyes, all trace of the ghoulish blue gone, although somehow still haunted. "You look yourself again, more or less."

Alex laughed; the sound raised the hairs on Josef's scalp. "More or less, yes." His expression darkened further. "There, you've seen how I am. Now you can go. I'm not fit for—"

"Company? Yes, Lottie told me you'd say that."

"She—? You've spoken to her?"

"Only way to find out if you were still alive, wasn't it? Look, are you going to let me in? You look like you're about to fall over."

"I'm fine," Alex grumbled, but he turned away from the door, leaving it open as he hobbled back into the flat, and so Josef followed.

The rooms were much as Josef remembered. That was no real surprise because it had been months, not years, since his last visit in those desperate hours after Alex had been bitten. What was a shock was the state of the place. The curtains were mostly closed, plunging the flat into gloomy half-light, and there was clutter everywhere: unwashed plates and cups stacked on the sideboard, discarded bits of clothing on the chairs, disarrayed newspapers and books splayed open on the floor. If Alex employed a maid, she hadn't been in for a long time.

Alex didn't seem to notice any of it, limping slowly through the chaos towards the cold, unlit fireplace. He turned, awkward with his stick, and lowered himself into one of the armchairs. A table stood next to it, a plate with an untouched slice of buttered bread, curling at the corners, sitting atop a pile of books.

Josef observed all this as he took the settee opposite Alex, pushing aside a sweater and cardigan to make room. "I tried to see you," he said. "I went to Belgrave Square five times, but they turned me away. Said you weren't accepting visitors."

"I wasn't." Alex rested his gaze on the floor between them. "I'm not."

"And yet here I am."

A flicker of Alex's gaze touched Josef's. "You never did know what was good for you."

Josef smiled slightly, but didn't argue. Dutta had been right. Alex wasn't the man he had been, but he wasn't the monster Josef had feared. He was in a hole, though, no doubt about that. Glancing around the room, Josef said, "Shall I open the curtains? It's gloomy in here."

"I don't need you to wait on me."

"Good, because I've no intention of waiting on you, or anyone else."

He went to the window to pull back the curtain, but Alex snapped, "Don't!" Startled, Josef turned around to find Alex scowling at him. "It's too bright. My eyes..." He gestured towards his face. "Sensitive to daylight."

Josef swallowed, letting his hand fall from the curtain; he didn't need to be told why. "I see. How about a lamp, then? Is that easier?"

Alex was still scowling, but after a moment, he nodded. "If you like. I don't need it."

There were two elegant gas lamps on the mantelpiece, so Josef found the matches and lit them. He kept the gas low, one eye on Alex to see how he reacted to the light, but he didn't flinch or shade his eyes. Just daylight that bothered him, then.

He wondered whether this was something that would improve, or remain a permanent legacy of Alex's infection by the ghoul. He wondered whether it was the only legacy. And he didn't dare ask either question. Instead, he sat back down on the settee and said, "How's the leg? It was a bad break, but I've seen worse."

"I'm sure you have." Alex gave him another of those flickering looks and added, gruffly, "There was an infection in the bone, but it's healing now. They say I'll always need the stick."

"You're lucky you didn't lose the leg."

Alex grunted; he didn't sound grateful. "I'd have rather lost the leg than—" He clamped his jaw on that thought and said, briskly, "Well, you've done your duty. Thank you for your visit. You'll excuse me for not showing you out."

Ignoring that, Josef said, "It's bloody cold in here. Why don't you have the fire lit?"

"I don't need it. Anyway, I can't..." He waved at his injured leg.

"What happened to your maid?" Josef said, rising.

"I don't need a maid."

Josef didn't bother arguing with that obvious untruth, just went to the fireplace where he saw that a fire had already been laid. All he needed to do was set a match to the kindling, which he did, crouching down and watching the flames dance along the dry wood. "Have you eaten breakfast?"

"What?"

He turned and looked at Alex slumped in his chair, lame leg stretched out before him. "Breakfast. The first meal of the day? Customarily eggs and bacon, toast, tea."

Alex didn't dignify that quip with a response.

"Well, I haven't eaten," Josef went on, "so I'm going to see what you have in your kitchen and—"

"What the devil are you playing at?"

"I'm not playing," Josef snapped, standing up. "I'm helping you."

"I don't want your help!"

Josef snorted. "Right, you're just fine sitting here in the cold and dark."

"For God's sake!" Alex snarled. "Won't you just go?"

His words rang in the silent room, challenge and accusation.

Heart thumping thickly, Josef made himself say, "I will, if that's really what you want."

Alex stared at him, eyes dark with anguish. "God help me," he rasped, "it should be..."

Blowing out a slow breath, Josef lowered himself into the other armchair. Close enough that their knees were almost brushing. "Tell me. Are you recovered from the infection?"

Alex spread his hands, clenching his jaw. "As you see."

Which, Josef noted with a journalist's ear, was not a yes.

In the doorway, Alex had looked dishevelled. Now, in the lamplight, Josef could see that he was still unwell. Grey shadows hollowed his cheeks, skin like milk save high points of pink on his cheekbones. Feverish, perhaps. Or agitated. "Christ," Josef said vehemently, "won't you just tell me what's going on?"

Alex looked away, towards the curtained windows. "What do you want to know?"

"The truth, what else?"

"I thought you'd be sick of the truth by now."

Josef laughed, but he wasn't remotely amused. "And I thought you'd be sick of hiding it, but here we are."

"I'm not hiding—" Alex glared at him. "Can't you see I'm trying to protect you?"

"From what? You?"

In the silence that followed, Josef locked his gaze on Alex's dark and angry eyes. Neither looked away. Roughly, his breath catching, Josef said, "Are you still...?" He tried to swallow the dryness in his throat. "Still infected? Tell me."

Alex held his eyes for a long time, then blinked once, slowly. "The infection has passed, but it left me ... altered. My eyes..." His gaze slipped away. "I can see extremely well in the dark, and poorly in daylight. I have troubling thoughts, and when I sleep—which I do rarely—the nightmares are worse. I can sense..." He closed his eyes, throat working as he swallowed, and when he spoke again, his voice was a hoarse rasp. "I'm closer to the Otherworld; I can sense its presence at the borders of our own. I can feel it all the time."

Josef had no idea what that meant, but he could see from Alex's grim expression that it must be fearful. "What about The Society?" he said. "Can they help you?"

His expression grew wry. "Saint thinks it makes me useful."

"'Course he fucking does. And what do you think?"

Alex's eyes lifted to Josef's. "I think it makes me dangerous."

"Ah," Josef said softly, finally understanding. "Which is why you've decided to live like a hermit, I suppose?"

"I'm not safe around people."

"Not even me?"

"Especially not you."

Josef leaned forward, elbows on knees, studying Alex. So close he could have reached out and touched Alex's leg. He didn't. "Because you blame me for refusing to end your life, for leaving you in the tunnels?" Alex's confused frown made him add, "You called me a fucking coward."

"I called you a coward?"

"A fucking coward, yes."

Alex's expression changed, softening into distress in a way that made Josef's throat ache. "I don't remember very much," he said roughly, "but I do remember you standing between me and Dutta's gun. And I remember you carrying me out of that place on your back. For God's sake, Josef, how could I think you a coward when you saved my life?"

Carefully, Josef said, "I suppose that depends on whether you think it's a life worth saving."

Alex frowned. "Do you think I'd rather be dead?"

"Dutta thinks so."

"He told you that?"

"Bumped into him outside. I think he was waiting for me."

Alex scrubbed a hand through his tangled hair. "Dutta doesn't understand. He's never been—I don't blame you for anything. You made a hard choice, a brave choice, and it was the right one."

Bowing his head, Josef was overcome. He hadn't realised how oppressed he'd been by Alex's shouted accusation, how deeply he'd taken guilt into his heart. "Thank you," he said, careless of the emotion in his voice. Let Alex hear it; he wanted him to know. Looking up, he said it again, "Thank you."

"It's the truth," Alex said quietly. "That's why you're here, isn't it? For the truth."

"It is, yes."

Their gazes tangled across the small space that separated them. Alex's hair, too long and falling over his ears, gleamed in the glow of the gas lamps, their golden light adding warmth to his pallid skin. His lips, though, were a determined line. "Then you have it," he said. "And now you should go."

Josef frowned. "But that's not what you want."

"It's for the best."

"Not for me, it isn't."

Alex was silent, then said, "What do you want of me, Josef? I've told you what I am."

"I want us to be friends—" He stopped himself. "No, I came here for the truth so here it is. I want us to be more than friends. I want us to be what we were a few months ago, and to see where that road takes us. And I came here to find out if you want the same."

Alex closed his eyes, his hands gripping the arms of his chair so hard his knuckles were turning white. "Of course I want the same. Christ, I've thought of nothing but you these past weeks. You've set my heart on fire. You're in my blood. In my bones. But—" He opened his eyes, the glitter of moisture on his lashes. "Can't you see it's impossible?"

Josef leaned forward, only inches left between them. "No. Why?"

"Because look at me!" Alex cried. "Look at what I am. Half monster!"

"Bollocks. The only monstrous thing about you is your bloody title, and if I can put up with that, I can put up with anything."

"My—" Alex seemed to run out of words, then choked out something that wasn't quite a laugh. "Damn it, Shepel, this is serious."

"Life or death," Josef agreed. "I choose life."

I choose you.

Alex said, "I don't know what..." He gestured at himself. "Things may improve; they may get worse. I could... hurt you."

"Like I said, life. What's your point?"

"My point is that being with me is dangerous."

Reaching out, Josef set his hand on Alex's thigh, thumb stroking. "For men like us, being together is always dangerous. You know that. But I think, if we face it together, it's a risk worth taking." He stilled his hand. "Question is—do you?"

There was a pause that felt eternal. Even the clock on the mantelpiece seemed to hesitate, breath held. And then, in a rush, Alex said, "Christ, of course I do," and reached out his arms.

Josef went to him, on his knees between Alex's thighs, hugging him hard, breathing in the scent of his hair, his skin, as he buried his face in Alex's neck, kissing him there. Feeling Alex shiver in his arms and give a single, stifled sob, Josef held him tighter. "Shh," he said, "it's all right."

"Sorry," Alex breathed, not letting go, speaking into Josef's shoulder. "It's just—I thought you were lost to me."

"No," Josef said fiercely. "Never."

Alex pulled away, far enough that Josef could see his face. His pallid skin had colour now, a pink flush that chased away the dark circles beneath his eyes—eyes that glittered dark blue and beautiful. "Josef," he said softly, lifting a hand to his face. "My Joe, can we truly have this?"

Josef smiled into those eyes, feeling his heart find its rhythm. The same as Alex's, beating in tandem. Together. Together against the world. "Yes," he said, cupping Alex's aristocratic, annoyingly perfect face in his palm. "Now kiss me, you idiot."

And he did, gently at first but swiftly igniting, burning away all the fear and trauma, consuming everything that had come between them until nothing was left but desire, untarnished by anything that had gone before.

Desire, and more.

Josef didn't dare name the feeling burning behind his breastbone, but it was there, nonetheless. Deep in his heart, beating steadily. And he understood that he stood at a fork in the road, that he was consciously choosing the path to a future that glittered bright and full of danger.

A future he could only have with Alex.

The only future he wanted.

THE END

Author's Note

The folklore drawn on in this book is all real.

Soldiers fighting in the Great War were very superstitious, and many believed that ghouls lurked in the disused tunnels and trenches of no man's land. This myth was first brought to life in 1920 by Ardern Arthur Hulme Beaman, a lieutenant colonel in the British cavalry. His memoir, *The Squadroon*, is set on the marshes of the Somme in northern France where wild men, deserters from all nations, lived underground "like ghouls among the mouldering dead, and ... came out at night to plunder and to kill."

And Victorian sewer-hunters, working alone in the dark and dangerous tunnels, believed the Rat Queen of London lived in the sewers and granted good or ill luck to those who hunted for treasure in her kingdom.

Also real is the Defence of the Realm Act, unaffectionately known as DORA. This law was passed on the 8th of August 1914, just after the outbreak of war, and granted the British government extensive powers to ensure national security and support the war effort. Among many other things, it allowed the government to censor newspapers and control the spread of information deemed harmful to the morale of the forces or the civilian population.

It also limited pub opening hours and watered down the alcohol they served—this was primarily to ensure that workers were sober enough to keep the munitions factories running. Although the bulk of DORA restrictions were repealed in 1921, pub opening hours remained limited until 1988...

About The Author

Sally Malcolm was bitten by the male/male romance bug in 2016 and hasn't looked back. She's also written tie-in novels, audio dramas, and video game scripts for the hit TV shows STARGATE: SG-1 and STARGATE ATLANTIS.

Sally lives in South West London.

For more information visit www.sallymalcolm.com

Readers are saying

"Pure delicious pleasure! This witty romance is full of toe-curling chemistry, slow-burn fun, and gasp-worthy plot twists. The drop-everything read of the year!" (Total Creative Control) - *NYT bestselling author Annika Martin*

"If you enjoy the way KJ Charles so skillfully weaves together romance, history and politics, then chances are you'll enjoy this book, too." (King's Man) - *All About Romance*

"I loved this book. It's a reading highlight of this past year ... gentle and lyrical but also engrossing and sexy." (Between the Lines) - *Cat Sebastian, author of* We Could be so Good

Books By This Author

HISTORICAL

The Last Kiss

When Captain Ashleigh Dalton went to war in 1914, he never expected to fall in love. Yet, over three long years at the front, his dashing batman, Private West, became his reason for fighting—and his reason for living. For Harry West, an ostler from London's East End, it was love at first sight when he met complex, compassionate Captain Dalton. Harry knew their friendship wouldn't survive in the class-bound world back home, but in the trenches there was no point in worrying about tomorrow...

King's Man

Had there been no war, Sam Hutchinson and Nate Tanner would have lived their lives together as intimate friends, and secret lovers. But when the revolution convulsed America, it threw them down on opposite sides of history...

Contemporary

Total Creative Control (co-authored with Joanna Chambers)

When fanfic writer Aaron Page landed a temp job with the creator of hit TV show, Leeches, it was only meant to last a week. Three years later, Aaron's still there... It could be because he loves the creative challenge. It could be because he's a huge *Leeches* fanboy. It's definitely not because of Lewis Hunter, his extremely demanding, staggeringly rude ... and breathtakingly gorgeous boss. Is it?

Best Supporting Actor (co-authored with Joanna Chambers)

After an ill-judged yet mind-blowing night together, Jay Warren and Tag O'Rourke part acrimoniously. So it's a nasty shock when they discover that they've been cast in a two-man play that could launch Tag's career and finally get Jay back onto the stage where he belongs. Sure, it's not ideal, but how bad can it be to work with your arch-nemesis?

Between the Lines

Luca Moretti travels light. Estranged from his parents, he vows this will be his last trip home to New Milton. His family's hotel is on the verge of ruin and there's nothing Luca can do to save it. He's given up on his family and on his future. Until he meets Theo. Prickly, captivating Theo. And discovers that one summer can change everything...

Printed in Great Britain
by Amazon